INESCAPABLE

INESCAPABLE

NANCY MEHL

BETHANY HOUSE PUBLISHERS
a division of Baker Publishing Group
Minneapolis, Minnesota

Published by Bethany House Publishers
11400 Hampshire Avenue South
Bloomington, Minnesota 55438
www.bethanyhouse.com

Bethany House Publishers is a division of
Baker Publishing Group, Grand Rapids, Michigan

Printed in the United States of America

Library of Congress Cataloging-in-Publication Data
Mehl, Nancy.
    Inescapable / Nancy Mehl.
        p.   cm. — (Road to kingdom ; bk. 1)
    ISBN 978-0-7642-0927-7 (pbk.)
    1. Young women—Fiction. 2. Stalkers—Fiction. 3. Mennonites—Fiction.
4. Kansas—Fiction. I. Title.
PS3613.E4254I54 2012
813'.6—dc23   2012002390

Scripture references are from the King James Version of the Bible.

Cover design by Paul Higdon

Author represented by Benrey Literary, LLC.

12   13   14   15   16   17   18   7   6   5   4   3   2   1

To my husband, Norman

Thank you for your strength, your encouragement,
and your love. You're my best friend. I can't imagine
making this journey of life without you. I truly
believe that "the best is yet to be."

CHAPTER /1

For the third night in a row the man stood under the streetlight, staring up at our apartment, his face hidden by a red ball cap pulled down to just above his eyes. I closed the curtain, trying to keep my movement slow so he wouldn't notice me watching him. But I couldn't keep my fingers from trembling.

"What's the matter, Mama?"

I turned to smile at Charity. Though only six, she knew when I was worried or afraid. Unfortunately, there'd been a lot of that lately.

"Nothing, honey. Did you finish your carrots?"

She grimaced. "They're too gooshy tonight."

I sighed and came back to the table, trying not to let her see my fear. "They're supposed to be gooshy. I cooked them."

She wrinkled her button nose. "I like them hard. You know that."

"You eat those carrots, Charity Lynn Engel. Right now."

I hadn't meant to sound harsh, but the strain I was under had frayed my nerves. Her dark eyes grew wide.

"Are you mad at me, Mama?" She sniffed a couple of times,

jabbed at her carrots with her fork, and stuck them into her mouth.

I pushed myself up from my chair, intending to put my arms around my small daughter and soothe her hurt feelings. But when I put my hand on the surface of our secondhand kitchen table, it wobbled horribly. Charity's glass of milk started to slide, and I barely caught it before it tipped over. I looked down and found that the paperback book I'd used to balance the table legs had slipped out again. I kicked it back under the uneven leg and went to hug Charity.

"I'm sorry, Cherry Bear," I said. "You don't have to eat the carrots if you don't want to."

She held out her soft, chubby little-girl arms. "It's okay, Mama. They're not really, really bad. Just kinda bad."

I stroked her soft black curls while I gazed around our small apartment. It wasn't fancy, but it had been home. Unfortunately, that wouldn't last much longer. I let go of Charity and forced a smile. "How about a fudge bar, honey?"

She looked up at me in wonder. "Instead of carrots?"

"Yes, instead of carrots."

She giggled, any trace of injured feelings gone like smoke in the wind. If only I could dismiss my own concerns so easily. She jumped down from her chair and skipped over to the refrigerator. "Can I have both halves?"

I usually broke the ice cream treat in two, not wanting her to eat too much sugar before bed. But tonight I didn't care. I reached into the small freezer and pulled a fudge bar out of the box, handing it to her without comment.

"Oh, boy. Thanks, Mama. Can I watch *Dora the Explorer* for a while before I hafta go to bed?"

I glanced at the clock. "You have thirty minutes, but when I say it's time to turn off the TV, no arguing. Promise?"

She bobbed her little head up and down with enthusiasm. "Promise."

I waved her on, and she scurried into the living room before I could change my mind. Not long after we moved in, I purchased a secondhand TV and a DVD player. We couldn't afford cable, but I'd found a stack of children's DVDs at a yard sale during the summer. At fifty cents each, they provided my daughter with hours of entertainment. Best ten dollars I'd ever spent. As soon as I heard the TV come on, I grabbed my cell phone out of my purse, which was on the kitchen counter. Meghan answered after the fourth ring.

"It's me," I said.

"Oh, Lizzie. I tried to call you earlier, but I guess you weren't home."

"I guess not," I said, trying to sound nonchalant. Not easy to do when you're lying. I'd been too upset to talk on the phone. It wasn't easy now, but I knew I'd have to face Meghan eventually.

"I still can't believe it," she said. "You've been such an asset at Harbor House. If Sylvia was still here—"

"But she's not. Reba's been almost impossible to work with from day one, but her attitude got really bad after her boyfriend showed a little too much interest in me."

Sylvia Martinez had been the director of Harbor House, a shelter for abused women, for twenty years. But after her second heart attack, she finally took her doctor's advice and resigned. Reba, her temporary replacement, didn't get along with anyone at the shelter, but she'd been treating me particularly bad ever since her city council boyfriend, James Webb, picked her up from work one night. There had been rumors about his ethics and under-the-table deals for as long as I'd been at Harbor House, and Meghan and I were pretty sure he was responsible for getting Reba the interim director's position. The evening Reba reluctantly introduced him to me, his eyes had lingered on me a little too long, traveling slowly up and down my body. By the next morning, Reba's already rancorous attitude toward me had turned toxic. Today, she'd finally taken revenge.

"If it helps, everyone knows you didn't steal that money, Lizzie."

"Well, I'm glad, but if she presses charges . . ."

Meghan gasped. "But she can't. There isn't any proof."

"The money's gone, Meghan. Over a thousand dollars out of petty cash. And Reba and I are the only ones with access. She showed me the books. They reveal months of bogus withdrawals with my initials by each and every transaction. Whoever copied my writing did a pretty good job. At first, even I thought it was genuine."

Meghan snorted. "I suppose the fact that Reba used to be an accountant and knows exactly how to doctor the records doesn't enter into this at all."

I sighed. "No, it doesn't, because I can't prove I didn't take the money, and she can prove I did. If she calls the authorities, I could lose Charity, and I won't take that chance. Besides, without a job, I can't pay for this apartment."

"You know that Jim and I would be happy to help you."

"Thank you, Meghan, but that won't solve my problems. I've got to get away from here in case Reba pushes this further. Besides, that man is still following me."

"No! Did you call the police?"

I sighed and glanced toward the kitchen window. *Should I risk another look?* "I've given up on them. They've been out here on four different occasions. The man is always gone by the time they get here. Besides, all they ever do is explain why they can't help me. It's not a crime to stand outside on a public street."

"But what about the threatening notes?"

"They barely looked at them. Not enough to go on, they said. If I find out who wrote them, then I'm supposed to give them a call."

Meghan grunted. "Our tax dollars at work." She paused a moment. "You're certain you have no clue who this guy is or why he's sending these notes?"

"I've racked my brain, and I can't figure it out. He can't be the husband of a client, because I don't work directly with the clients."

"I know you're not dating right now, but what about someone in the past? A man you don't see anymore?"

"No one who would be doing something like this." I took a deep breath and let the air out slowly. "I've got to get away from here, Meghan. I have no choice."

"But . . . but where will you go?"

I bit my lower lip, not wanting to say the words out loud. Meghan noticed my hesitation.

"Oh, Lizzie. No. You can't go back to . . . to Kingdom."

"There's no other option open to me. At least no one can find us there. Listen, you can't tell Reba where I am, Meghan. I mean it."

She laughed. "I couldn't, even if I wanted to. I have no idea where Kingdom is. Besides, didn't you say that its location is so remote even people who live in the area have a hard time finding it?"

My mind was spinning, trying to find another way out. Kingdom, Kansas, was the last place in the world I wanted to be. I'd grown used to living in Kansas City. Going back to a town of barely three hundred people would certainly cause severe culture shock. Unfortunately, there didn't seem to be any other answer. We had to find someplace safe, away from Reba and from the man in the red cap who had been stalking us for the past few weeks.

The man had never approached us. But right after he first appeared, the notes had started coming. Although I couldn't prove he was sending them, it just made sense. What I couldn't figure out was what he wanted beyond trying to frighten me. The police informed me that his behavior wasn't all that unusual for a stalker and cautioned me to stay away from him. Great advice. Of course I was trying to avoid him. But I worried he would get bolder and follow through on his threats.

"What about your degree, Lizzie?"

I glanced over at my ancient computer, my college books stacked up next to it. "I won't be able to work on it in Kingdom. Kinda hard to take online courses in a town without electricity." I suddenly became aware that I was twirling my hair around my finger and immediately let it go. My mother's voice echoed softly in my head. *"Leave your hair alone, Elizabeth Lynn. You want your father to shave your head? He will, you know. He says a woman's hair is her vanity."* A feeling of shame washed through me. I angrily pushed it away.

"When will you leave?" Meghan asked.

"As soon as I can. I've got to talk to my landlady. My lease isn't up for another couple of months. I hope she doesn't try to hold me to it."

"I'm sorry, Lizzie. You shouldn't have to deal with all this.

NANCY MEHL

You're a good person who deserves better. I wish I could help you."

I rubbed my eyes with my other hand as weariness seeped through my body. "Hey, just having someone to talk to makes a big difference. I know you're busy with the kids and all. Jim is probably getting really tired of me."

She chuckled. "Yeah, he's so tired of you he offered to wait outside your apartment and beat the crud out of your friend in the red cap. He's as concerned as I am."

"I guess you've got the only good guy in the entire world," I said, sighing. "I'd better get going. I have a lot of planning and packing to do, and I'm almost asleep on my feet."

"Promise me you'll call me before you leave. Don't disappear without saying good-bye."

"I promise, Meghan. You're my best friend. In fact, you're pretty much my only friend."

"Good night, Lizzie."

I said good-bye and hung up the phone. Then I carried it back to the counter and plugged it into its charger. After that I watched the rest of Charity's DVD, even though I couldn't concentrate on it at all. When it was over, I helped her get ready for bed. We shared a bedroom, but that didn't bother me. I liked having her near. Her soft snoring at night lulled me to sleep. It was the one time of the day I didn't worry about her.

I made a cup of tea and sat down on the couch, gazing around our small apartment. I'd really believed Charity and I would spend many years in Kansas City. Although our start had been rough, life had gradually improved.

The first job I landed here was at Betty's Café, a small greasy spoon down the street. I didn't have a car, but it was within walking distance. Betty, an older woman with a drinking problem, taught me the business from the ground up. I'd been hired as a waitress, but many times she didn't come to work, saying she was "sick." It didn't take long before I was able to run the place by myself.

Then one day, Sylvia came in to eat. We bonded immediately. She was really interested in me, and I poured out my story between slinging hamburgers and serving coffee. Not long after that, she offered me a job. I gave my notice to Betty and started at Harbor House two weeks later. I'd been there for the past four years and, until Sylvia's heart attack, had finally begun to feel hopeful about the future. That hope was shattered and lying in so many pieces that no one could possibly glue it back together. Why had I allowed myself to think things could ever be good in my life? Being positive had only set me up for disappointment. I wouldn't make that mistake again.

As I tried to figure out my next move, a familiar feeling of fear wriggled around inside me and wouldn't be still.

CHAPTER / 2

I spent the next day packing and explaining to Charity why we had to move. I tried to make it sound as if we were getting ready for a great adventure, but I could tell she wasn't completely buying it. I didn't want to worry her, but no matter how hard I fought to calm my fears, tears kept filling my eyes.

My grandmother's voice whispered inside me. *"There isn't anything too big for God, Lizzie girl. You gotta cast your cares on Him. He loves you so much."*

Yeah, right. He loved me so much He gave me a father who did nothing but use terror and intimidation to control me—and a mother too timid to stand up for her only child. He allowed me to be threatened by some crazy person, and to top things off, He allowed me to lose my job and possibly face jail. *Save me from all this love, God.*

My father would have called it sacrilegious, trying to talk one-on-one with God. Supposedly, God only listened to the church leaders in Kingdom. And He was certainly too busy to fool with a nobody like me.

Although Reba's accusation and threats felt even larger than my fear of the man in the red ball cap, the two combined to create a storm of anxiety. My mind couldn't seem to wrap itself around everything that was wrong in my life. If I tried to deal with one problem, another crisis waited behind it. It was too much for me. Too much for anyone.

That afternoon Meghan called to tell me that my final check plus two weeks' severance pay was waiting for me. With Charity in the backseat, I immediately drove over to Harbor House. Pulling an old knit hat on my head and hiding most of my face behind a wool scarf, I slipped in unnoticed. It was clear Meghan had pulled some strings to get the check cut so soon. After retrieving it from the woman who worked at the front desk, I snuck off like a prisoner escaping from her cell.

Before getting in my car, I stopped and took one long, last look at the big brick building that housed Harbor House. How was it possible for me to belong there one day and not belong the next? How could such a refuge of safety chew me up and spit me out like unwanted garbage?

My father's face kept drifting into my mind. His expression when he'd found out I was pregnant still haunted me. He never said a word, just stared at me with disappointment and contempt. The way I'd felt then echoed my emotions now. I was trash. Something to discard.

I finally climbed back behind the wheel of my car, checked on Charity, who was coloring in the backseat, and drove away. Thanks to my final check, I had enough money to pay all my bills and just enough left to get us to Kingdom. I had no intention of leaving a forwarding address or contacting anyone in Kansas City once we were safely out of town. Lizzie Engel would disappear completely. It was the only way Charity and I would finally be safe.

Though I knew it might be useless in Kingdom, I couldn't

bring myself to part with my cell phone, so I planned to pay that bill two months in advance. The phone was my lifeline to the outside world, and the thought of cutting it off made me feel insecure.

After I paid all my bills, my biggest concern would be my car. The 1991 white Chevy Caprice had over one hundred and fifty thousand miles on it, and the engine light had been on for at least two months. Since I couldn't afford to put it in the shop, I'd simply ignored the warning. Sylvia had sold it to me for five hundred dollars not long after I started at Harbor House and allowed me to make payments whenever I could. It took me a year and a half to pay it off, so now I owned it free and clear. Remembering Sylvia's kindness made me weep. I missed her so much, but the staff had been told in no uncertain terms that she couldn't be disturbed. Her health was at stake. As much as I wanted to call her and tell her what was going on, I couldn't take the chance. Better for everyone that I just slip away.

On the way home, big white flakes began to drift down from the sky, and by the time we were three blocks from our apartment, the wind had picked up, and blowing snow made it a little difficult to see. Something about the weather made me feel nostalgic for snowy days in Kingdom when Mother would make a big pot of soup. I didn't have the ingredients for soup, but I suddenly wanted something special for dinner. Although I usually watched our money like a miser, a strange urge came over me. A feeling of reckless abandonment. What did it matter? Working hard and pinching pennies had gotten me nowhere. On a whim, I pulled into the drive-through of a local burger joint that made the best cheeseburgers in town. The last time I'd picked up any kind of fast food was last spring when I had the flu and couldn't cook.

"Oh, Mama," Charity said breathlessly when she realized we were having cheeseburgers for dinner, "this is the best day of my whole life."

I had to look away, pretending to read the menu. When Charity was little, too young to realize how tough life really is, she used to claim that almost every day was her favorite day. I hadn't heard her speak those words in quite some time. Hearing them again made me happy and sad all at the same time. By the time we got home, she was chattering nonstop, full of little-girl excitement.

In our apartment, we parked ourselves in front of the TV, scarfed down cheeseburgers, watched two different *Dora* DVDs, and then switched to *Sleeping Beauty*. I'd fallen in love with the story of the sleeping princess and sometimes played the animated movie at night after Charity went to bed. No one except Meghan knew I'd never seen a movie of any kind until after I left home at eighteen. And I'd only discovered *Sleeping Beauty* two years ago. For some reason, the tale of the beautiful princess Aurora, who slumbered as she waited to be rescued by her prince, touched something deep inside me. I never got tired of watching it.

At the same yard sale where we'd found all our DVDs, Charity had discovered a Sleeping Beauty doll that was still in its box and priced at ten dollars. Ten dollars might as well have been a thousand back then, and it almost broke my daughter's heart, as well as mine, when I had to say no. Charity had learned not to ask for things we couldn't afford, and when she begged for the doll, I realized how important it was to her. The woman hosting the sale noticed her obvious distress and got up out of her lawn chair.

"Please," she said, "I'd like to give her the doll as my gift."

When I objected, the woman explained that she'd purchased it as a surprise for her granddaughter's birthday. But the child had gotten upset and thrown the doll on the floor because she'd wanted a Barbie doll.

"The look on your daughter's face is the one I'd hoped to see on Stephanie's," she'd said. "Please. I'd really like the doll go to a little girl who will appreciate it." The second she put the doll in Charity's arms, it became her best friend. Now "The Princess," as she called her, went everywhere she did. The doll, with long blond hair, a gold crown, and a beautiful pink dress, was like the third member of our ragtag little family. Charity couldn't go to sleep at night without The Princess beside her. It had been a real struggle to get her to leave the doll at home during the day when she went to school, but she finally agreed when I explained that The Princess would be safer in our apartment, where she wouldn't get wet, dirty, or stolen.

I left Charity watching the movie and quickly finished packing. Then I called Meghan and told her we were leaving in the morning. It was hard to say good-bye because, although I told her I'd keep in touch, I actually had no plan to do so. It was better to make a clean break. I couldn't risk having anyone trace a call or find out where I was. I'd already called Charity's school to tell them we were moving. They'd asked for a forwarding address. I'd told them I didn't have one yet but would be in contact so they could forward Charity's records. Another lie. I had no intention of phoning them. Charity could start the first grade again. It was better than putting her in a position where she might be taken away from me.

I was packing the last of our dishes in the kitchen when Charity called out, "Mama! *Sleeping Beauty* is all done."

I walked out into the living room. "Why don't you get ready for bed, Cherry Bear? I'm going to run downstairs and get our mail. I'll lock the door behind me. Don't open it for anyone except me. You hear?"

"I hear you, Mama."

I hurried out the door and into the hall. The mail could have waited until morning, but I wanted a few minutes alone to gather my thoughts. Leaving Kansas City was hard, and going back to Kingdom was even harder. I walked slowly down the stairs to our mailbox, trying to rein in my wounded emotions. Our box was just one in a long row of identical metal boxes with numbers etched on them. Most apartment buildings like ours had inside mailboxes. Leave it to me to find an apartment with mail delivered outside.

When I turned my key in the lock, I found several pieces of mail waiting for me. Flyers. All of them. Except for one. A light blue envelope with my name on it and no return address. Perfect. Another one. Just what I needed. I stuck the flyers back into the box and pulled out the blue envelope. As snowflakes blew chaotically around me and the wind cut through the thin material of my dress, I ripped it open.

I'm watching you. It's just a matter of time before I get you and your little girl. You'll never get away from me.

I jogged out to the curb, the icy wind pushing me back as if trying to stop me from what I was about to do. My body trembled from the cold, and I scolded myself for leaving my coat upstairs. Sure enough, there he was. Standing next to a small orange car with a smashed left front bumper. I held the note up in the air. "Why are you doing this?" I yelled.

"What do you want? If you don't leave me alone, I'm going to call the police." Hopefully, he didn't know how useless my warning actually was.

He looked surprised and took a step back.

"You'd better get it through your head, you jerk. No more!" I took a step off the curb, trying to look threatening, though I had no intention of getting close enough for him to grab me.

Before I had a chance to say anything else, I heard the squeal of tires, felt a big jolt, and everything went black.

CHAPTER/3

"Lizzie, are you all right?"

A voice filtered through the fog. I slowly opened my eyes to see Doris, my landlady, standing over me. With her were several strangers, all of them staring at me with wide eyes and worried expressions. I struggled to sit up. What was I doing in the street?

"Maybe you should wait for the ambulance," Doris said, trying to push me back down.

"No. I . . . I'm okay. What happened?"

Even as she started to explain that I'd been hit by a car, I remembered. I pushed myself up to a sitting position, running my hands over my arms and legs. The only pain I felt was in my left hip and the back of my head.

"I'm all right," I insisted, feeling embarrassed to be the center of attention due to my sheer stupidity. I could hear Father's voice. *"I swear you don't have an ounce of sense in your head, Elizabeth Lynn."* "R-really, I'm not hurt at all."

"Are you sure, miss?" An older man knelt beside me, his face pale and his voice unsteady. "You ran out in front of me. I tried to stop but couldn't."

"It's not your fault. I wasn't watching." I struggled to my feet, feeling flushed by all the unwanted interest. "Please, I'm fine. I really am."

"I still don't think you should get up until the ambulance arrives," Doris said, frowning. "You could have internal injuries."

"No. Just a bump on the head." I glanced quickly across the street. The man with the red cap was gone.

In the distance, the sound of a siren began to grow louder. I glanced up at my apartment window. "Charity's alone. I need to get back. . . ."

"You stop worrying about that little girl of yours," Doris said. "Wait here and let the paramedics look you over. I'll take care of Charity." She looked over at her husband. "Charles, you stay here with Lizzie. If they decide she needs to go to the hospital, you come let me know." She smiled reassuringly at me. "We'll keep Charity until you're released, honey."

Go to the hospital? A blanket of fear fell over me like a shroud. Although Harbor House carries insurance on all their full-time employees, it's not very good. A trip to the hospital could cost me a lot of money and create bills I had no way to pay. "No, I'm not going to the hospital. It's not necessary."

Just then an ambulance pulled up, and two men in uniforms jumped out.

"Someone get hit by a car?" one of them asked.

"Right here," a man said. "She's right here."

"I'm okay," I said to the first paramedic who reached me. "I was knocked down, but nothing's broken. No damage done." I could feel beads of sweat form along my hairline. "Please," I pleaded, "I've got to get back to my little girl."

The other paramedic, who was very good-looking, said,

"Why don't you just let us check you out? It won't take long. Better safe than sorry."

"No thank you. Really." I knew I sounded manic, but the idea of more bills terrified me. Was my insurance even in force? Would being fired for theft disqualify me from benefits? I couldn't risk finding out.

The first paramedic, who was a little older, folded his arms across his chest. "Ma'am, are you refusing treatment?"

I nodded quickly. "Yes, I'm refusing." I glanced back and forth between the two men, who appeared irritated that I wouldn't allow them to toss me in the back of their ambulance and cart me off to the emergency room "So I can do that? Refuse, I mean?"

"Yes, of course you can. It's a free country." The first guy looked at his partner. "Grab a release form."

The younger paramedic jogged back to the ambulance, muttering something about wasting everyone's time.

"You really should let them look you over," an elderly woman said harshly. "It's irresponsible to call an ambulance and then refuse treatment."

"I-I didn't call the ambulance," I said defensively. "My landlady must have called."

The paramedic corrected me. "The person who called was a man. Dispatch said he was very upset."

I swung my gaze around the quickly diminishing crowd that had gathered around me. No one took responsibility for coming to my aid. The attendant who'd fetched the form held it out in front of me, and I quickly signed it.

"Thank you. I'm sorry I caused you so much trouble."

"Me too," he said in a disgusted tone.

His partner reached out and patted my shoulder, concern

written on his face. "If you have any problems with double vision, develop a bad headache, or experience any pain in your body that seems abnormal, you call us. We'll come back, okay?"

His kindness brought a degree of comfort to an extremely awkward situation. "Thank you. Thank you very much." I turned from the small crowd still waiting to see my final outcome. The man who'd hit me hurried to his car and took off, probably grateful to get on his way without being further involved in my careless actions.

Pain shot through my hip as I hobbled to the mailboxes and grabbed the junk mail I'd left in my box. I looked briefly in the street for the note sent by the man in the red cap, but it was gone. Probably blown away in the cold wind that had gusted past me. Fine by me. I didn't want the hateful thing anyway.

I slowly entered the lobby of our apartment building. I usually took the stairs but decided this once to use the elevator. It seemed to move slower than molasses and had a strange smell. Like disinfectant. By the time I reached the fifth floor, the sickly sweet aroma had intensified my headache. I limped down the hallway and pushed open the door to my apartment. Charity was sitting on the couch with Doris beside her.

"So you're all right?" Doris asked with a frown. "They let you go?"

"Yes, I'm fine. Thank you for watching Charity."

My daughter stared at me, her eyes big. "Are you okay, Mama? What took you so long?"

I breathed a sigh of relief. I had been afraid she'd be frightened silly by the time I returned, but obviously, Doris hadn't told her I'd been hit by a car. "Just had to take care of something, Cherry Bear. Everything's fine."

Doris stood up. She hesitated as if she wanted to say something else, but instead she told me to let her know if I needed anything else.

I went over and hugged her. "Thank you. Thank you so much for everything. I really appreciate your kindness. I'll miss you."

She hugged me back. "You two take care of yourselves. And let me know how you're getting along, okay?"

Once again I agreed to stay in touch without planning to ever honor my promise. *"Liars go to hell, Elizabeth. Do you want to spend eternity in hell?"*

I got Charity into bed, trying to reassure her that everything was okay. It took a while, but she finally fell asleep. I took several aspirin, but my discomfort continued to intensify. I limped into the bathroom and looked at my hip. It was swollen and red. I knew from past experience it would turn purple quickly. *"Spare the rod, spoil the child. Those bruises will cleanse your soul."* I raised my knee up and down several times. Pain shot through the inflamed area, but at least there was easy movement. Hoping nothing was broken, I stared at myself in the mirror and gingerly felt the knot on the back of my head. It was tender to the touch.

"How could you be so stupid?" I whispered to my reflection. "How could you possibly be such an idiot?"

"How could you be so stupid, Elizabeth? How could a daughter of mine be so ignorant?"

"I guess you were right, Father." I said quietly to the girl with the sad, dark eyes who stared back at me. "Maybe you were right about everything."

Even though my childhood had been wrapped up with pain and insecurity, I suddenly had the strangest longing for home. That was a first. Up to that moment I'd been glad to get away from Kingdom. Why was I thinking about it now? Of course, there wasn't much difference between being a screw-up in Kansas City or a screw-up in Kingdom. My mother's troubled eyes seemed to look back at me through my own. I'd never doubted she loved me, but she'd never stood up to my father. Never protected me from his wrath.

Without warning, another voice seemed to rise up from deep within me. A voice that didn't sound like my father. *Go home, Lizzie. Everything will be all right.*

My eyes swam with tears. How could things ever be all right in Kingdom? I'd been an outcast. The girl who got pregnant out of wedlock. The fallen daughter of an elder in the Mennonite church. How could it have happened? In my mind I could see Clay Troyer's handsome face, his hazel eyes full of sincerity. *"It's okay, Lizzie. This is what people do who love each other. Trust me."*

It had felt so good to finally hear someone tell me they loved me that I'd given in. Just once. That was all it took. A moment that seemed to be over before I even knew what had happened. And then came the morning sickness. The bloated feeling. At first I'd thought it was the flu. But before long the truth was evident. Not long after Clay and his family learned I was pregnant, they left the area. No good-byes. No forwarding address. All that was left was Father's silence, Mother's sadness, and the looks of disapproval from church members. I couldn't go through that again. "I won't allow anyone to treat Charity like some kind of mistake," I said softly to my own image. "I just won't."

Go home, Lizzie. Go home.

Whose voice spoke to me? Was it the God I refused to

acknowledge, or was it the devil, trying to finally destroy the last little piece of Lizzie Engel that still remained? I couldn't tell, but it was clear there was nothing left for me in Kansas City. No job, no money, no choices, and no peace as long as the man in the red cap continued his campaign of terror. I had to get Charity away from his threats, and I had to protect her from Reba. Her lies had the power to land me in jail. Either one of those situations could cause me to lose the only thing left in my life I cared about: my daughter. It was abundantly clear that there was only one road left open for me.

And it led to Kingdom.

CHAPTER / 4

The next morning Charity and I loaded up our meager belongings and filled the car with gas. My hip still ached, but I chose to ignore it. Before driving away from our apartment, I checked the street carefully, making certain there were no small orange cars in sight. There weren't. Nor did I see the man in the red cap anywhere. As I pulled onto the road, a feeling of relief washed over me. We were traveling toward the one place where no one could find us, a small town nestled in the northern part of Kansas, only ten miles from the Nebraska border. Surely we would be safe there.

We left Kansas City around ten o'clock with almost two inches of snow on the ground. The roads in town were slippery, but when we reached the highway, they were in pretty good shape, despite the continuing snowfall.

"Where are we going again, Mama?" Charity asked from the backseat. I looked in the rearview mirror. She was settled in her booster seat, The Princess clutched in her arms.

"We're going to the place we lived when you were a baby," I said for about the third time, trying to be patient with her. "Your grandma and grandpa live there."

There was silence as she considered my response. Finally, she asked, "Will I see my daddy?"

My heart skipped a beat. Charity had never asked about her father before. I knew she'd thought about it as she watched other children at school with their fathers, but she seemed to view them only as an oddity. Not something that pertained directly to her.

"No, honey. Your daddy doesn't live in Kingdom. He lives a long way away."

"But why?" A frown darkened her heart-shaped face. Although Charity looked very much like me, with curly black hair and dark brown eyes, I could certainly see Clay in her too. Clay's coloring was lighter than hers, but he was clearly displayed in the tilt of her head, her turned-up nose, and the widow's peak that framed her face.

"He . . . he had to go away a long time ago, Cherry Bear. I don't think we'll ever see him again."

She locked eyes with mine in the mirror. "Is he dead, Mama? Missy said my daddy was probably dead just like her daddy that got killed in the war."

So she'd been talking about her father at school. I felt a sense of shame, knowing I should have addressed the subject long ago, but I had been afraid, unsure how to explain my failure to provide her the kind of family she should have had.

"I'm sure he's not dead, honey."

Her frown deepened. "But how do you know?"

I sighed. "I *don't* know. That's just what I think." I screwed up a smile. "Let's not worry about it anymore right now. Okay? We'll talk more about it after we get ho . . . after we get to Kingdom."

She nodded slowly, but I could tell I hadn't satisfied her

curiosity. How would I ever be able to clarify it for her? Would she be ashamed of me too? The disgrace and humility I'd felt in Kingdom washed over me, and I almost pulled over. What was I doing? I was twenty-three years old. Someone who should have her life on track. Why was I going back to a place I'd promised to never set foot in again? Would there be a friendly face anywhere in the entire town? A moment ago I'd almost called Kingdom *home*. But it wasn't home. Not by a long shot. What if we were run out of town? Not allowed to even enter the place I'd grown up? I hadn't considered such a possibility until that moment. How would something like that affect Charity?

"Mama, I don't have any friends in Kingdom, do I?" I almost didn't hear her, she spoke so softly. Her question made my heart ache. I didn't know how to answer her.

"Not yet, Cherry Bear. But once people meet you, you'll make lots of friends." Was that true? Had I just lied to her?

Charity was quiet for a minute or two. I kept checking the rearview mirror, watching her face. She was obviously thinking hard about the situation. Finally she looked at me, our eyes making contact in the mirror again. "Who are your friends, Mama? Maybe they'll like me too."

Feeling a sense of panic, I tried to recall some of the residents in Kingdom who had been kind to me. Funny, but I'd spent so much effort the last five years purposely *not* thinking about the small Mennonite town, that pulling up memories now was rather difficult. Memories buried beneath years of pain and repression began to drift into my mind like tendrils of smoke released from a candle that had just been blown out.

"Well, let's see. There's Hope Kauffman. She makes beautiful quilts." Hope ran Kingdom Quilts. Her shop sold finished quilts and quilted pieces fashioned by the female residents of Kingdom. She also offered lessons to young women who needed to learn how to succeed at the age-old craft perfected by our Amish and Mennonite ancestors.

"I like quilts," Charity said happily. "Tell me something else about her."

"Like what?"

"Like does she have a daddy?"

The *daddy* question again. I stifled a sigh of frustration. "Yes, she has a daddy. His name is Samuel."

"Is he a nice daddy?"

I wanted to tell her that he was certainly nicer than *my* daddy, but I didn't. "Yes, he's a nice daddy." Actually, Samuel was a good father, although just like most of the men in Kingdom, he was serious about his religion. At least Hope never had to gain the favor of the church to work in the shop, since Samuel oversaw the daily business. Samuel had kept a tight rein on his beautiful daughter in many ways, yet she'd had freedoms most of the other women in Kingdom didn't enjoy.

"Do you like Hope Kau . . . Kau . . ."

"Kauffman," I finished for her. "And yes, I like her very much. She was a very good friend to me." I'd been in awe of Hope, since she was occasionally allowed to travel alone to a fabric store in Washington, Kansas, for supplies. Usually, only the men drove buggies past the borders of town. If women wanted to go, they would ride with their husbands. But once a month, Hope would hitch up their horse, Daisy, and ride out of town by herself. I liked to watch her go, pretending I was in the buggy, traveling away from the place that held so much misery.

And then, one day, it *was* me. Hope saw my distress and

the unkind way my father treated me after Charity was born, and she agreed to help me get away. I had waited in a grove of trees near the edge of town, holding my child, a cloth bag containing a few clothes, and a little money my mother had kept hidden in a jar in her kitchen. Hope picked me up and drove me to Washington, where she helped me buy a bus ticket. It took several bus rides to get to Kansas City.

The Salvation Army took us in, and the kind staff there gave me a job cleaning and cooking for the women housed at the shelter. They also helped me get my GED and find my first apartment. I worked at Betty's Café for a while, but then Sylvia met me and changed my life, teaching me how to use a computer and training me to be her administrative assistant at Harbor House.

Hot tears pricked at my eyelids. Maybe someday I'd get the chance to thank Sylvia and let her know I was okay. I couldn't believe she would suspect for a minute that I'd taken that money. But even as I tried to reassure myself about Sylvia's faith in me, doubt nagged at my mind, making me feel sick inside.

"How much longer, Mama?" Charity's words were slurred, and she could barely keep her eyes open. She'd be asleep before long.

"Just a little while, Cherry Bear. I'll let you know when we get close."

She blinked several times and nodded. Soon I could hear her quiet little snores. The sound brought me peace while the tires pounded out a steady rhythm against the road. Thankfully, the car seemed to be running well. If I still prayed, I would have been praying with all my might that it would get us to Kingdom without breaking down.

As I drove, more and more people from Kingdom began to flood my mind. Good people. It slowly became apparent that my father's unkindness had flooded out quite a few positive memories.

I tried to find something on the radio to keep my mind occupied. I searched for music that would soothe the apprehension building inside me, but stations were becoming faint and full of static. A sign we were approaching Kingdom. The modern world was beginning to fade away. Once again, I considered turning back. But the desire to protect my daughter drew me—along with some strange force that compelled me to keep going. If I hadn't walked away from the church, I'd have thought it was God's leading. But my father had made it crystal clear that God doesn't listen to people like me. Sinners. I'd been told that over and over as a child. And I'd tried so hard to be good. To be worthy of His love. Eventually I gave up. It was evident I'd never be perfect enough for my earthly father *or* my heavenly Father. Some people seemed born to always be on the outside looking in. If this was my destiny, I might as well embrace it. Fighting against it had proven useless.

Finally, I saw the turnoff that would eventually lead me to the only road that led to Kingdom. A little over an hour later I reached the city limits of Washington. I first met Clay there, at school, although we didn't really get to know each other until after my father made me quit school after eighth grade. The thought of Clay brought a familiar deep aching pain that had lived inside me ever since he'd abandoned me and his daughter. I quickly pushed him out of my mind. That was a door I was determined to keep closed for good.

Pulling off the main road, I parked in front of a popular

local deli. My father never knew that some of the "Kingdom kids," as we were called, left the school grounds during lunch and bought sandwiches there if we had money. I'd usually share a sandwich with Mary Yoder, a girl my age whose father was a lot like mine. Mary was a quiet child who did everything she was asked to do but without ever showing a spark of enthusiasm. Going to the deli was the one rebellious thing she ever did, and it was also the only time I ever saw her smile. As soon as she took a bite of that forbidden meatball sub, her expression changed and her blue eyes twinkled.

Unfortunately, before the year was over, I lost my sandwich partner. Someone tattled on us, and her father pulled her out of school for good. I'd still see her around Kingdom and in church, but she never spoke to me again. I was certain she was forbidden to have anything to do with me, since I'd been her partner in crime. I never saw another smile on her face.

I turned off the engine and checked out the deli. It looked exactly the same as it had back then—as if frozen in time. I turned around to check on Charity. She was still asleep, so I called her name softly. Her eyes fluttered open. At first she was drowsy, but when I told her we were stopping to eat, she sat up straight in her booster seat.

"Do they have cheeseburgers, Mama?" she asked, clutching her doll.

"I don't think so, honey. But they make the best sandwiches I've ever tasted." A look of disappointment flashed across her face. "But you know what? Their meatball sandwich is a lot like a cheeseburger. I think you'll like it."

With this encouragement, she smiled. "Can I have a pop too?"

"Yes, you can have a pop too."

Her happiness restored, we got out of the car and went inside. It felt good to stretch my legs. The pain in my hip had lessened, had turned from a deep ache to a small twinge, confirming my belief that there wasn't any serious damage. I breathed a sigh of relief.

There were a couple of tables open, so we grabbed one. The shop's only waitress hurried over and cleaned off the tabletop while I ordered two meatball sandwiches. About ten minutes later, Charity and I were happily munching away. The sub was as good as I'd remembered. The sliced meatballs were spicy and covered with thick red sauce. And the cheese was gooey and rich.

"This is the best cheeseburger I ever ate," Charity said, shaking her head. "I want all my cheeseburgers like this for-ever, Mama."

Her comment brought laughter from a family seated at a nearby table, as well as from our waitress. "How about some more?" she asked, motioning to our almost empty glasses.

I nodded. "Thank you."

She picked up our glasses and walked away, returning a couple of minutes later with refills. "You folks aren't from around here, are you?" she asked. She looked to be about my age, her long blond hair pulled back into a ponytail.

"No . . . Well, I used to be. It's been a long time since I've been back."

"You used to live in Washington?"

I shook my head. "I lived in . . . Kingdom."

"Kingdom kids, Kingdom kids. Watch 'em as they flip their lids." The taunts of some of the schoolchildren came back to me. Especially those who liked to rip the bonnets and hats from our heads. I watched the waitress's face for a sign of rejection. There wasn't one.

"Kingdom. Heard of it, but I don't know much about it." She smiled at Charity and me. "Hope you two have a real nice reunion."

"Thank you," I said, feeling relieved. As she walked away I reminded myself that I wasn't a child anymore. I was an adult who didn't have to worry about what other people thought. So why were nervous butterflies slamming into each other in my stomach?

We finished our lunch, and I paid the tab, thanking our kind waitress once again. As we were going out the door, a man was coming in. He held the door open for us, and I thanked him without actually looking at him. Charity and I were halfway to our car when I heard the door slam and a voice call out, "Elizabeth? Elizabeth Engel?"

I turned around, surprised to hear my name. The man who'd opened the door came toward us, a puzzled look on his face.

"I-I'm Elizabeth Engel. Do I know you?"

He smiled. "It's Roger. Roger Carson. You know, from Washington Elementary?"

Although his bright red hair had turned darker and his freckles weren't quite as noticeable, he still looked the same. *"Kingdom kids, Kingdom kids. Watch 'em as they flip their lids."* I suddenly remembered one of Roger's personal favorites. *"Lizzie Engel, Lizzie Engel. She's so ugly she'll stay single."*

"Hi, Roger," I said, without smiling. "It's been a long time."

His face lit up, and he grinned widely. Was he going to taunt me again? In front of Charity?

"Well, it certainly has. How are you? And who is this?"

As he looked at my daughter, I saw a look of bewilderment cross his face. Roger had been best friends with Clay. Was he seeing the similarities?

"This is my daughter, Charity. Charity, say hello to Mr. Carson." I tried to keep my voice steady, but I failed. It shook like an old woman's.

"Hello, Mister Carson," Charity said shyly. Actually, she said "Hello, Mistah Cawson." Charity had trouble with the letter *r*.

He smiled at her. "Nice to meet you, Charity. What a beautiful little girl you are. You look just like your mother."

"Thank you," I said. I felt my face flush while I tried desperately to come up with something else to say. I wanted to leave, wanted to get away from this man before he said or did something that would stir up old wounds. "So . . . so you still live in Washington?"

He nodded. "Yep. Never left. That probably sounds silly to someone like you who made it out, but I actually like it here. I took over my parents' dairy after Dad passed away. I still live in the same house with my wife and two sons. Mom is in the nursing home."

"Oh. Did you marry a girl from our school?"

He grinned. "Yes. Do you remember Mary Yoder?"

I'm sure my expression matched my shock at this revelation. "Mary Yoder? From Kingdom?"

"Yep. I snagged a Kingdom girl. Quite a feat."

I was so surprised I couldn't respond. How in the world did Mary and Roger end up together? I couldn't imagine a more unlikely pair.

"Where are you headed?" Roger asked.

"We're going to Kingdom to see my grandma and grandpa," Charity said proudly, her earlier shyness gone.

"Really?" he said with a smile. He looked at me. "Have you been back lately?"

I managed to shake my head.

He zipped his coat open and pulled a card out of the pocket of his jeans. Then he took a pen from his shirt pocket. "Listen, Lizzie, I know Mary would love to see you. I'm writing down our telephone number." He scribbled for a moment and then handed me the card. "I believe there are several phones in Kingdom now. Cora Menlo has one in the restaurant you can use."

I took the card from him and stared at the number for several seconds. Finally I said, "Thank you, Roger. I'll keep it in mind." I grabbed Charity's hand. "Now, if you'll excuse us, we need to get going." I turned and almost ran back to the car. Charity pulled at me, telling me I was walking too fast, so I scooped her up in my arms and carried her. I opened the back door and quickly fastened her into her car seat. As I pulled out into the street, I looked in my rearview mirror.

Roger still stood in the parking lot, staring at our car. I wasn't a little girl anymore, but I hadn't lost the terror of being bullied. Surprised that those raw feelings still existed in my psyche, I focused on beating back the shame that made my heart beat faster and my breathing speed up. The thought occurred to me that I was driving away from one source of pain in Kansas City and right into another. Would Kingdom be even worse?

CHAPTER / 5

I drove until the pavement beneath me changed to dirt. About ten miles later, my car bumping on uneven surfaces, I found the road to Kingdom. Almost hidden from sight, it cut through a large grove of trees. Anyone not knowing what to look for would surely miss it. I turned off onto a small lane not made for automobiles. As soon as I was certain my car couldn't be seen from the road I'd just left, I pulled over and got out.

A strange sensation had come over me when I'd made the last turn toward Kingdom. For the first time since I'd left the town I grew up in, I felt a twinge of homesickness. Not for my mother or for the friends I'd left behind. For the town itself. I stared down the road, wondering what awaited me. How would I be greeted? It was impossible to know unless I gathered up the nerve to complete my journey.

I'd stuck my keys inside the pocket of my jeans, and when I pulled them out, the card Roger had given me came out with them. After staring at it for a moment, I crumpled it up, jogged to the other side of the road, and tossed it down into the deep ravine that bordered the other side. It was a dangerous drop, and more than once horses and buggies had needed rescuing when drivers were careless about navigating the narrow path. I watched the card land in a snowdrift at the bottom. Roger had been so cruel to me and to the other children from Kingdom that I had no desire to call him or ever see him again. Besides, he reminded me too much of Clay. I briefly wondered if he and Clay were still friends. Probably not. Clay had been gone a long time.

I hurried back to the car and checked on Charity. She'd fallen asleep again not long after lunch. I smiled at her angelic face and wondered how my decision to come back to Kingdom would affect her. Charity had always been loved by the only parent she knew. If she experienced rejection because of me, what would that do to her? Even as I asked myself these questions, I was reminded that I had no other choice. I had to protect her from the known threats, and I couldn't afford to worry about what *might* happen.

The tiny town wasn't on any map, so surely no one from the outside world could find us there. Perhaps my father and the church might try to turn us away, but no matter what lay ahead, I'd find a way to make it work. At least until I could come up with another plan. I got back in the car and drove as slowly as I could, trying to miss all the ruts, but it was almost impossible, since snow covered everything. After hitting one rather large hole, the car jumped violently and Charity woke up.

"Are we there yet, Mama?" she asked, rubbing her eyes. "This sure is a bumpy place."

Cherry Bear, you have no idea how right you are. "We're almost there, honey. If you look out your window you'll soon see the town just over that big hill."

I glanced back at her in the rearview mirror, taking only a quick look, since watching the road was vital to our safety. The snow began to drift down from the sky again, and I feared that our journey would soon become even more treacherous.

Although the ground was now white, I could remember walking down this path in the spring, wild flowers covering the ground below the tall trees. Purples, blues, yellows, and reds had anointed the area like colorful patchwork quilts. I'd pick the flowers and bring them to my mother, who put them in a jar, decorating her drab kitchen with various shades of the season. Even Father seemed to like them, though he was opposed to almost everything beautiful or colorful. This attitude especially applied to our clothing. Our dresses had to be dark blue or black, with aprons in the same shades. In the winter we wore dark bonnets, and in the summer, black prayer coverings.

Not long before I left, Pastor Mendenhall introduced the idea of pastel-colored dresses for the women and white prayer coverings for the unmarried girls. The young women in Kingdom buzzed with excitement about the idea, but a few weeks later, the elders, under the direction of my father, quashed the notion. "This is the beginning of the world's leaven," Father had said in response to the pastor's suggestion. "It will introduce vanity and encourage impure thoughts in the minds of our young men. This idea has no place in Kingdom, and we will not have it."

The kind pastor, not wanting to start strife in the church, backed off. However, the pastor's wife, Bethany, quietly got up and walked out of the meeting when the elders' decision was announced. Since I took Charity and ran away not long after this incident, I never heard what fallout resulted from her rebellion, but her bravery helped me to make the decision to leave.

Although Kansas was known for its flat plains, the terrain around Kingdom was very hilly. The large hill that hid the town from prying eyes also made the last mile of our trip somewhat dangerous. My tires slipped and skidded up the sharp incline. As we finally made it to the top, the snow was falling more heavily, making it hard to see more than a few feet in front of the car. We were almost at the edge of town before the place I'd known as home so many years ago became visible through the misty white veil of winter.

"What's that, Mama?" Charity called out. She pointed to the large white structure on the corner as we approached the heart of the town.

"That's the church, Cherry Bear," I said. Kingdom Mennonite Assembly Church looked exactly as it had when I'd left. It was as if I'd only been gone a few days. The surprise came as I drove farther into town. Several of the shops on Main Street had been painted. Charity asked about almost every building we passed, so I tried to tell her about them.

A few of the businesses I remembered were gone, and there was at least one new sign painted on the front of another building, but the snow prevented me from reading it. The quilt shop was a lovely blue, and the café was crimson with white trim. Eberly's Hardware was yellow, and Menninger's Saddle and Tack, although it was still white, was trimmed with green. Green shutters, a green door, and green window boxes. The blacksmith shop, where my father worked when he wasn't at the church, looked exactly the same—bare wood weathered by time, and it still leaned slightly to the right. Some of the men in our church used to tease Father that in a strong wind the entire building would fall down. However, offers to help rebuild the structure were turned away. Father always said he would do the work himself, but somehow it never got done. Obviously nothing had changed. The large wooden sliding door was shut, meaning he wasn't there. I sighed with relief, since I really wasn't ready to deal with him yet.

"Mama, is this Kingdom? I think it's pretty."

I had to agree with her. But the biggest shock of all was the discovery that I wasn't driving the only vehicle in Kingdom. There were four others parked amid the horses and carriages hooked up to hitching posts in front of various stores. I saw two pickup trucks and two cars. One dark-colored car with its bumper painted black and another car that was bright yellow with shiny chrome bumpers. It was parked right in front of Cora's Corner Café. Some brave soul had certainly broken ranks with the status quo. I pulled over and gazed at the brightly colored restaurant.

Cora Menlo. I'd forgotten how kind she'd been to me. It had been very hard for her to get the approval of the elders to open her small business. In Kingdom, the elders basically ran everything. No one could make a move without first getting their permission. And anyone who wanted to become a part of our community had to seek an audience with the elders before putting down stakes. Of course, not everyone was considered holy enough to join our ranks. And God help the citizens who displeased them. Even though Cora had lived in Kingdom since she was very young, I could still remember how she trembled the day she petitioned my father all those years ago. Just as the elders could vote to allow someone to live in Kingdom, they could also vote to expel them.

"Women should stay home and feed their husbands,"

Father had insisted. "We have no need of a restaurant in this town."

"My husband is dead, Elder Engel," she'd said, standing in the kitchen of our small home, addressing my father. "I have no way to make a living."

"The church provides for you, Sister," he'd replied gruffly. "That should be good enough."

"But I'm a good cook, Elder. As you know, many of our men are without wives. They work in their fields but have no one to come home to. No one to cook them a good meal. This would be a service to the community. A ministry. I . . . I think there are a lot of lonely people in Kingdom who need companionship. And a place that feels like home." She'd cast her eyes to the floor. "And when a wife is sickly or with child, I could assist them. I see many ways my restaurant could benefit our people."

"Our people are benefited through the church, Sister. This is God's way. If you want to help our community, you may do so by joining the other women from our congregation who cook for others without expecting to be paid. I find it sad that you will only do a good deed if you are given money for it. Surely this does not please God." Father's dark, bushy eyebrows had knit together in anger. He wasn't used to being challenged, especially by a woman.

I'd watched Cora's expression as she faced my father. She jutted out her jaw and met his eyes without fear. Something I'd never been able to do. "Pastor Mendenhall said he thought it was a fine idea." She spoke these words quietly but with obvious strength, knowing the effect they might have on my father. He was frequently at odds with the pastor he and the other elders had elected. Our pastor, in my father's opinion, was trying to mix the world's leaven into the church by talking too much about love and forgiveness. Father saw these as bywords of the world, using them as excuses to wink at sin.

In my mind's eye I could still see his face as he glared at poor Cora. "I see you have already gone over my head. Why come to me then? Is it your plan to stir up strife so we will give in and agree to your proposal?"

Cora continued to meet Father's furious expression. "No, Elder Engel. I came hoping to receive your blessing. I have no desire to create strife in the church."

My father had taken two steps closer to the frightened woman. She immediately moved back. "I will take the Christian way and be a peacemaker," he'd thundered. "I will not contest this plan of yours. But do not expect to see my family cross the threshold of this . . . this restaurant." He spit the last word out as if it were rancid food.

Cora, obviously feeling as if she'd won the battle, scooted out of our house before her victory, albeit small, could be snatched away. I happened to catch my mother's quick smile as she returned to stirring a pot of beef stew simmering on our stove. That smile bothered me for a long time. It had never occurred to me before that my mother might actually disagree with my father about anything.

Cora got her restaurant. At first only single farmers and widows came to eat. But eventually, families drifted in and Cora's business was a success. True to my father's word, our family never stepped foot inside Cora's Corner Café.

I looked around at a place where change had always been unwelcome. But something had obviously happened in Kingdom. Change had come, welcome or not. Two women hurried out of the quilt shop, capes protecting them from the cold.

The dresses that peeked from underneath their winter cloaks were adorned with colorful printed flowers. One dress dark green, the other a deep pink.

"Mama," Charity said rather breathlessly, interrupting my musings, "this place looks like it's been here forever."

I laughed. "It hasn't been here forever, but it sure has been here a long time." After living in Kansas City, my daughter was certainly taking a step back in time. The buildings in Kingdom were old. Some of them going back to the very foundation of the town. The first settlers who called the area home were part of a thriving settlement called Mason City, named after its founder, William Mason. Mason had been instrumental in bringing the railroad to Kansas. Unfortunately, many years later the route was changed, leaving Mason City miles away from the railway line. That decision eventually turned the city into a ghost town.

Twenty years later, a disgruntled group of Old Order Mennonites, uncomfortable with what they saw as worldly and unrighteous changes to their faith and not willing to unite with their Amish brothers, discovered the abandoned city. They decided to build their own "Kingdom of God," the first name they gave their new town. Eventually, it simply became Kingdom. The aim was to mold the place into their vision of what God's kingdom on earth should be. They developed a sanctuary, hidden from the unwelcome attention of a sinful world.

Although people in nearby towns knew about Kingdom, almost everyone left them alone. Kingdom residents preferred anonymity, as did their neighbors. Folks who lived in the reclusive town weren't known for their welcoming attitudes. As a girl I recalled several occasions when a hapless fisherman or hunter accidentally wandered into town. None of them stayed long after being greeted by a resolute committee of Mennonite elders, dressed in their plain clothes, wide-brimmed hats, and obligatory beards, demanding to know their business.

A couple exited the hardware store carrying satchels and wearing the darker and more traditional clothing that I was used to. They got into a buggy and headed down the street toward the residential part of town. The business area was very small, but many of the people who live in the area were farmers, so the actual vicinity designated as Kingdom stretched out for several miles all around.

I drove to the middle of town and turned down Paradise Road, toward my family home. Apprehension caused my heart to beat wildly inside my chest, but, as I watched the houses pass by me, memories of childhood friends and fun times began to come alive in my mind.

Two blocks away from my house, a group of small children ran around in the front yard of a home where the Hoffmans had once lived. Their daughter, Callie, had gone to school with me. But these children couldn't be hers. Most of them looked several years older than Charity, and when I left, Callie had still been single. As I drove past they stopped their playing to stare at me. There might be a few cars in Kingdom now, but it was obvious they were still a novelty.

Several of the houses on Paradise Road had been painted colors other than white, the only shade once approved by the elders. I was seeing the seeds of a revolt. It was certainly about time.

My house finally came into sight—still white, of course, and looking in need of some attention. There was peeling paint, and a screen was off one of the front windows. The two-story structure was only a shadow of what I remembered, and I was amazed by how much smaller it looked.

I pulled the car over and stared at the place where I'd been born, trying to gather courage to go inside.

"I want outta the car, Mama," Charity whined. "I need to go potty."

"Okay, Cherry Bear. But wait just a minute, okay? I have to make sure Grandma and Grandpa are home. I'll be right back."

She wasn't happy about it, but my daughter nodded her assent. I wasn't being totally honest with her. I could see our horse in the corral and the buggy in the shed. But until I knew we wouldn't be turned away, I didn't want Charity anywhere near my parents.

I left the car running, even though the heater was almost useless, and I hurried up to the front door, dreading the response that might be waiting for me on the other side. I knocked lightly, and a few seconds later the door swung open. My mother's face registered shock.

"Hello, Mother. I—" was all I got out before she threw her arms around me.

"Lizzie," she said between sobs. "Lizzie, you are home."

I hugged her back, trying to blink away tears that sprang into my eyes. "I . . . I was afraid you wouldn't want to see me. . . ."

She put one hand on each of my cheeks. "You are my daughter, Elizabeth Lynn. There will never be a day when I do not want to see you." She studied my face as if trying to memorize it. "Are . . . are you home for good?"

"I don't know, Mother. I lost my job, and I need a place to stay for a while."

She bit her lip, and her already pale face turned even whiter. "Your father . . ."

"I know. But I had nowhere else to go."

"Shush." Mother took her hands away and dabbed at her eyes with her apron. "Your father is not at home now. We will talk and try to find a way."

"But the buggy . . ."

"He has ridden with Elmer Wittenbauer to a special meeting. He will not be back for a while." She looked out toward the street. "Is Charity . . . Is she with you?"

I smiled. "Of course she is. I'll get her."

"Oh my. Yes, please. I want to hold my granddaughter."

I hurried back to the car and helped Charity out of her car seat. "That's your grandma, honey," I told her. "And she can't wait to give you a big hug."

Charity looked past me and saw my mother standing in the doorway. She stared up at me, her eyes big. "Mama, why does Grandma look so funny?"

I knelt down next to her, pulling her red wool coat tight to protect her from the cold. "People dress a little different in Kingdom, honey. But it's okay. Your grandma knew you when you were just a baby, and she has always loved you."

Charity gazed silently at me for a moment. Something in my expression must have reassured her, because she suddenly beamed. "Okay, Mama. If she already loves me, then I should love her back."

I shut the car door and took her hand. As we walked up the stone path to the house, she suddenly let go of me and ran to my mother, her little arms flung out wide. Mother knelt down and waited for her, wrapping her up in a big hug.

"It's really cold out here," I said when I reached them. "Let's hug each other inside, okay?"

My mother nodded and stood up. "Please come in. I will heat up some cider."

Charity and I followed her into the house I'd left behind so long ago. It looked the same but shabbier. The wood floors were scuffed, and the furniture was in need of refinishing. My mother had obviously re-covered the couch and a chair. But a rocking chair that had once belonged to my grandmother sat broken and pulled to the side of the room. And an ancient bookshelf where religious books were kept was short one of its shelves.

"Why hasn't Father taken care of the house or fixed the furniture?" I asked. My father was a harsh man, but he'd always been faithful to keep our home and furnishings in good repair. He had prided himself on being able to fix anything that was broken, although he would never admit he had any kind of pride. Instead, he considered himself to be a good steward of the blessings he believed God had bestowed on him.

Mother gently removed Charity's coat and hat and held her hand out for my jacket, not meeting my eyes. "Things are a little different from when you left," she said quietly.

"I definitely noticed some changes in Kingdom, but that doesn't explain why Father has neglected our home."

Mother took our coats over to the coatrack on the wall near the door and hung them up. Then she pointed toward the kitchen. "Let us go into the kitchen, where it is more comfortable."

I glanced over at the fireplace. It was cold, and the wood basket kept nearby was empty. In the winter, it had always been stocked with wood.

I took Charity's hand and led her to the kitchen, where an old woodstove provided needed warmth. Mother's carved oak table and chairs, also once my grandmother's, looked the same. The tablecloth my grandmother had made for her beloved daughter was slightly more threadbare, but the stitched flowers were still vibrant. The middle of the cream-colored tablecloth contained a ring of blossoms in light pink and blue with yellowish green leaves, thin vines connecting each flower. All four corners were decorated with small bunches of blossoms, and on each end, hanging over the side of the table was a big blue flower.

Mother loved it so. When Grandmother Bessie Lynn passed away, it became even more special to her. Every stitch had been done with love, and I'd always been very careful not to spill anything on it. Right after Grandmother died, Mother tried to store the precious cloth in a trunk in an attempt to preserve it, preferring to use the old oilcloth covering we'd had on the table for many years. But my father had forbidden her to put it away. "Tablecloths are to be used, Anna. It is pride that makes you want to ignore the reason it was created." As was always the case, Mother didn't argue, just left it on the table. But every time a stain appeared, I watched her cringe.

I ran my hand lightly over the old tablecloth, wishing Grandmother were still here. She'd died a couple of years before I left Kingdom. I'd been named after her. Even though everyone called her Bessie, her actual name was Elizabeth Lynn. Frankly, I was surprised my father had allowed Mother to pass down the name to me. But she'd told me once, in a moment of unusual candor, that Father hadn't always been the harsh authoritative figure I'd only known. He'd actually been close to my grandmother at one time. I could still see

Grandmother's kind smile. She was the one who nicknamed me Lizzie when I was a child. Mother and most of my friends called me by that name, but Father refused to call me anything except Elizabeth. He never explained why, but to me it was just one more sign of his contempt for me.

"Mama, I need to go potty," Charity reminded me. "Real bad."

"I'll take her," Mother said. "You warm up. We'll be right back."

I watched the confusion on Charity's face as my mother led her outside to the outhouse. The day was going to be filled with new experiences for my daughter.

Some of the houses in Kingdom used generators to pump water through pipes, but my father had never seen the need to bother with that. Having to go outside on harsh winter nights was solved another way. I couldn't help but giggle when I thought of trying to explain a chamber pot to Charity.

A few minutes later they walked back up the path. Charity looked somewhat stunned.

"Mama," she said with dramatic emphasis when she came inside, "the potties here are just like the ones at the lake."

I nodded, having forgotten the trip we took to a state park once. It had taken me a while to get Charity to use the outdoor commode. She'd had a hard time believing there wasn't a regular toilet hiding somewhere nearby. "This is a bad potty, Mama," she'd said, wrinkling her nose. "It smells bad, and you can't flush it."

"You two sit here," Mother said, smiling. "I'll get the cider on the stove." She took an old pot from under the sink and filled it with cider from the propane refrigerator. Then she set the pan on top of the woodstove.

Mother had been cooking on this stove ever since she and Father married. It had two dampers. One that moved smoke out of the house and another that controlled how much heat went to the burners. Even though I'd loved my electric stove in Kansas City, I had to admit that this ancient cousin did a fine job. Mother was a whiz with it, creating wonderful meals with a minimum of fancy kitchen equipment.

I watched her as she worked. She seemed thinner. Mother had always been rather frail, but I'd never seen her back down from hard work. She was the kind of person everyone took for granted, because she never complained, never admitted to being tired or ill. Although I could remember her taking care of me when I developed colds or the flu, I couldn't actually recall her ever being sick herself. Mother had quiet strength and a graceful, ethereal beauty about her. Her large blue eyes were certainly mirrors to her soul. I'd always been able to tell how she felt by looking in her eyes.

"How about some butter cookies?" she asked Charity.

My daughter frowned. "I don't know what those are."

Mother opened the old cookie tin on the counter and withdrew several cookies, which she placed on a plate. "You try these, Charity. I believe you will like them."

I smiled and nodded at her. "Your grandmother makes the best butter cookies in the world. Trust me."

Charity picked up a cookie from the plate, still unsure about this plain-looking treat. She gingerly took a bite, and her face lit up. "These are really good, Mama. I love them."

My mother pushed the plate toward me. "Here, Lizzie. You have some cookies too."

It didn't take any additional prompting. I bit into one, the familiar taste igniting memories of sitting in this kitchen, warming in front of the stove, eating cookies and drinking cider before Father came home. The pleasant memory vanished at the thought of my father, and my stomach tightened the same way it had all those years ago when he returned from the shop or the church.

"So when will Father arrive?" I asked after finishing one cookie and as I reached for another.

"He should be home shortly." She frowned as she ran a finger down the stitching on the tablecloth. "Kingdom is different now, Lizzie. Your father . . ." She sighed and looked up at me, her smile tight. "There are younger people in the church who . . . well, who are pushing for change. They say the old ways are too restrictive, and that the love of God should be emphasized more than His judgment. Pastor Mendenhall is very supportive of this opinion. He has said that the true tenets of the Mennonite church stress grace, as does God's Holy Word. But your father and several of the elders do not agree." She hesitated, her eyes searching my face. "Your father insisted we leave the church, Elizabeth Lynn."

I couldn't hold back a gasp. "He . . . he's left? I don't understand. He's no longer an elder?"

She shook her head slowly. "No, and two of the church's other elders have gone with him. Three others remain and three new elders have been appointed. That is where your father is today, meeting with the men who departed. They seek to find a way to remove Pastor Mendenhall from office."

"How can they do that if they're no longer part of the church?"

"I do not know. But since Kingdom Mennonite Church was founded without the oversight of a larger governing body, there is no one to intervene." A tear rolled down her cheek.

"Your father is determined to start a war in Kingdom. I do not know what to do."

"And where do you stand, Mother? On which side do you find yourself?"

Her face turned pale and she looked away. I really didn't expect her to contradict my father, so her response took me by surprise. "I hate the way people have been treated in this town," she said, her voice trembling. "And I hate that my daughter had no choice but to run away." She reached out and took my hand in hers. "My Bible talks of a God of love and forgiveness. This is not the God your father purports to know so well. I do not want to be disobedient to his headship in our home, but I believe he and his friends are wrong."

I was shaken by her words. For some reason the smile I'd seen on her face when Cora defied my father drifted back into my mind. "So what are you going to do, Mother?"

She let out a long, tortured breath. "There is nothing I can do, Daughter. My job is to stand by your father even if I disagree with him. I am his helpmeet." Even as she spoke of acquiescence, a look of defiance painted her delicate features. "But I pray every day, Elizabeth Lynn. I ask God for His help to change our church and our community into a place that honors Him.

"My parents raised me in the Mennonite faith, and I was proud to be a part of such a wonderful, caring group of people. Our congregation was small, but we were a family. We loved each other because God loved us, and we forgave each other because He became forgiveness for us. Our modest dress was beautiful and worn out of respect for our God. It was not a prison uniform. But then we came to Kingdom, and everything changed. Here, we have become hateful and critical under the rule of men like your father. And I believe it stinks in the nostrils of God!"

Her sentiments were spoken with more emotion and passion than I'd ever seen from her. I was so shocked, at first I could only stare at her. It took several seconds for me to respond.

"Why didn't Grandfather and Grandmother leave Kingdom, Mother? Why did they stay if they disagreed with the way the church was run?"

Mother sighed. "My father died, and Mother had nowhere to go. So we stayed, and I married your father. But your grandmother never stopped trying to teach me the reality of who Christ really is. Her words of love still ring in my heart."

"They ring in mine too," I said softly. "I have to say that I'm surprised to hear you say these things. But I'm also happy to know that you don't agree with the meanspirited teachings that have caused so much pain in this town. Have you ever voiced your opinion to Father?"

"I have no intention of speaking my mind," she said with a sigh. "Especially now. If I anger him, he certainly will not allow you to stay. He is a man obsessed, Lizzie. That is why he does not take care of his duties at home or at work. I dare not cause more antagonism by challenging him about his view of our town's spiritual path. It would only destroy the uneasy peace that still exists in our home."

In all the years I'd lived in this house, she'd never stood up to my father. Not when he spoke hurtful words to me, not when he punished me for breaking one of his many rules by locking me in my room without dinner, and not even when he spanked me for things I hadn't done. It still hurt inside, remembering how she stood by in silence, never challenging him. Never standing up for me. I wanted to ask her why, but I wouldn't. Not because of any nobility in my own soul, but because I sensed her emotional fragility. No matter what I'd been through, I couldn't hurt her. The pain she'd already suffered through Father's lack of compassion had already pushed her to the limits of her strength—yet somehow she'd endured. I wouldn't be the one to push her over the edge.

"I understand." I glanced nervously toward the front door, wondering if I'd heard the knob rattle. Why was I still so afraid of him? I tried to remind myself that I was a full-grown adult and a mother myself. "What do you think Father will do when he comes home and finds me here?"

"I do not know. He is so bitter and resentful these days. I must admit that I am afraid."

"You don't need to be afraid for me—or for Charity. Father can't do anything to hurt me now. Nor would I allow him to harm Charity. I'm not a child anymore, Mother." I searched her face, seeing the fear etched there. "I won't allow him to hurt you either."

Her eyes widened. "He has never struck me, Daughter. And the discipline he applied to you was never violent. Your father believed it was entirely scriptural."

It took effort for me to swallow the anger that rose inside me. My father's discipline was never administered with love or concern for me. I fought to bring my emotions under control. I grasped my mother's hand with both of mine. "I'm out of options, Mother. Please try to convince him." I hoped she'd never think to ask me why I hadn't stayed in Kansas City and simply found another job. I didn't want to tell her about my stalker, nor did I want her to know about the charges of theft. Although I tried to convince myself that she would never believe I'd robbed the shelter, I couldn't be sure. She had to know I'd taken her money when I'd left town. Would she believe I'd also taken money from my employer? Even if she didn't, I had no desire to worry her.

She gently pulled her hand away and rose from the table. She took a pencil from a holder near the cookie tin and quickly scribbled a note on a piece of paper. "Take this message to Cora Menlo at the café. Tell her you need a place to pass the time for a while. I will remain here and wait for your father. Let me tell him of your return before he finds out another way. After that, I hope he will allow you and Charity to move back in with us." Her fingers shook as she handed the paper to me. "You must leave now, though. Hurry, before he arrives."

I got up and helped Charity down from her chair. When she begged for another cookie, my mother wrapped a couple of them up to take with us. We hurried to the door, quickly pulling our coats on. Before we stepped outside, Mother hugged us both so hard Charity said, "Grandma, you're loving me too much."

Even though my mother and I couldn't keep back our tears at having to say good-bye again, we both laughed at her comment.

"Go quickly," Mother said. "I will come to you when I have an answer from your father." She kissed my cheek. "And pray, darling girl. Pray very hard."

I picked Charity up and almost ran from the house, fear of my father's wrath filling me with a sense of alarm. Down the street, barely visible through the snow, I could see a buggy coming down the road. Knowing it could be one of my father's cronies giving him a ride home, I quickly started the car and pulled away from the house. I turned at the first corner, confident that even if Father had seen my car, he would have no reason to suspect his wayward daughter had returned. Then I drove back to town and pulled in next to the yellow car in front of Cora's Corner Café. The small restaurant seemed to be doing a brisk business. Buggies were lined up in front, their horses tied to the hitching post. Two trucks remained parked near the entrance door.

My emotions tumbled around crazily inside me. I was happy to see my mother again and thrilled she was glad to have me back. Yet I worried about her. How would my father react to her news? Maybe she was telling the truth—that he had never hit her. But I wasn't sure I believed her. Although I'd never seen him abuse her, I worried that if he was becoming angrier than he used to be, she could be in danger. As far as I knew, she'd always obeyed everything he said. Today, however, I'd seen a new fire in her. And even though she said she'd never confront my father's judgmental beliefs, the possibility worried me.

I got Charity out of the car, and we walked up the wooden steps to the café. I couldn't help but admire the difference the red paint had made to the old faded brick exterior. And the gleaming white paint on the door and the window trim set the color off beautifully.

Entering, we found the place nearly full. Tables and booths filled the room, and the wood floors gleamed. The walls were a mixture of wood paneling halfway up and red-and-white-checked wallpaper from the edge of the paneling to the ceiling. Quilts and painted plates hung on the walls, along with hand-stitched samplers. A fire crackled in the stone fireplace on one side of the room. Families in Old Order garb mixed in with farmers in overalls. Several women wore the lighter-colored dresses and white prayer coverings I'd noticed earlier.

The room was filled with the sound of folks talking and laughing together. However, several people stopped their conversation to turn and stare at me and Charity. I heard someone cry out, and Ruth Fisher rose from a nearby table. She hobbled toward me, one arm outstretched, the other holding onto her cane.

"Lizzie child, is it you?" she asked as she approached. She leaned her cane against the side of a table and put her hands on my shoulders. "My Lizzie," she said with tears running down her weathered cheeks, "are you finally home? *Ach,* I have prayed so long."

Ruth had been such a blessing to me as a child. I'd visit her house almost every Sunday afternoon between our morning and evening church services. She would bake soft white cookies topped with coconut in her ancient oven while she sang hymns in her native German tongue. Then we would eat her wonderful cookies and talk about the Lord. Her view of a loving God was just like my grandmother's, and so much different from Father's that I almost felt guilty listening to her. I never told anyone else what she said to me, fearing my father would find out and Ruth would get called before the elders. I didn't want her to get in trouble or risk losing the shelter her house had become.

"It's me, Ruth," I said with a smile. "And yes, I'm home. At least for a while."

"Bless my soul. And here is our Charity." She smiled at my daughter. "*Ach,* she was such a beautiful baby, but oh my, she has only grown even more lovely, *ja?*"

Charity grinned at the attention and didn't stare at Ruth's Old Order garb. It seemed she was getting used to the different clothing styles in Kingdom.

"Thank you," I said. "I'm so glad to see you, Ruth."

"How long will you be here? You will certainly come soon to visit me, *ja?*"

"I'm not sure yet how long I'll be in town," I said, "but I will definitely come by before we leave."

"You promise this, my Lizzie?"

"Yes, I promise."

Ruth's daughter, Myra, came up and took her mother's arm. "We must get home, Mother," she said, "before it gets worse outside."

"*Ja, ja.* I am coming." She leaned over and kissed my cheek, her eyes crinkling as she smiled. "You have made an old woman very happy today."

Myra smiled at me. "It's wonderful to see you, Lizzie. Please do stop by and visit Mother. She's mentioned you almost every day since you left. It would thrill her to spend some time with you."

I nodded. "Are you still living in the same house, Ruth?" At Ruth's age, I imagined she'd gone to live with her daughter by now.

"Of course I am, dear," she said. "Myra no longer tries to talk me into moving into her home. She has given up."

Myra shook her head and rolled her eyes. "My mother is nothing if not obstinate."

Ruth was renowned for her stubbornness, but those who knew her were aware that it was sparked by an indomitable spirit. Something she'd needed after losing her husband at an early age and having to support three children on her own. She came to Kingdom not long after he died because the church promised to help her and make certain her children were well cared for. Even though the original church was strict and watched over the old rules, they were true to their word. Ruth's family never went hungry, and her two boys and one daughter had everything they needed to live a comfortable life. The boys had moved out of state many years ago, but they had come back to visit whenever they could.

I hugged her one more time, and she and Myra left. The sound of chatter in the dining room, which had become subdued when Ruth called out my name, started up again with a vengeance. It wasn't hard to guess that Charity and I were probably the main topic of conversation.

I was leading Charity to a table across the room when someone grabbed my arm. I turned to find Abram and Miriam Zook standing behind us. I cringed, preparing myself for a sharp rebuke. Their reaction toward me after the community became aware I was pregnant still stung. Although the Zooks hadn't actually confronted me, they'd stopped speaking to me and even crossed the street when they saw me walking toward them on the sidewalk.

"Elizabeth," Miriam said, squeezing my arm. "We are so glad to see you. Abram and I have kept you in our prayers all these years, hoping God would lead you back to us." She put her arms around me. "We are so sorry for our behavior toward you. We should have supported you, should have been there to help you." She let go of me and shook her head. "I am ashamed to say that we were afraid, my dear. Afraid of the elders. Of your father. Can you find it in your heart to forgive us?"

I nodded dumbly while Charity watched us, a bewildered look on her face. We didn't usually garner so much interest.

After the Zooks went back to their table, several other people approached us. Some of them just expressing joy that we were home. Two more people admitted to remorse for not being more supportive toward me. It was overwhelming. Finally everyone returned to their seats.

"Why, if it isn't Lizzie Lynn Engel!" a voice rang out. "What in the world are you doin' here?"

I turned to see Cora Menlo's round, smiling face. She wore a dark blue dress with yellow flowers and green leaves, and over her dress was a red apron. I wasn't sure there was a color she'd forgotten. But even more surprising was her complete lack of a head covering. Her hair had been cut short and curled around her plump face. To my further amazement, I realized she was wearing makeup. I could only suspect that she had fallen away from the church, like me. She toddled up to us, clutching an order pad in one hand.

"My . . . my mother told me to give you this." I took Mother's note out of my pocket and handed it to her.

She read it quickly. "You poor little lamb," she said when she'd finished. "You come over here with me."

Charity and I followed her to a table in the corner, where she motioned for us to sit down.

"How about some dinner?" she asked. "What kind of food does this gorgeous little lady like?" She winked at Charity, who giggled.

"Cheeseburgers!" she said with glee.

Cora laughed. "I can fill that order. And how about you, Lizzie? Everything I'm servin' is on the menu board. Did you check it out when you came in?"

I shook my head. "I'm sorry. I didn't even see it."

She clucked her tongue. "Seems I remember whenever we had church dinners you always gobbled up my fried chicken. How about some nice fried chicken, mashed potatoes, and gravy?"

"That sounds wonderful," I said gratefully. "Thank you so much."

"No problem, honey." She glanced around the room. "I'll get it to you as fast as I can. Things are really hoppin' tonight, and my only waitress is too pregnant to help out anymore. How about startin' off with some nice hot coffee?"

"Please. But let me get it, Cora. You're too busy."

She studied my face. "Honey, you look exhausted. You stay right where you are and let me take care of you. I sure appreciate the offer, though." She grinned at Charity. "And a glass of milk for you, little miss?"

Charity shook her head. "Pop!" she declared with enthusiasm.

"Milk," I responded firmly. "You've already had your pop limit for the day."

Charity's bottom lip stuck out. "But I want pop."

"You know what?" Cora said. "Your mama always was the prettiest girl in Kingdom, and I heard tell it's because she drank so much milk."

Charity mulled this over, her mouth pursed in thought. "Okay, milk," she said seriously.

I flashed Cora a thumbs-up, and she scurried away to fill our order. I glanced around the room, feeling rather conspicuous but thankful that almost everyone had gone back to their meals. Those who met my gaze smiled warmly at me. This was a much different reaction than the one I'd received after Charity was born. The town really *was* changing.

But then I spotted John Lapp sitting at a table across the room. His expression was far from welcoming. After one angry glance, he refused to look my way again. He and his wife, Frances, had been my chief accusers. I could still remember Frances's scathing diatribe condemning me and my "ungodly behavior." I'd never denied that I'd sinned, and I'd told her how repentant I was. But that wasn't enough for Frances. I had a feeling that tarring and feathering me still wouldn't have fulfilled her need to see me punished. John was an elder in the church, cut out of the same cloth as my father. I'd bet everything I owned, which wasn't much, that John was one of the elders who'd left with him.

I looked the other way, ignoring John the same way he chose to disregard me. As a rather large family got up to leave, I noticed a young man who had previously been hidden from my view. He was sitting alone in the corner staring intently at me. His brownish blond hair curled over the collar of his blue denim work shirt.

For a moment I didn't recognize him, but it only took a few seconds before I realized the handsome man who seemed to find me so interesting was Noah Housler. I took a sharp intake of breath. He was even better looking than I'd remembered. I was so surprised to see him I couldn't seem to think clearly. What was he doing here? He'd left Kingdom a couple of years before I did, headed for college and life somewhere else.

It struck me as odd that, until that moment, I hadn't thought about Noah for years. He had been my best friend. We'd shared many happy times together, running around Kingdom, laughing and talking about almost everything. He'd been the most popular boy in the Washington school. Although Kingdom children weren't allowed to go further than the eighth grade, Noah's father had rebelled against the church elders and demanded that his son stay and graduate.

The main reason I liked school was because it gave me time away from Father and allowed me to spend time with

Noah. As we got older he spent most of his time at his family's farm, and in church, the boys and girls were carefully kept separated. But at school we had special classes and assemblies together, even though he was a year ahead of me.

Without warning, a memory popped into my mind that I hadn't thought about since I'd left Kingdom. My father had spanked me with a branch after some small infraction. I was eight years old and Noah was nine. He found me behind the church, crying. Instead of asking me what was wrong, he just came over and sat down next to me, holding out his arm so I could nestle against his shoulder. I'd never been that physically close to a boy before. It felt strange yet exhilarating. He smoothed my hair with his other hand.

"It will be all right, Lizzie," he'd said gently. *"I promise you that someday everything will work out. Don't be afraid. I'll watch over you."* We never talked about it again, but I knew he was looking out for me from that moment on. No one bullied me at school again without Noah warning them to leave me alone. I suddenly remembered the time he beat up Roger Carson not long before I left school. Roger had been teasing me, and Noah lit into him without a moment of hesitation. It was the only time I ever saw Noah lift a finger to another human being. He got in a lot of trouble for it, both at school and in church. He apologized, but I knew he wasn't really sorry. There were many times before I left when I wished he'd hold me again like he did the day after my father's whipping. But he never did. No boy did. Until Clay.

"Whatsa matter, Mama?" Charity said loudly. "Are you sick?"

The sound of Charity's voice made me jump. I'd been lost in my thoughts and was horrified to realize I'd been staring at Noah. I quickly looked away. "Hush, Cherry Bear," I said under my breath. "I'm not sick."

She screwed up her face with concern. "But you look all funny."

I frowned at her. "If you don't be quiet, I'm going to—"

"Lizzie?" a deep male voice said.

I looked up and found Noah standing next to me. My heart leapt into my throat. His emerald eyes bore into mine, and I couldn't find my voice.

He smiled. "It *is* you. I thought so."

I nodded like an idiot, unable to tear my eyes from his. They were even greener than I remembered. "Yes . . . yes it's me," I said finally, my voice squeaky. "How are you, Noah?"

His hands clasped his wide-brimmed black hat. "I'm fine. Still living at home, farming wheat and raising milk cows."

"But you went to college. I didn't think you'd ever come back to Kingdom."

"I did go for a couple of years, but my father died not long after you went away. That left my mother alone with my brother, Levi. He's a good man, but he's not a farmer. Never was. So I came home to help out."

"Oh, I'm sorry." And I was. Even though I was thrilled to see him, he was someone who'd had a chance at a better life. And here he was, trapped in Kingdom against his will, his dreams left unfulfilled.

He chuckled, a deep throaty sound that made my face feel warm. "I was glad to come home, Lizzie. You may find this hard to believe, but I never wanted to leave Kingdom in the first place. That was my father's plan, not mine. I happen to love it here."

If seeing Noah again hadn't been enough of a jolt to my system, hearing him say he actually wanted to live in this small backward town certainly completed my sense of disorientation.

"I don't understand."

He nodded slowly. "No, I guess you wouldn't. I heard that this town wasn't kind to you. But I believe those attitudes can change, and I'm determined to make that happen." He smiled shyly. "My brother and I were recently asked to accept eldership positions at church, and we're both working hard to bring a new spirit to Kingdom." He shook his head. "Unfortunately, your father doesn't understand. He believes our goal is to destroy what he and others have tried so hard to build." He gazed down at his hat, turning it round and round in his long fingers. "I won't say anything bad about your father, though. He's a good man who sees things in a different light than I do. I'm just sorry he dislikes me so much."

"I . . . I don't know what to say, Noah." I looked at my daughter, who was talking softly to The Princess. I swung my gaze back to Noah. "I truly hope you can make a difference here. This town has been a bastion of rules and regulations all my life. And God help those of us who prove too weak to measure up to the standard."

"I know, and I'm sorry, Lizzie. Sorry for your pain, and sorry that I wasn't there for you. If I'd only known . . ."

I tried to pull up a smile. "You had your own life to live. Fighting my battles was never your job, even though you seemed to think it was."

His eyes sought mine. "I liked fighting your battles," he said softly. "And I never forgot about you. When I came home and found out you were gone, I tried to find you. But no one here knew where you were."

I nodded. "I didn't tell anyone." I glanced over at Charity, who was still busy with her doll. I couldn't tell Noah I'd left town because of her. If she overheard me and understood, it would hurt her and devastate me.

Noah followed my gaze and seemed to understand. He quickly changed the subject. "So you're here visiting your parents?" he asked.

I didn't answer right away, trying to figure how to tell him we were here for more than a visit without going into details.

"I'm sorry. It's not my business . . ."

"Oh no. It's not that. I'm afraid there's no simple answer, Noah. Maybe one of these days when you have time, I'll tell you all about it."

He smiled at Charity, who had forgotten her doll and was now gawking at him with her mouth hanging open. I felt a rush of embarrassment.

"I'd like that, Lizzie. Maybe we could get together some-time soon?"

I nodded, trying to quell the nervous fluttering of anxious butterflies in my stomach. "Sure. That sounds good."

"Well, I'd better get back to the house. My mother will have dinner waiting."

I frowned at him. "If your mother's making dinner, what are you doing here?"

He laughed. "Cora makes the best apple pie I've ever tasted. I could never tell my mother that, so I sneak in here a couple times a week and order a piece. You just happened to catch me."

I grinned at him. "I won't tell. I promise."

"Thank you." He put his hat back on his head and said good-bye to Charity, who continued to stare at him with wide eyes. She didn't say anything in response to his gesture.

I started to chastise my daughter for being rude, but before I could get a word out, she took a deep breath, turned toward me and said, "Mama, this man looks just like Prince Phillip . . . from *Sleeping Beauty*." She fastened her gaze back on Noah, staring at him with an expression that bordered on adoration. "Are you Prince Phillip? My mama has been waiting for you such a long, long time."

CHAPTER 6

I tried to choke out an explanation of my daughter's fascination with the story of the sleeping princess while feeling the most mortified I've ever been in my entire life. Noah seemed to take it well. He just laughed, patted Charity on the head, and left. I could hear him chuckling all the way to the front door.

A family I didn't know, sitting at a table near us, found the entire episode very entertaining. I, however, did not.

"Charity Lynn, don't you ever say something like that again," I whispered to her. "Prince Phillip is a character in your movie. He isn't real."

"I'm sorry, Mama," she said, totally unconcerned about my severe humiliation. "But that man looks just like Prince Phillip. I really think it might be him."

I sighed, wondering how in the world I could explain to my little girl that there weren't really princes in the world who ride in on white horses and rescue sleeping princesses. But as I stared into her cherubic face, I just couldn't do it. "Please don't say that to anyone else, Cherry Bear. Okay? We'll have to keep that secret between us."

That seemed to satisfy her—for the time being. My daughter

loved secrets. The idea of having one would keep her quiet for a long time. I wondered if Charity's inappropriate remark had scared Noah away. I longed for the friend I'd had as a girl. The boy I could tell almost anything to. But Noah wasn't a boy anymore. He was a man, and I was a woman with a child. That old friendship was gone, replaced with polite banter. An almost overwhelming sense of sadness overtook me.

Cora brought our food, which was absolutely delicious. My first bite of her fried chicken reminded me how much I'd loved it when I was younger. Her meatball sub forgotten, Charity proclaimed Cora's cheeseburger to be the best she'd ever eaten. I'd noticed that she seemed much happier since we'd left Kansas City. I'd expected her to be somewhat insecure about leaving her home and her school, but that hadn't happened. Thinking about school made me realize that I'd need to make a decision about her education before too much time passed. Since I had no idea how long we'd be in town, I had no choice but to wait for circumstances to guide me in an appropriate path.

I glanced up at the clock on the wall as I finished my last bite of chicken. We'd been in the café for over an hour and a half. Where was my mother? As if answering my silent question, the front door of the restaurant swung open, and she came in, her black cape wrapped tightly around her. As she approached our table, I could tell she'd been crying. She sat down next to me, pulling her chair close.

"I am so sorry, Lizzie," she said quietly, trying to keep her voice soft so no one else could hear. "Your father refuses to allow you to come home."

Cora had come up next to us, probably to see if she could get my mother anything. She frowned at my Mother's statement.

"Charity," Cora said, "would you like to come and see my kitchen? I can show you where I cook all the food. And I might be able to find a nice piece of chocolate cake if your mother will allow you to have it."

"Chocolate cake," Charity said breathlessly. "My favorite food in the whole world."

I could have pointed out that whatever she was eating at the moment was her favorite food in the whole world, but instead, I just nodded. "That sounds great, Cherry Bear. You go with Cora, and I'll wait here with Grandma." I gave Cora a look of gratitude, and she smiled.

I waited until Charity was gone. "He's never going to forgive me, is he? Doesn't he even want to see his granddaughter? She was only a baby the last time he laid eyes on her."

"Oh, Lizzie," my mother said, wiping her eyes with a napkin she picked up from the table. "He is so embittered. Much worse than he was when you left. Truthfully, it would not be good for either one of you to be in our house right now."

"Well, that's great. Now I have nowhere to go." This turn in the road made it perfectly clear that the voice I'd heard telling me to come back to Kingdom wasn't God. I felt foolish for believing for a minute that He might be interested in my life.

"I do not know what to say, Daughter, but perhaps we can find somewhere else for you and Charity to lodge."

I grunted. "There aren't any hotels in Kingdom, Mother. And if Father won't take me in, I doubt anyone else will."

"Actually, they would."

I jumped, not realizing Cora had returned. She stood on the other side of my chair. "Charity's in the kitchen with her chocolate cake. She's fine." Cora sat down in the chair where my daughter had been only a few minutes earlier. "I overheard you say you have no place to stay." She patted my shoulder. "I have an offer for you, Lizzie. There's room for you here. In fact, there's an entire floor upstairs. Most of it's used for storage right now, but there's also space for bedrooms. My sister's stayed there when she's come to visit. There's only one bed up there now, but I have a cot in another room. You and Charity should be very comfortable. And with a little cleanin' and some additional furniture, we can turn that space into a very nice apartment."

"I-I don't have much money," I said slowly. "I'm not sure I can afford it."

Cora chuckled. "I'm not chargin' you anything, dear."

I shook my head. "I'm sorry, I don't understand. You're offering us a place to live rent free?"

Cora grinned at me. "And you want to know what the catch is?"

I nodded while the wind rocked the building with its bluster. I had no desire to take Charity out in the middle of a winter storm, but at the same time, a familiar sense of suspicion stirred inside me. It fought tooth and nail against that old saying about not looking a gift horse in the mouth.

"The catch is that you'll work for me, Lizzie. Since Julie left I've been tryin' to run this place by myself, and it's just too much for me. So I'm offerin' you a job and a place to live. All your meals will be free, and there aren't any other bills for you to think about. I can't pay you much, but since you won't be buyin' food, payin' rent, or worryin' about utility payments, I'm confident you'll do just fine." She frowned at me. "I don't suppose you've had any experience workin' in a restaurant."

I burst out laughing. "Yes, lots in fact." I briefly told her about my stint at Betty's.

Cora clapped her hands together. "How wonderful." She reached over and grabbed my hand. "It was meant to be, Lizzie. Isn't God good?"

I nodded dumbly, not knowing what else to say. So God had brought me to Kingdom to be a waitress? Great. That sounded about right.

Then, realizing that Charity and I weren't going to be thrown out into the snowstorm, I instantly felt ashamed of myself.

"Thank you, Cora. I'll gladly accept your offer. You have my gratitude."

She smiled. "And you have mine. I know we'll become great friends. And it's actually fun workin' here. There are still residents in Kingdom who refuse to darken my door . . ." She hesitated a moment. "Like your father," she said finally. "But for the most part, I've been accepted by the entire town. Even those who are a little more strict in their beliefs."

My mother sighed, looking around the charming, cozy restaurant. "This is the first time I have been inside in all these years. Not quite the den of iniquity my husband made it out to be."

Cora nodded. "Just families comin' in to eat. I wish Matthew would give us a chance. He might actually enjoy gatherin' together with his neighbors."

My first thought was to ask Cora if she'd ever actually *met* my father, but I let it go. He certainly wasn't the "gathering together with his neighbors" type. Not unless someone was being burned at the stake.

"I hope he will do that someday, Cora," Mother said. "But this is not a good time for him. Or for our church."

Cora raised one eyebrow. "I have to say I'm hopin' these

changes will actually bring us closer to God. To who God really is."

Mother shook her head. "I am afraid my husband does not see it that way. He believes the influence of the world will destroy us—that those who are promoting change will ruin Kingdom from the inside out."

"And what do you believe, Anna?" Cora asked.

Mother's eyelids fluttered at the question. She wasn't used to being asked her opinion. Was she already regretting her honesty with me earlier? Would she speak her mind in front of Cora?

Mother stared down at the table, running her fingers, reddened by work and weather, along the grain pattern in the wood. "It is my job to support my husband in whatever he does," she said softly. "But . . ."

She was silent for a moment, while Cora and I waited for her to continue. When she spoke, her voice trembled with emotion. "I lost my daughter and my granddaughter because of my husband's beliefs." She looked up, her eyes shiny with tears. "I must confess that I cannot believe that was God's will. I have been praying . . ." She gave me a tremulous smile. "I have been asking God for a sign that it isn't too late to have Elizabeth Lynn and Charity back in my life, and now they are here." She shook her head. "I must believe this is God's answer. That He has heard me."

She covered her face with her hands and took a deep breath. Then she put her hands down and glanced up at the clock on the wall. A look of panic crossed her face, and she quickly rose to her feet. "Matthew will be furious with me if I do not get home and make his dinner." She rested her small fingers on Cora's shoulder. "Thank you, my dear friend, for being an answer to prayer. I will never forget your kindness."

She looked at me, a single tear running slowly down her cheek. "I will find some things from the house to bring to you. Warm blankets, sheets, towels, whatever you might need." She straightened up to her entire five-foot height, her back ramrod straight, her expression determined. "I cannot come back on Monday because I have promised to work on a quilt with some of the ladies in the church, but I *will* return on Tuesday, Lizzie, no matter what your father says. And I will spend time with you and my granddaughter. In fact, we will have lunch together in this wonderful place. That is, if you will have me, Cora."

Cora's smile almost split her face in two. "I would be honored, Anna. And since your daughter now works for me, all meals for her family are on me."

My mother looked puzzled.

"'On me' means your meals are free," I explained.

Mother looked aghast. "Oh no. I could not—"

"Now, Anna," Cora said, standing up and facing her, "your daughter will earn every meal she and Charity eat, as well as yours. Trust me."

Mother considered this. "I will accept," she said with hesitation. "You have my thanks. I do not have many funds of my own and know that asking my husband for money to spend here would certainly bring a rebuke."

A sense of guilt swept through me when Mother spoke of money. I still hadn't apologized for taking what she'd managed to scrape together when I left. I couldn't do it now, with Cora listening, but I planned to apologize the first chance I got.

Mother came over and kissed me on the cheek. Then she hugged Charity.

"Bye, Grandma," Charity said. "Can you bring more butter cookies when you come back?"

Mother laughed. "Yes, I will do that." She smiled at all of us. "I was so distraught when I first arrived, and I feel so much better now. God's hand is evident, and I will thank Him for His provision tonight in my prayers. May He bless you all."

She hurried toward the front door, but the wind made it hard for her to pull it open. A man I didn't know rose from his table and held the door for her, shutting it after she was safely on the sidewalk.

"I hate to see her drive that buggy all the way home in this weather," I said to Cora.

"She'll be fine, child. Besides, there's no other way for her to reach her destination. You know she won't accept a ride in your car or mine. Trust me, I've offered transportation many times to some of these folks when the weather was bad. People like your parents just won't take it."

"So one of those cars outside is yours?"

She nodded. "Yep, that canary yellow job. Bought it from a guy in Washington about a year ago. And don't think there weren't some terse statements from folks in the church when I drove it home."

"Cora, do you mind if I ask you a question?"

"Sure, honey. You can ask me anything."

"Do . . . do you still believe in God?"

She chuckled. "Do you think buyin' a yellow car means I don't love God anymore?"

"No, of course not. But you're obviously living your life outside the boundaries of the church."

She smiled kindly. "Lizzie, I didn't lose God when I quit livin' the way a group of men told me to. God is bigger than that. I follow Him now without any help from the elders, and I've never been happier."

"Really?"

"Darlin', I may not walk into that building at the end of the block on Sundays, but I found out that God is much larger and more gracious than most folks give Him credit for." She frowned at me. "Look, people can act however they want; I don't make that my business. But I don't intend to allow anyone except the Holy Spirit to tell me how to run my life. I've discovered that God loves me just the way I am. And He doesn't care if I drive a car or ride in a buggy. He cares about my heart. You know, John the Baptist wore camel skins. Maybe I oughta serve folks locusts and wild honey while I'm prancin' around in animal skins. Think that would generate some interest from the elders?" She guffawed like she'd just said the funniest thing in the world.

Charity giggled along with her, although I was certain she had no idea what she was laughing about.

Cora's jovial expression gradually turned more serious. "Honey, one of these days you'll figure out that your heavenly Father isn't much like your earthly father. I'm sorry to say somethin' harsh about your daddy, but it's just the plain truth. God loves you, and He's not judgin' you." She reached over and patted my arm. "In fact, I like to think God carries around our pictures in His wallet and shows them to the angels every so often. 'Why, look at my Lizzie,' He says to them. 'Isn't she the most wonderful daughter any father could ever have?'"

I shook my head. "I doubt that's what He'd say about me."

Cora stood to her feet. "And that's where the problem is, isn't it?" she asked softly. "If you don't mind, I'm gonna pray that one of these days you'll understand how powerful the love of a good Father really is."

I didn't answer her, but her words struck something raw in my heart. More than anything I wanted to believe that God still loved me, but I'd done many wrong things and spoken rebelliously to Him more than once. I had no faith that He would listen to me even if I decided to talk to Him again.

"God is a righteous God, Elizabeth Lynn. He can't hear the voices of sinners."

"Looks like someone's gettin' sleepy," Cora said. Sure enough, Charity's eyelids were drooping, though she was fighting the approach of bedtime for all she was worth. I, for one, couldn't wait to close my eyes.

"Let me help you clean up," I said. The last of Cora's customers had gone, but several tables still held dirty dishes.

"Nonsense," she huffed. "You two are goin' to bed. Tomorrow is Sunday and the restaurant is closed, so sleep late. We'll do some work upstairs after a good night's rest. You've both had a long day."

I wanted to argue with her, but my tired body won out over my good intentions. "I appreciate everything you're doing for us, Cora. There's no way I'll ever be able to repay you."

She threw her head back and laughed. "You'd better wait until the Friday-night dinner rush is over. You may not feel the same way."

I got up and helped my sleepy daughter out of her chair. "If you had people lined up for a mile, waiting to get in, I'd still feel very fortunate."

"Oh, Lizzie," Cora said, putting her arm around my shoulders, "I'm only a vessel. God sent you here for a good reason. And before you leave this place, you'll know why. I'm just honored to be a part of it."

Charity and I followed her upstairs. My mind kept playing her words over and over. *"God sent you here for a reason. And before you leave this place, you'll know why."* Was it possible God really hadn't deserted me? Had He actually led me to Kingdom? I prayed silently as we mounted the stairs to our new home. *Please, God. If you're listening, and if you care anything about me at all, please help me to find my way. I'm not asking just for me. I'm asking for Charity too.*

For the first time in years, a small flame of hope ignited deep within my heart. But with it came a warning. Hoping for good things had brought only pain in my life. Would the path I was on lead to even more disappointment?

CHAPTER 7

I woke up Sunday morning when something soft brushed my cheek. My eyelids felt as if they weighed a pound each. I started to drift off again when I heard my daughter's voice.

"Mama, we're in a very strange place."

That got my attention, and I struggled to sit up. Charity leaned over the edge of my bed. She touched my cheek again.

"Are you up yet, Mama?"

"I am now," I said with a smile. "Why don't you change your clothes and let me try to wake up a bit more?"

She scooted out of the room while I attempted to find the willpower to put my feet on the floor. The bed Cora had prepared for me was so comfortable I didn't want to leave it.

The four rooms above the restaurant were in surprisingly good shape. Cora had explained that the building had been a hotel when Mason City was in its prime. And before Cora put in a restaurant, it had been used to store farm equipment and horse supplies. Avery Menninger, who ran the Saddle and Tack, purchased it and allowed other residents to use it for storage.

When Cora presented him with the idea of starting a

restaurant, he moved his and everyone else's things out. Avery, who'd never been much of a fan of my father or his friends, bravely went against the wishes of the church elders. Not long after Cora had stood in our kitchen, asking my father for his blessing, I overheard Avery tell James Hostettler, a local farmer, that it gave him a great deal of satisfaction to put a "burr under Elder Engel's saddle."

Avery, James, and several other men in Kingdom repaired, painted, and installed kitchen equipment for Cora. The rooms upstairs had also been cleaned up, but that was ten years ago. Now the wood floors needed to be polished, and the walls would certainly benefit from some fresh paint. But all in all, the entire area looked to be in better shape than I'd hoped for.

Last night, Cora pulled out the cot she'd stored in a closet and put fresh sheets on both it and the bed. After showing Charity and me around, she declared, "I only need one storeroom. That will not only give you and Charity your own bedrooms, it will also provide you with a living room. The kitchen downstairs is yours, as is the main bathroom. And there's a shower in the basement along with another small bathroom. Right now our electricity is run by a good-sized generator, but we got word that the electric company will reach Kingdom in the spring. Anyone who wants electricity can have it. I intend to be the first in line."

I was surprised that the electric company even knew Kingdom existed. Cora didn't elaborate, but I was fairly sure she was behind the move of modern technology to the small Mennonite town.

As I pushed myself out of bed, I couldn't help but think about Cora's incredible offer. Our own bedrooms, a living room, a fully stocked kitchen, and an indoor toilet. What else did we need?

Coming to Kingdom had been a journey made out of fear, yet I was beginning to think it might work out on a long-term basis. Reba and her cohorts would never find me in Kingdom, nor would the man who had stalked us in Kansas City. Charity and I were finally safe.

I sat on the edge of the bed and put my head in my hands. I'd have to give the situation some time to see how it worked out, but at that moment I didn't want to think about what might happen tomorrow. At least for now we were out of harm's way, and that felt wonderful. Today, Kansas City felt a million miles away.

I checked my watch. It was just now nine o'clock. As if on cue, the big bell in the church began to ring. Most of Kingdom's faithful would be finding their seats in the building's large meeting room. Although some churches would call that room their sanctuary, the term had been rejected by the elders as too worldly. As far as I was concerned, it was a good choice, since under the direction of my father, the church had never felt like a safe haven anyway.

Cora, who lived in a small one-bedroom house a couple of blocks from the restaurant, planned to meet us at the café sometime around noon. That gave me time to unpack and poke around a bit. Last night I'd brought our suitcases in from the car and tossed them on the floor, too tired to unpack. Cora had asked me to pull the car around back and park it in an empty shed so it wouldn't take up space in front of the café. It had taken several attempts to get it started. After the engine finally turned over, it belched and wheezed all the way to what I fear might end up being its final resting place.

I unzipped our suitcases so Charity and I could begin to sort our things and find a place to put them. There was a small dresser in the room I'd slept in, so we put what we could in it. I was delighted to find quite a few hangers in the closet, since I hadn't thought to bring any. They'd probably been left behind by Cora's sister. I wondered what would happen if she decided to come for another visit. Would we have to leave? I gazed around the apartment, reminding myself that the arrangement could be temporary. Maybe it wouldn't pay to get too comfortable.

Charity and I gathered our clean clothes and headed downstairs. A look out the window revealed several inches of snow on the ground. Although the wind still gusted, the sky was clear. There was absolutely nothing moving outside. The little town looked deserted. However, the deep ruts on the streets made it clear that many members of Kingdom's Mennonite church had climbed into their buggies and made the frigid trip to Sunday meeting.

Charity and I climbed down a narrow set of stairs that could only be accessed through the kitchen. They led us to the basement, where a metal shower stall had been installed in one corner. Charity and I took turns showering. It took a while for the water to heat up, so it was challenging at first. But all in all, the experience wasn't too bad. When I was a child in Kingdom, bathing meant waiting for water to be heated up on the stove before it was poured into a large tub in the middle of the kitchen floor. Most of my friends took baths only once a week, but my mother made me bathe twice a week. Discovering showers after I got to Kansas City was a revelation and a joy.

After washing, we went upstairs for breakfast. A previous

tour of the kitchen had availed me of all the pertinent information I needed to whip up a meal. Within thirty minutes Charity and I were eating scrambled eggs, bacon, and toast. I brewed coffee for me and poured milk for my daughter.

"I never had breakfast in a restaurant, Mama," Charity said. "But I like it."

I smiled at her. "I like it too, honey."

She turned her head sideways and gazed at me with a puzzled look. "Do we live here now?"

I stuck a forkful of eggs in my mouth to give me a moment to frame an answer. Then I swallowed and put my fork down. "I don't know, Cherry Bear. We'll probably stay here for now. How do you feel about that?"

She pondered my question for a few seconds before answering. "Well . . ." she said finally, drawing out the word. "I like Grandma very much, even though I don't like her potty. Not one little bit." She scrunched up her face to show her displeasure. Then she relaxed her expression into something more amenable. "But I do like her butter cookies. She hugs me too hard, but that's okay." She took a deep breath as she considered the rest of her answer. "I'm not sure about the funny way some people dress here," she said, "but I *love* all the horses. And I like this restaurant—and Miss Cora. She's a really nice lady. And I really, really, really like our rooms upstairs."

The look on her face suddenly turned serious. "There's nobody next door like in our other apartment. Sometimes they said bad things to me if I bounced my ball in the hallway. I'm glad no one's mad at me here."

I chuckled. "Well, you won't be able to bounce your ball in the restaurant when it's open, you know. And you'll have to find a way to keep yourself busy while I'm working."

"Miss Cora said I could help her. She's gonna give me a whole quarter a day." She searched my face to see if I was impressed. I tried to look properly amazed.

"When did you start calling her *Miss* Cora?" I asked.

Her brow furrowed with the gravity of her explanation. "Well, she *is* like your boss, and you told me to call your other boss Miss Sylvia. So I decided it was the right name for her." She raised her eyebrows. "Is that wrong?"

I shook my head. "Absolutely not. I think she looks just like a Miss Cora. Don't you?"

She giggled. "Yes, she does. I think we'll be very good friends."

"I do too, honey."

"Mama?"

"Yes," I said, chomping on a piece of bacon.

"If you start working here, do you have to dress funny like some of the other ladies?"

"You mean in long dresses?"

She nodded slowly. "And funny hats."

I shook my head. "Miss Cora told me I can wear whatever I want, so I'll just wear jeans and a nice blouse or sweater. And my comfortable shoes."

She thought for a moment. "What about an apron like Miss Cora?"

I laughed. "Yes, I forgot about the apron. I'll have one of those too."

"Good. I like them. They look cool."

I winked at her. "They are cool, aren't they?" I found it funny that my modern daughter liked aprons.

"Mama?"

"Yes?"

"Where is the TV? I'd like to watch cartoons now."

I swallowed hard. *This should prove to be interesting.* I explained to her that the TV was still in the car. I'd bring it in, but there might not be any TV channels available in Kingdom. However, I quickly reassured her that the DVD player would still work, and she would be able to watch all her movies. I had to explain the concept more than once, since in Charity's mind, anytime a TV is plugged in, shows just magically appear. But after going around several times about airwaves and cables, she finally decided that as long as she could watch her DVDs, Kingdom was still a good place to be. Our TV only got three channels in Kansas City anyway, so it wasn't really a big loss.

We cleaned our dishes and headed back upstairs. I'd gotten a broom and dustpan from the kitchen, along with some disinfectant and clean cloths. By the time Cora arrived, we had everything pretty well straightened up. I put out some of my pictures and a few knickknacks from home. And in the storage room we found a large wooden box that could serve as a toy box for Charity. Since it was empty and shoved in a corner, I hoped Cora would be okay with it. And she was.

"My, it's beginnin' to look pretty good up here," she said when she came up the stairs. "I have a few things in my car that should help. Why don't you two help me carry them in?"

We made several trips to bring in some colorful rugs, a couple of quilts, and a small mahogany bookshelf.

"Cora, this is wonderful. Perfect for our books. Thank you for letting us use it."

She waved her hand at me. "I'm not lettin' you *use* anything. All this stuff is yours—if you want it."

I hugged her. "Thank you. I know I keep telling you how

much I appreciate what you're doing for us, but I truly don't know where we'd be if it wasn't for you. You're an absolute angel."

She blinked her eyes and sniffed. "Don't remember ever bein' called an angel before. You're gonna make me cry if you don't knock it off." She wiped her eyes with the back of her sleeve. "I told Avery Menninger about you stayin' here, and Monday afternoon he plans to bring you some furniture that used to belong to his daughter before she moved away. It's nice stuff, Lizzie. And there's a proper bed for Charity."

She gazed slowly around the room. "Why don't we clean up these floors today before we move that furniture in? They could sure use some polishin'." She frowned at the walls. "We don't have time to paint, but I think if we wiped these walls down really good, we might get them lookin' a whole lot better." She grinned at both of us. "Are you girls game?"

We both said yes and spent the rest of the afternoon working to make the upstairs of Cora's Corner Café a livable space. We were able to fit all the extra items into the storage room. Then we polished the floors, cleaned the walls, and put rugs down. By the time we finished, it was beginning to look like a real home. As we'd moved all the things we couldn't use out of what would be our living room, we'd uncovered a large wood-burning stove sitting in the corner. It hadn't been fired up in a while, but it was in great shape and had been properly vented.

"I had that put in about three years ago," Cora said as we surveyed our handiwork. "I was hopin' my sister might think about movin' here, and I wanted to make things nice for her. But she won't leave Oregon. It's been her home all her life."

"Maybe she'll change her mind someday."

Cora shook her head. "No, I'm afraid not. She has multiple sclerosis, and travelin' that far is out of the question for her now. It's only her and me left. We had a brother, but he died a couple of years back, and our folks have been gone for a long time."

"She's not married?"

"No, she never did find anyone, but she's the kind of person who's happy livin' alone. Now me, I hate it. I miss my husband every day."

"You never had children, Cora?"

"We wanted them, but it just never happened. We didn't let it get us down, though. We had each other, and that was enough."

Cora and I carried logs from the large woodpile just outside the back door and placed them in a box next to the stove. I love fireplaces and could hardly wait to get some furniture in the room so we could start a fire and enjoy the cozy atmosphere. I also fetched our TV and DVD player from the car. Charity looked relieved to see them. We all went downstairs for dinner, tired but pleased by our efforts.

"You two sit here while I make supper," Cora said.

"Heavens, no," I said. "You worked too hard to be waiting on us."

She laughed. "I'm makin' some grilled cheese sandwiches and heatin' up some chicken noodle soup that's in the refrigerator. Not much work to that. I'll be back in a flash."

I gave up and stayed where I was. Sitting down for a while felt good. Within fifteen minutes, we were eating gooey, buttery, grilled cheese sandwiches. Cora's chicken noodle soup was the best I'd ever had. Much better than the soup from a can Charity was used to. She kept telling Cora how much she loved it. I was pleased that she enjoyed it, but I also felt a little guilty about not making more meals from scratch for my daughter. Of course, I'd been working a full-time job, studying for my degree, and taking care of Charity without the help of a husband. At the time I believed I had good reasons to cut a few corners, but in the end, the sacrifices I'd made hadn't paid off. My job was gone, and I had no way to continue my studies. It had all been for nothing.

Cora left around eight o'clock, and Charity and I went upstairs. We sat on the floor and played games for about an hour, and then I put her to bed in her new room. Her toy box was there, along with a beautiful rug and an incredible quilt that Cora had insisted we hang on the wall. A snowman stood in the middle, its stick arms held out to its sides, and a colorful scarf wrapped around its neck. Cups of hot chocolate with marshmallows on top decorated the corners. More marshmallows lined the quilt borders. A big black hat sat on the ground next to the snowman, and next to the hat was a carrot and lumps of coal. It was as if he wasn't quite finished yet. The whimsical quilt had been crafted by Hope Kauffman, and Charity fell in love with it at first sight. "Look, Mama," she said dreamily, "it makes me want hot chocolate with marshmallows."

I kissed her on the nose. "Me too. If you can stay awake a little bit longer, maybe I can make some."

Her dark eyes grew wide. "Oh, Mama. That would be . . . like magic."

I had to swallow the lump in my throat. There hadn't been very many *magical* moments in Kansas City. Bedtimes were strictly followed because I had to study every night and then get up early to take Charity to school or the baby-sitter.

On weekends, I'd spent almost all my spare time in front of the computer. Having hot chocolate together after she was supposed to be in bed was certainly a break in our routine. And as I gazed at my beautiful daughter, I knew beyond a shadow of a doubt that it was long past due.

I hurried down to the kitchen and easily found all the ingredients for homemade hot chocolate. A quick search of the pantry revealed a package of marshmallows. In almost no time at all I was carrying two large cups of hot cocoa up the stairs.

Charity had left her bed and was sitting on the floor in what was now our living room watching the snow drift down outside. I stopped for a moment and stared at her with a lump in my throat. She looked so sweet and innocent waiting for me, the glow from a nearby oil lamp highlighting her features. More than anything else, I wanted to capture that moment and keep it in my heart forever.

Finally I sat down next to her, and we watched the snow together, drinking our chocolate. We didn't talk much, just enjoyed the cozy room and the feeling that, at least for a little while, we were safe and everything was right with our world.

As Charity got back into bed, she smiled at me. "This was a good day, Mama. The best day of my . . ." Those were the last words she said before she drifted off.

I sat next to her, watching her sleep for a while, grateful that Cora had brought a couple of chairs from the restaurant upstairs so we'd have something to sit on. When I left Charity's room, I pulled the other chair up next to the window where we'd just been. I gazed out on a quiet, snow-covered town, no one stirring, the snow coming down lightly now. The only illumination came from a porch light installed next to the front door of the café. It was hard for me to believe I was back in Kingdom.

As I wondered what the future had in store for us, I soaked in a feeling of peace—something I hadn't experienced in a long time. But would it stay? Could I trust it? Or would the evil I'd sensed in Kansas City find a way to follow us here?

I left my spot by the window, headed toward my bedroom, and crawled into bed. That night I dreamed I was walking down a road bordered on both sides by bright wildflowers. But I was afraid to pick them, afraid of the deep, dark, and bottomless ravine that lurked somewhere behind their beauty.

CHAPTER / 8

Monday morning passed quickly. I was kept busy trying to learn Cora's way of doing things. All in all, it was easier than I'd anticipated, thanks to my training with Betty. Who knew I'd end up owing her so much? But as much as I appreciated Betty's help in my time of need, working with Cora was much more enjoyable.

Cora was like a calm tornado, cooking food, training me, and joking with her customers. Amazingly, she managed to do it without a hint of stress or strain. And although I didn't have access to all the modern conveniences available in Kansas City, the morning flowed without a hitch. Since there wasn't an electronic cash register, I figured change in my head. I actually enjoyed it more than dealing with the cash register at Betty's. Always on the fritz, it had definitely made my job harder. Checking customers out the "old-fashioned way" was refreshing.

One thing became apparent as I watched Cora run her kitchen. Even though she had a large generator, the building itself had a minimum of outlets, and they were used sparingly. Besides making coffee in old-fashioned metal coffeepots, she toasted bread on the grill instead of in a toaster. None of this appeared to cause her a second of concern.

However, this situation presented us with some interesting challenges upstairs. With our bedroom space heaters plugged in, we didn't have many outlets left for lamps. This was problematic, since we had no ceiling lights. In my bedroom, I used one of Cora's old oil lamps. I'd been brought up using them so it was no problem for me, but I forbade Charity to touch them. It was too dangerous. Fortunately we were able to plug in Charity's favorite bedside light. Another yard-sale purchase, it was adorned with pink butterflies and flowers, and my daughter loved it. Because it had three bulbs and we could select different levels of illumination, we kept one bulb on at night for her. Our living room had only one outlet for our TV and DVD player, so unless we wanted to plug it in and out all the time, we had to use the second oil lamp in that room.

Having to go downstairs to the bathroom at night was a problem too. I'd told Charity to wake me up if she needed to go, and I would light the lamp in my room and carry it with us. It was a lot of hassle, but it was obvious the situation wouldn't be resolved anytime soon.

When they set up her restaurant, even Cora's number one supporter, Avery, refused to help her with the electrical issues. Church members dared defy the elders only so much. Since no one from Kingdom would help, she hired someone from Washington to set up the generator and put in the outlets. The same electrician also helped her find good deals on used restaurant equipment. One of his customers had just gone out of business, so Cora was able to pick up a large refrigerator, freezer, grill, and dishwasher for a song. "When that nice man drove into Kingdom with my appliances, you'd have thought I invited the devil himself to town," she'd told me. "And when I had a phone installed here and at home . . . some folks stopped speakin' to me for a while." She'd shrugged. "Business fell off for a couple of weeks until my customers forgave me and started comin' back. A couple of the men told me they couldn't stay away 'cause their wife's cookin' wasn't anywhere near as good as mine." She'd covered her mouth with her hand, her eyes sparkling. "Now that's the kinda stuff we have to keep between us. Okay?"

I'd promised to keep her secrets, which wasn't hard, since I didn't have anyone to tell anyway.

"Funny thing is," Cora said after securing my vow of discretion, "now Avery has a phone himself. A lot of the farmers got 'em 'cause they need to be able to order supplies and things they can't get in Kingdom." She'd grinned widely. "I feel kinda responsible for helpin' them by bein' the first rebel." She'd chuckled. "You'll be surprised at all the folks champin' at the bit for electricity now. I may be the first one to sign up, but I won't be the last."

After the lunch rush, things slowed down long enough for a sandwich and a cup of coffee. I ate in the kitchen so I could visit with Charity, who'd been having a ball watching Cora cook.

"This is a very exciting place, Mama," she said. "I love it here, and Miss Cora is so nice to me."

"I'm glad, honey. So you're not bored?"

She shook her head. "Oh no. Miss Cora tells me stories, and I'm drawing all kinds of pictures." She gave me a very serious look. "I don't have time to be bored, Mama. I'm way too busy."

I smiled at her. "I guess we're both pretty busy."

Cora pushed open the door to the kitchen. "Avery's here with your furniture," she said. "Will you hold the front door open for them? And flip that Open sign over, will you? Don't need no one botherin' us for a while."

"Sure." I told Charity to stay put so she wouldn't get in the way. Then I jammed the last bite of my turkey sandwich into my mouth and hurried out front.

There were only a couple of customers left in the dining room when I got there. I turned the sign over on the front door and held it open. The cold December air rushed in, and I wished I'd grabbed my coat. The red apron Cora had given me to wear over my clothes might keep me safe from food stains, but it didn't offer much protection from freezing temperatures.

I stuck my head around the door to see Avery Menninger pulling a mattress out of the back of his truck. Someone else was assisting him, but he was on the other side, and all I could see were pant legs.

"Open it wide, Lizzie," Avery called out. "We got a lot of stuff to bring in."

I found it funny that Avery didn't say hello, just got down to business, even though I hadn't seen him in five years. He'd always been a very pragmatic man, and it was evident he hadn't changed much. I nodded at him, still trying to swallow my sandwich while wishing I hadn't shoved such a big piece of food into my mouth. Trying to chew it was proving more difficult than I'd anticipated. I pulled the door back as far as I could. There were several pieces of furniture on the truck, including a beautiful green couch, a dark wood dresser, and something that looked like a headboard for a four-poster bed. I hoped he had the footboard too.

Avery came up the stairs and backed into the dining room, his hands holding tight to the bottom and side of the mattress. He looked over at me. "Be obliged if you could keep that door as wide as possible, Elizabeth Lynn."

I smiled, unable to talk with my mouth full. At this point, I wanted nothing more than to spit out the uncomfortable piece of food. But I needed a napkin, and the closest table was still too far away for me to reach.

Avery pulled the mattress in almost all the way, but it seemed to get stuck. Whoever was on the other end was obviously having a problem. Wanting to help, I came around in front of the door, holding it open with one leg while I tried to help pull the mattress the rest of the way inside. Suddenly, something went horribly wrong. When I yanked on it, the mattress shot through the door, flipped over, knocked me down, and landed right on top of me. I took an involuntary deep breath, and the bite of turkey sandwich in my mouth lodged itself in my throat.

"Get that thing off of her," Avery hollered.

The mattress moved, and as I lay there choking, I found myself looking up into a familiar pair of green eyes. Noah Housler stared down at me, his expression a mix of alarm and amusement.

Although I realized I might possibly be lying at death's door, ridiculously, I couldn't help but think about how great he looked.

"Are you okay, Lizzie?" he asked.

I shook my head and pointed at my throat, wondering if anyone in Kingdom had ever heard of the Heimlich maneuver. I needn't have worried, because Noah pulled me up off the floor, wrapped his arms around me from behind, and pushed hard under my rib cage. The piece of sandwich lodged in my windpipe came flying out, almost hitting Avery in the face. Grateful to be able to breathe again and self-conscious beyond description, I tried to dislodge myself from Noah's arms.

"You can let go now," I said, my voice raspy from my near-death experience.

"If you insist," he said in a low voice.

I would have found having Noah's arms around me rather appealing if it hadn't been for the almost-dying-and-spitting-out-my-food thing.

Cora had come running out of the kitchen when she heard the commotion and was quietly retrieving the remains of my lunch from the floor while Avery stared down at it with something akin to disgust.

I wiggled away from Noah and turned to face him.

"Thank you," I rasped, certain my face was as red as my apron.

"You're welcome," he said, grinning. "But if you wanted my arms around you, all you had to do is ask."

I was so flustered I couldn't seem to form coherent words. "If I . . . ? If I . . . what?" was all I could manage to squeak out.

"Maybe we better get someone else to take care of the door," Avery said with a frown, looking concerned.

I cleared my throat. "I-I can hold a door open, thank you. I have no idea why . . ."

"My jacket was stuck on a nail outside," Noah interjected. "I'd set the mattress down so I could get free. That must be when you decided to grab it."

"I guess so. I was just trying to help."

Noah gave me a lopsided grin. "I appreciate that. But maybe next time you decide to . . . um . . . help . . . you could wait until we ask you?"

I glared at him. "I think I can handle that."

Avery's grunt signified that he wasn't as confident about my door holding abilities as his partner, but he grabbed the mattress once again, and the two of them carried it upstairs.

It took about thirty minutes for them to get all the furniture into our apartment, and after recovering somewhat from almost terminal humiliation, I was thrilled with the results.

"You two sit down and have some pie on me," Cora said when they'd finished.

Avery started to say no, but Cora insisted. "For crying out loud, Avery," she declared, "you give Lizzie all this stuff, and Noah saves her life. A piece of pie isn't too much to accept, is it?"

"I'd love some pie," Noah said before Avery could turn Cora down again.

"Then that settles it," she said. "You two have a seat." She pointed at me. "Why don't you help me, Lizzie? See what these two men want to drink."

Noah and Avery sat down at a nearby table, both of them asking for coffee. As soon as I reached the kitchen, I slumped against the wall where they couldn't see me.

"That may have been the most mortifying moment of my whole life," I said to Cora. "And believe me, I've had experience with all kinds of indignities."

Cora laughed loudly. "And just who are you worryin' about? Me? Avery? Or could it be that you're thinkin' about Noah?"

Charity, who thankfully had no idea she'd come close to

becoming an orphan, perked up immediately. "Is Prince Phillip here, Mama? Can I see him?"

I pushed away from the wall and pointed at her. "Charity Lynn Engel, you stop calling him that. And no, you can't see him. Not right now." I softened my tone somewhat when I saw her bottom lip start to push out. "He's in a big hurry, Cherry Bear. You can see him next time, okay?"

"Okay, Mama. But I still think . . ."

She caught my warning look and went back to her drawing. Of course, the piece of chocolate cream pie Cora handed her certainly helped to distract her from her illusion about Noah. All I needed was for her to run out there and start that prince stuff again. We'd definitely have to leave town after that, no matter what fate awaited us outside the borders of Kingdom.

I ignored Cora's question and grabbed the coffeepot. She chuckled as I pushed the door open and headed back into the dining room.

"Cora will have your pie ready in a minute," I said. "I hope you'll excuse me while I—"

"Here we go," Cora hollered. "Pie for everyone." She promptly slapped down four plates on the table. "Sit down, Lizzie," she ordered. "You need somethin' to make up for the lunch you lost."

My escape thwarted, I couldn't do anything but slump down into a chair next to Noah. To make matters worse, I heard the kitchen door swing open again. Charity came skipping out, holding on to her small plate.

"I'm comin' too, Mama," she called out. She immediately set her sights on Noah and headed straight for the empty chair on his other side. Before I had a chance to head her off at the pass, he got up and helped her into it. The entire time she never took her eyes off of him.

"How's that?" he asked when she was settled.

"Just lovely, thank you," she said, her eyes shiny with admiration. "You are a very nice man."

He grinned. "Why, thank you very much. And I think you are a very nice young lady."

Charity beamed as if she'd just been given a compliment from the real Prince Phillip. Somehow I needed to point the conversation away from anything *princely* before my daughter said something else I'd have to live down.

"So, Avery," I blurted out, "your daughter, Berlene. Where is she living now?"

Avery launched into a long story about Berlene marrying a man from Summerfield and moving there. It was just the kind of distraction I needed for Charity, who still hadn't taken her afternoon nap. As soon as her pie was finished, she started nodding off. Avery had just begun explaining why his new son-in-law, Herman, was a chucklehead for trying to grow soybeans instead of grain sorghum, when I was able to extricate myself by taking Charity upstairs for her nap. After I got her settled, I waited a while. By the time I ventured back downstairs, Avery and Noah were gone.

I checked the kitchen, where Cora was working on the evening's dinner specials. "You missed Noah and Avery," she said when she saw me. "Noah left this for you." She took a folded piece of paper out of her pocket and held it out.

"Thanks." I took it but didn't open it.

"You and Noah used to be such good friends," Cora said, "but you seem to be so uncomfortable around him now. Why is that?"

I cleared my throat and stared down at my shoes. "I don't know. It's just not the same. We're not children anymore."

"That young man cares deeply for you, Lizzie," Cora said. "I remember you two runnin' all over this town together. Seems to me it wouldn't be too hard to pick up where you left off." She didn't look at me, just kept stirring something that looked like gravy.

"I feel like I don't know him anymore," I said softly. "It's like we're strangers."

She smiled. "I don't think he sees it that way." She finally stopped stirring and turned to frown at me. "Maybe I'm wrong, but you don't seem to know how folks feel about you. I wonder if it's because you don't like yourself too much."

She waited for me to respond, but I was wiped out from making it through my first morning working in the restaurant, almost being smothered by a mattress, and nearly choking to death.

"I have no idea. But regardless, I'm sure he's not the least bit interested in any kind of relationship with me. No man in his right mind would want to spend time with someone who acted as goofy as I did today."

She shrugged and went back to her gravy. "I'm not tryin' to tell you your business, honey, but I hope you won't shut the door to possibilities. Life is full of 'em, you know."

Yeah, and so far all of mine have been bad. "Let's concentrate on tonight's dinner, okay? What do you want me to do?"

She sent me out to the dining room to clean up the tables, stock the condiments, refill the salt and pepper shakers, and make sure every table had sugar. I was about halfway through before I remembered the note from Noah. I pulled it out of my pocket and unfolded it.

Lizzie,

I'm so glad you've come back to Kingdom. If there's anything you need, I'm here for you. When you're not too busy, maybe we could spend some time together.

I've really missed you.
Noah

I reread the note several times before putting it back in my pocket. The idea of spending time with Noah stirred up something inside me I couldn't completely comprehend. But the thought of being near him made me feel happy. Maybe I'd take him up on his offer. I put the note back in my pocket and tried to concentrate on my work. But the rest of the day, I couldn't get Noah's emerald-green eyes out of my mind.

CHAPTER/9

The next few days passed quickly. Keeping my vow to Cora about not sharing her secrets proved to be one of the easiest things I'd ever done. I learned quickly that listening to her customers was a lot more interesting than talking about them. Exchanges between residents brought me a whole new perspective on Kingdom. Although being Matthew Engel's daughter caused some of Cora's customers to immediately halt their banter when I appeared at their table, most of them weren't quite quick enough. I caught several snatches of conversation before people had a chance to change the subject.

The number one topic of interest in Kingdom was the current upheaval going on in the church. Many of the older members were distressed about it, to say the least, but a majority of folks seemed to be all for it. Little by little, I began to understand that my father and his friends were in the minority, and that the rejection I'd felt when I'd gotten pregnant probably wasn't because people felt unkindly toward me. Most likely it was because they'd been too afraid to speak their minds and cross the elders. Many who had stayed silent back then began reaching out to me.

Except John and Frances Lapp, of course. Frankly, I was surprised they frequented the restaurant at all, seeing how my father felt about the place. Cora finally explained that Frances had been sickly for quite some time, and John couldn't cook. Although several of the women in the church helped them when they could, Frances and John relied on Cora's Corner Café to fill the gap. We didn't see them on Monday, but Tuesday, they walked through the door. Neither one of them seemed surprised to see me working. I was confident that by then news of my arrival and job at Cora's had spread throughout the town. When I started to approach their table, Cora, who had come out of the kitchen to see if I needed help, grabbed my arm.

"I'll take their order, honey," she said. "You don't need to put yourself through that."

I shook my head. "No, if I'm going to work here, I need to be able to serve everyone. I'll be fine."

She grinned at me. "You got guts, girl. But if you change your mind, all you gotta do is let me know. I don't expect you to deal with folks that are just plain rude."

"Thanks, Cora, but it's okay."

And it was. I casually walked over to take their order. Talking to me seemed to put them in so much pain they could barely move their mouths, but we got through it. And to my surprise, once when I brought them fresh coffee, Frances even let a thank-you slip out. It may have been accidental, but I told her she was welcome and gave her a smile. Maybe it was only a small victory, but I counted it as a real step forward.

True to her word, my mother came back on Tuesday around eleven. She brought all kinds of towels, sheets, and blankets with her. She also brought an entire tin of butter cookies.

Charity clapped her hands when she saw them, but I was mortified. The tin she used was the one I'd taken money from when I left Kingdom. After Charity left with Cora to take the cookies into the kitchen, I confessed to my mother.

"I knew you took the money, Daughter. It was saved for emergencies, and you had an emergency. My only regret is that it wasn't more."

"Thank you, Mother," I said, my voice catching. "I've felt guilty about it all these years. You were always good to me, and I took it without asking."

She was silent for a moment before saying, "I was not a good parent, Lizzie. If I had been better, I probably would have gone with you." She shook her head slowly. "The way your father treated you broke my heart. I challenged him about it more than once and asked him repeatedly to show you some compassion. I even went to Pastor Mendenhall, and he spoke to your father too. Our pastor believes in strict discipline, but he believes even more in love. However, our words fell on deaf ears."

I was surprised by the revelation that my mother had tried to help me. "I thought you turned a blind eye to his treatment of me."

She shook her head so violently, her bonnet almost slipped off. She reached up to adjust it. "Absolutely not. But I was raised to believe that married people should not air their disagreements in front of their children. It can cause confusion. This is why I confronted your father privately."

"But he continued to treat me like dirt, Mother. I never felt a moment's love from that man."

Tears spilled down her cheeks, and the anger I'd felt toward her turned to pity. My mother had been just as trapped as

I'd been. She'd tried to find a way to protect me without being disobedient to her husband, but it had been a war she couldn't win. Her visit today was in direct rebellion to my father. He'd clearly told us we were not to step foot inside Cora's restaurant, and Mother was purposely ignoring his mandate. I could only surmise that he'd also commanded her to stay away from me, but I had no intention of asking her if that was true. No sense in stirring up something best left alone. For the first time, it seemed that my mother had chosen me over my father. It made me feel wonderful and guilty all at the same time.

"Elizabeth Lynn," she suddenly blurted out, "I am going to say something that you may not believe, but I cannot keep silent about it." She clasped her small hands together as if she were preparing to pray. "Daughter, your father *does* love you. He loves you very much."

My mouth dropped open at her comment. "You've got to be kidding. He's never cared about me one day in his life."

She wiped her eyes with her napkin and daintily blew her nose. "Matthew was brought up by a very stern father himself. You never met your grandfather Engel because he died before you were born, but he was the hardest man I have ever encountered. He drove a spirit of severity into your father, and he has not been able to rid himself of it. I never heard your grandfather say a kind word to his son. Not one." She sighed. "It is sad, Daughter, but Matthew believes to this day that he has been a good parent. He has a difficult time understanding why you rebelled against him."

I was dumbstruck—but only momentarily. "He told me more than once that I was going to hell, Mother. What parent tells their child something like that? There's no excuse . . ."

114

She put a hand to her heart, as if she felt pain there. "You are not going to hell, Elizabeth Lynn Engel. You are loved by God and loved beyond description by your mother. I am so proud of you."

Her words, meant to comfort, only caused anguish. "How can you say that? I got pregnant, Mother. I knew better. I had a child out of wedlock. You can't be proud of that."

"Yes, you sinned, Daughter. But God still loves you. Do you not see this when you look at Charity? Is she not a blessing from Him? Our heavenly Father gives us beauty for our ashes, Lizzie."

I stared at her without responding. My daughter *was* the greatest blessing of my life. Why would God give her to me if He had rejected me?

The question rolled over and over in my mind the rest of the day. And that night before going to bed, I didn't actually offer another prayer, but I did manage to whisper, "Thank you for Charity," before I drifted off to sleep.

My first few days at the restaurant also brought some wonderful surprises. On Tuesday Ruth Fisher ate at the café. She and I tried to talk, but the restaurant was very busy. She invited Charity and me to her house Thursday night for dinner, so we could catch up without interruption. Cora quickly gave me permission to go, since Thursday night was always slow and she usually closed early. I could hardly wait to spend some time with my old friend and found that I'd missed her even more than I'd realized. She was a lovely substitute for my grandmother.

Wednesday morning, Noah came in for breakfast. We were so busy, there was no time to visit, but I gave him a note I'd written in response to his. I didn't want to seem too eager to accept his invitation, but at the same time, I really wanted to convey feelings that were a little stronger than just a casual friendship. I must have accomplished my goal, because when he read it, he smiled. Although we didn't have a chance to plan a time to meet outside work, the anticipation excited me.

Hope slipped in the door Wednesday afternoon. I was so happy to see her I almost spilled the coffee I was pouring for Harold Eberly, who owns the local hardware store and comes in for lunch every day. Thank goodness he caught my attention seconds before his coffee cup ran over. I apologized profusely, set the pot on his table, and hurried over to where Hope stood, just inside the door.

"Hope," I said, "I'm so glad to see you. I was going visit the quilt shop if you didn't make the first move."

"Oh, Lizzie," she said, "I heard you were back, and I could hardly believe it. Should I be glad or sad that you have returned to us?"

I smiled and gave her a quick hug. "Long story. Why don't you come over and sit down? As soon as I take care of Ebenezer Miller's egg salad sandwich, we can visit."

Hope's eyes darted nervously around the almost empty room. "My father doesn't know I'm here, and I'm not sure how much time we'll have."

"It will only take me a minute." I grabbed her hand. "Please. Just sit down and wait. I'll be right back."

She smiled and allowed me to lead her to a nearby table. I hurried to the kitchen, where Cora had just finished putting Ebbie's sandwich on a plate.

"Hope's here," I told her. "Do you mind if I take a few minutes to visit with her? After delivering Ebbie's sandwich, everyone will have been served."

"You go on," Cora said with a smile. "You're doing great and deserve a break. Charity and I are thinking about taking an apple pie break ourselves."

I smiled at my daughter, who was having a wonderful time learning how a restaurant kitchen runs. "Just a small piece, Cherry Bear. Okay?"

"Sure, Mama," she said, returning my smile. "But it's gotta have ice cream."

"Okay, but just a little bit."

She grinned happily. "Just a little bit."

I picked up Ebbie's plate and had just started to open the kitchen door when Charity called out for me.

I stopped and turned around. "Yes, sweetie?"

She stared solemnly at me. "I like it here, Mama. And Miss Cora really, really needs our help. I think we might have to live here forever."

"We'll talk about it later, honey. Okay?"

She nodded, not satisfied by my answer but willing to put the subject on hold while she ate her pie.

As I left the kitchen, I had to fight emotions that swung wildly back and forth between joy and fear. I knew she was as serious as a six-year-old child could possibly be, but I couldn't make her any promises yet. I was thrilled she was happy, but until I knew for certain we would be safe in Kingdom, I couldn't tell her what she wanted to hear.

I gave Ebbie his sandwich, checked his coffee, and hurried over to where Hope waited for me. As I sat down next to her, I noticed Ebbie watching us closely. Hope smiled shyly at him once before turning her attention to me.

"How about some coffee, Hope? Or a piece of pie?"

She shook her head. "I don't have much time, Lizzie, but thank you."

I marveled at how little she had changed. Her alabaster skin was still flawless, and her violet-blue eyes just as striking as I remembered. She looked a little paler, but it was winter and that could certainly account for it. Her blond hair, so light it was almost white, was wrapped in a bun and stuffed under her black bonnet. Wisps of hair that had escaped captivity framed her lovely face.

"Hope, I never got the chance to thank you for helping me leave Kingdom. I hope you didn't get in trouble over it."

"Papa wasn't very happy, Lizzie. Nor was your father. But I've never regretted my decision." Her eyes kept darting toward the front door. Hope's father was strict, but unlike mine, he was a just man. Why was she so nervous?

"How did the church react?"

She smiled. "Well, I was reprimanded by the elders, but I guess it could have been worse."

"I'm sorry, Hope. I didn't mean to cause you problems."

"Lizzie, if I had it to do all over again, I would do exactly the same thing. You were so unhappy." Her forehead creased in a frown. "I truly believe most of our residents wanted to support you—to comfort you. But many were too afraid of retribution. I regret we weren't braver."

I shook my head. "You were very brave. You have nothing to regret. And I'm learning that there is more love and understanding in this town than I realized. It's too bad we were all too timid to communicate better."

"I completely agree."

"So you and your father still run the quilt shop together?"

She nodded. "Yes, but since Papa has become more and

more involved with church business, I'm usually alone in the store."

"Church business? I understand my father and some of his friends are challenging the leadership."

"Yes, and I'm worried about it. My father has been friends with Pastor Mendenhall for many years, yet like your father, he also fears that if we relax our standards our way of life may suffer." She leaned in closer and lowered her voice. "Papa is meeting with your father and Pastor Mendenhall right now to try to bring some peace to our church. Even moments before he left, he still wasn't certain just where he stood on the issues being discussed."

I frowned at her. "And what's your view, Hope?"

Her eyes widened at my question. Were there any women in Kingdom besides Cora who had a mind of their own? I was beginning to wonder.

"I . . . I honestly don't know. I see both sides." She sighed and shook her head. "I have felt for a long time that we should show more love and forgiveness to the people in our congregation. Your situation is a perfect example. I'm still distressed that you felt you had to leave town to find peace."

"But?"

She stared down at her long, slender fingers. "*But* before this current unrest, our town was serene. There was no conflict. How can our current state of affairs be God's will? Would He want us to be at odds like this?"

"You mean the way the people were stirred up against Jesus? Didn't He say something about not bringing peace but a sword? That neighbors would be stirred up against neighbors?"

She looked startled at my statement, but not as much as

I was. Where had that come from? It was as if my mouth just opened of its own accord and the words tumbled out. I fought to remain calm and appear as if I'd meant every word I'd just said, but I felt a real sense of confusion. God and I weren't on speaking terms, and explaining His motives wasn't something I would attempt to do even on a good day.

"Oh, Lizzie. I never thought of it that way." Hope sat back in her chair and studied me. "Maybe trying to keep the peace isn't the best thing after all. Standing up for what is right is more important sometimes."

"Maybe," I mumbled, still baffled by my strange outburst.

I noticed Hope exchanging another quick smile with Ebbie Miller.

"Hope, is there something going on between you and Ebbie?" I asked. "You two keep looking at each other."

She blushed. "Papa and Ebbie's father are trying to arrange a marriage between us."

"Arrange a marriage? I know parents must approve unions in the church, but I had no idea they were actually being arranged. When did this start?"

"Perhaps I shouldn't have used the word *arranged*. I don't mean to give the wrong impression." She stared down at the tabletop for a moment. "My father and Ebbie's father are friends. They approached us with the idea of marriage, and we are both in agreement."

I frowned at her. "Do you love him, Hope?"

"We're getting to know each other, but only under supervision. You know how it works, Lizzie. You lived here for eighteen years."

"Yes, I know. But in every case I'm aware of, the boy and

girl fell in love first and then asked for permission. Seems to me that you and Ebbie haven't even fallen into *like* yet."

She laughed. "You have such an interesting way of saying things. But you're wrong. I like him very much." She held her delicate hands up. "What does *being in love* mean anyway? My mother and father were good friends and respected each other, yet they certainly weren't comfortable with public displays of affection. And they had a wonderful marriage."

I'd known Hope's mother before she passed away. Maybe they did have "a wonderful marriage," but I couldn't tell it by watching them. They were always very formal with each other—more like brother and sister than man and wife. Of course, what did I know? I'd only been in love once, and look how that turned out.

"Well, I hope things work out the way you want them to, Hope. Any man who marries you will be very blessed."

She blushed. "Lizzie, I've missed you so much. Talking to you is good for my soul."

"Look, I know you're concerned about your father's meeting, but it's liable to take a while. Why don't you let me make you something to eat?"

She glanced nervously out the window, toward the church. Then she nodded. "All right. You've talked me into it. How about a piece of Cora's wonderful peach cobbler and a cup of coffee? It sounds perfect on a cold, snowy day like today."

"Great, I'll be right back." I glanced out the window as I headed toward the kitchen. After the last storm, the temperatures had dropped even more, keeping the snow we already had from melting. So far, it had snowed every day since we'd arrived. Not so much that it added much accumulation, but just enough to let us know it hadn't moved on. I'd loved snow as a little girl, but after living in Kansas City and having to drive to work in it, I'd almost forgotten its ethereal beauty. I was suddenly filled with a deep sense of gratitude that long trips to work on icy streets were behind me—at least for a while.

Hope and I spent the next hour talking about Kingdom and its residents. She named those who had died since I'd left. I was sad to hear about the people who were gone. She also shared other events that had occurred in the lives of townspeople over the last five years. There were tragedies, but there were also reasons to celebrate, including marriages, births, and baptisms.

"I noticed that you painted the outside of your shop," I said. "How did that happen?"

She smiled. "I'd been begging Papa to let us paint it for quite some time. Then one day last summer, he suddenly walked into the shop and declared, 'If God thought enough of the sky to paint it blue, I don't see why we can't do the same with this old quilt shop.' And that was it. The next day he went to Washington and bought the paint. A couple of his friends joined in to help, and when they were done, we had a blue quilt shop." She laughed. "Papa may take a little time thinking things out, but when his mind is made up, no one except God himself can stop him. After he painted our shop, a few of the other business owners painted their buildings too."

I grinned. "So your father is the rebel behind the changes in Kingdom?"

Hope laughed. "No, the first person to paint was Cora. Papa was next."

"Well, he was still very courageous."

She nodded. "I'm so proud of him, Lizzie. He's not afraid to stick up for what he believes." She sighed. "That's what he's trying to do now, with the situation in the church."

"Hope," I said, changing the subject, "tell me about the school-age kids. Are parents still taking their children to meet the Washington bus?"

"We have our own school now," she said with excitement. "Leah Burkholder teaches classes in the old feed store that August Gretz used to own."

I frowned. "The state allows it?"

"It was very easy to set up. All we had to do was register. They've never questioned us."

"Does school stop at the eighth grade?"

She shook her head. "Although there have been decisions that allow some communities like ours to remove children from school after the eighth grade, our elders decided that trying to challenge the law might bring unwanted attention to our town. Their priority is to keep Kingdom away from the eyes of the world."

"And what is the law?"

"In Kansas children are supposed to be educated until they are eighteen. At that time, they should either receive a diploma or pass a GED test. It's not unbendable, though. Parents can give permission for their child to leave school at sixteen or seventeen if they want to. It's up to them. As you know, many of our people farm and need their children's help. But with a long summer break and flexibility when it is needed during harvest, there haven't been any major problems. So far, everyone has elected to complete their education. Leah has proved to be a very effective teacher, and the children love her."

"She always was very bright. Does she charge for her services?"

"The church provides her a salary so the parents don't have to pay. It isn't a lot, but it's enough for her to take care of herself."

"She doesn't live with her parents anymore?"

"No, she has a room in the back of the school building. She's more comfortable there. If you remember, the Burkholders' farm is located quite a long way from town. In the winter, it was very difficult for her to ride back and forth."

"So she and I are both living in the center of town," I said with a smile. "When I get the time, maybe I'll pop over and visit her. If we end up staying in Kingdom for a while, I'd like to enroll Charity." A thought jumped into my head. "Will the church allow my daughter to attend classes if we're not church members?"

"Yes, the church now supports the school for all the townspeople, not just for church members. It wasn't this way until your father left the church. So his leaving makes it possible for his granddaughter to attend school. Strange turn of events, isn't it?"

"Yes, more than strange." Figuring out how to get Charity in school had been my last major hurdle. Since the Washington bus didn't come to Kingdom when I was young, we had to ride two miles in buggies until we reached the nearest bus stop. I could still remember frigid mornings, sitting in a buggy and praying the bus would hurry because it was so cold I could barely stand it.

Parents took turns carting us to the stop. Everyone had a closed carriage except for Leah's folks. The days her father drove were the worst. There was no protection against the freezing temperatures except to huddle underneath the comforters we covered ourselves with. My favorite ride was with Isabelle Martin's father, a jolly man who liked to make us laugh. He hung a key on a string at the front of the buggy, next to window. He told us it was the key to his ignition. Although we took it as a joke, every time he carried us, we would keep our eyes peeled to see if he really used that key. In the summer, he'd brag that his buggy had air-conditioning and then roll up the side flaps. In the winter, his wife would put hot water into large, plastic milk containers. These would be placed on the floor at our feet, and they helped to keep us warm.

Since leaving Kingdom, I'd convinced myself that our trips to school were a hardship. As I thought about them now, I realized I'd completely forgotten how much fun we had.

Hope finished her cobbler and went back to the shop, promising to visit again soon. I was so glad she'd come by. Having someone like Hope in my life might help to fill the empty spot caused by saying good-bye to Meghan. Anyway, I hoped it would.

Everything seemed to be falling into place for me and Charity. A job, a place to live, a new school. Almost as if our coming back to Kingdom really was meant to be.

By the end of the workday on Wednesday, I felt I was getting a good handle on the restaurant and was actually enjoying my new job. Even so, I could hardly wait to go upstairs to our apartment after Cora closed for the night.

The furniture Avery brought was gorgeous. I found it surprising. Kingdom was known for its commitment to plainness, yet Avery's daughter, Berlene, had bucked the trend and purchased some pieces my father would not have approved of. The couch was huge and covered in dark green brocade with stitched flowers and carved wooden arms. A matching chair with an ottoman sat near the couch, and a creamy beige occasional chair with carved arms and legs took up a place in the corner. A mahogany accent table held our TV/DVD player, and a decorative trunk stored our DVDs. The beautiful four-poster headboard I'd spotted in Avery's truck had indeed come with the footboard. The white French Provincial bed was gorgeous, and Charity loved it.

When I lit the fire in the evening, our makeshift living room was so cozy and comfortable it almost brought tears to my eyes. I'd never had such a beautiful room before. Over the fireplace, Cora had hung a painting she had stored in the basement. Paintings were looked upon with suspicion in Kingdom, but there were a few rebels who had them in their homes. This painting was one that Cora's sister had created. It was of a Kansas prairie. Dark gray storm clouds rolled across the sky, but a ray of sunshine had managed to push its way through. Its unearthly glow turned the wet wheat field below into a shining blanket of gold. It was beautiful and powerful. I'd tried to turn Cora's gift down, explaining that her sister would want her to hang it in her own home.

She'd chuckled. "My house is full of Georgia's paintings. And besides, I have a feeling this picture is just for you. I know there have been storms in your life, Lizzie, but God's love is still shining through. Maybe when you look at this picture, you'll remember that."

I had to admit that since coming to Kingdom, my soul was beginning to change in ways I hadn't anticipated. Maybe I wasn't ready to start teaching Sunday school yet, but my hard heart was softening. I'd even begun to miss church. With my father and his supporters gone, would Charity and I be welcome? I had no intention of donning a prayer covering or wearing a traditional black dress to the service, though. Cora had been thinking about attending church again too. After talking about it, we decided to wait until the current situation came to a conclusion. If my father and his friends won, Cora and I would never be embraced by the church. If they didn't come out on top, there was still no guarantee we would be allowed to darken the doors, but at least there was a chance.

Charity ate dinner with Cora Wednesday evening, but I'd been so busy I'd missed out. So before climbing the stairs to our apartment, I went to the kitchen and made myself a meatloaf sandwich. With my plate and a glass of iced tea, I was ready to enjoy our night. I'd been so tired from work on Monday and Tuesday, I'd just stuck a DVD in the player and slept while Charity watched one of her favorite movies. But tonight I felt more lively and decided to read to my daughter.

Charity's favorite book was *Dragonspell* by Donita K. Paul. I found it at a used book store not long after we moved to Kansas City. Charity loved the adventurous story of the slave girl Kale, and I did too. I'd promised myself that I'd find the other books in the series, but I hadn't done it. Instead we'd enjoyed the first book over and over and over. It had been well read and well loved. You could tell by its dog-eared pages and torn cover.

I read several chapters until Charity's head began to nod. With a promise to read more another night, I carried her to her room. Her beautiful new bed had a thick rose-colored comforter and pink sheets. Cora had painted the large wooden box in Charity's room a gleaming white. Then she added pictures of a beautiful princess dressed in pink, a dragon, and a handsome prince.

Oddly, the prince looked a lot like Noah. Charity loved it so much she couldn't keep her eyes off it. There wasn't a dresser for her yet, so we kept her clothes in the box and her toys in the chest in the living room along with the DVDs.

After tucking her in, I wandered back to the living room, feeling a sense of belonging I couldn't remember experiencing before. Maybe my life was finally on track. Even if my father never spoke to me again, I had my mother and Cora. And Hope. It was more than I'd had in Kansas City. I was actually starting to understand my mother's motives, and it seemed that almost everyone in Kingdom I'd thought was against me really hadn't been. Had I been at fault in believing the town wanted nothing to do with me? Was I the one who closed doors that could have stayed open?

I was turning these questions over in my head when I drew back the drapes in the living room to see if it was still snowing.

An orange car sat parked across the street. The porch light outside the restaurant illuminated the driver's-side window. I could see the smashed-in front bumper and the man who sat inside, wearing a red ball cap.

CHAPTER / 10

I watched the man from behind my curtain until he drove out of town. Trying to push back the terror that gripped me in its cold grasp, I was extremely thankful my car wasn't still sitting out front. There was no way he could be sure I was in Kingdom. I was certain he hadn't followed us here. I would have seen him at some point along the trip.

Was he really a stalker, or could he have something to do with the missing money in Kansas City? He'd shown up right about the time Reba took over her position at Harbor House. Was it possible that Reba had been planning to set me up even before I met her boyfriend? The man in the red cap certainly didn't look like anyone in an official capacity. Frankly, he was pretty scroungy. But what other explanation could there be? Yet if he was connected to Reba, why send those terrible notes? It just didn't fit. The idea that someone else had mailed them didn't make much sense. It seemed like too big a coincidence.

The questions rolling around in my head were giving me a monstrous headache. What did the man want? How had he found his way to Kingdom? Only Meghan knew the name of my hometown, but she had no idea how to find it.

I thought about some of the recent changes in town. To start a school, Hope said they'd had to register with the state. That meant there was a record somewhere. Maybe information from Meghan and the records from the state could lead someone to my door. But why would Meghan tell anyone at Harbor House where I was? Had she been pressured for information?

I couldn't stop the tears that slid down my face as I weighed my options. Actually, there weren't any. There was really only one thing I could do. Charity and I had to leave before the man in the red cap found us. If someone from Harbor House *had* sent him, I could lose my daughter. And if he was here for another reason . . . Well, that outcome could be even worse.

A little after two in the morning I rolled out of bed. It only took me thirty minutes to get dressed and pack our suitcases. Focusing on the task at hand, I refused to allow myself to think about the comfortable rooms that had begun to feel like home.

I left Charity sleeping. Might as well warm up the car first instead of dragging her out into the cold. Carrying two of our suitcases out the back door in the kitchen, I trudged through the snow to the shed, where our car sat. I slid the big door open, unlocked the car, and put the suitcases in the trunk. Then I turned the key in the ignition, hoping it wouldn't make too much noise and wake anyone up who might be nearby. Nothing. No grinding, no popping, nothing. I turned the key again, stomping on the gas pedal and commanding the car to start. No spark of life. It was completely dead, and I had no idea how to get it started. All I could do was sit in the cold, dark interior and cry.

For a split second, I wondered if I could borrow a car, but as soon as the thought popped into my mind, I dismissed it.

This wasn't Kansas City. This was Kingdom, a place where transportation options were bleak at best. There weren't many cars in Kingdom, and all of them belonged to people who really needed them. Besides, even if I could get my hands on a car or truck, how could I ever bring it back?

"What are you doing to us?" I cried out to God, my voice echoing in the silence. "You send us here for this? You gave us a home to take it away? You know I didn't take that money. Why don't you help me?" My sobs made it impossible to speak for several minutes. Finally I prayed the only thing I could. "Please, God, help me. I don't know what to do. Please show me mercy. Unless I find a way out of this mess, I could lose Charity, and she's all I have left. You're my only hope, God. There's no one who can save us but you."

When I got so cold I couldn't feel my nose any longer, I got out of the car, grabbed our suitcases, and went upstairs. Charity was still asleep. I unpacked and climbed back into bed, lying there until the front door opened at five o'clock. I closed my eyes as Cora trudged up the stairs to wake us.

"Lizzie, honey," she said softly, when she opened the door to my room, "time to get up."

I mumbled something as if I'd been asleep and waited for her to leave. After the sounds of her steps faded on the stairs, I got out of bed, got dressed, and woke up Charity. We were both downstairs by five thirty. The café opened at six, so while Cora fired up the grill and mixed up the pancake batter, I turned on the lights, filled the small cream pitchers, made sure the sugar, salt, and pepper shakers were full, and then put out eating utensils, napkins, and water glasses. The sun was still an hour away from rising, and the low lights in the restaurant gave the place an eerie glow.

I couldn't help glancing out the front windows. Would the man in the red cap walk in the door this morning? If he wanted to catch me, I was certainly making it easy for him. I'd thought about telling Cora I was sick and hiding upstairs, but I couldn't do that to her. Besides, the situation was out of my hands. There was no way of escape that I could see. All I could do was hope that God had heard me and that somehow He would save us.

Right at six o'clock, people began filing in. Even though it was winter, farmers still had to feed their livestock and maintain their equipment. They were always our first customers. After that, other residents would filter in little by little. I got busy serving everyone while keeping my eyes on the front door. By lunch the man in the red cap still hadn't shown up. Around two, Mother came in and I took my lunch break, leading her over to a corner table in the back. I made us both sandwiches and sat down across from her.

"Mother, I need to talk to you," I said, keeping my voice low. There were only a couple of customers on the other side of the room, but I couldn't take a chance that anyone would overhear us. As she listened silently, I told her everything. About the man in the red ball cap and the real reason we left Kansas City. "So we really did come here because we needed a place to stay," I said finally, "but I've been a lot more concerned about losing Charity than I've been about losing my job."

"And you believe this man has followed you because of the missing money?" She grasped the edge of the table like a drowning person clinging to a lifeboat.

"I don't know. Unless he's just some kind of crazed stalker, there's no other reason I should be attracting his attention." I sighed. "To be honest, I'm so confused right now. I can't think straight. This morning I started wondering if I shouldn't just confront him—ask him what he wants. At least that way the truth would finally be out in the open."

Mother shook her head, her eyes frightened. "Oh no. Please do not speak to him, Daughter. He must not know for certain that you are here." She let go of the table and held out her right hand. I grasped it in my own. "When strangers come to our town, the elders approach them to find out why they are here. Would this not be a better way to handle the situation? Your presence in town would not be uncovered this way."

"I . . . I don't know. You mean the current elder board? You certainly don't mean Father. He'd sooner turn me in than look at me."

She let go of my hand. "Elizabeth Lynn, your father would not betray you. You two may not see eye-to-eye on everything, but he does not appreciate strangers who come to our town to cause trouble."

"No, Mother. I don't want Father involved. As far as the current elder board . . . Let me think about it. The problem with your suggestion is that if this man asks them if I'm here, they won't lie. I'm afraid your plan won't really help me much."

"Then what *can* we do, Lizzie? I do not want to lose you again."

I sighed. "I don't know. If I had an answer, I'd tell you. I tried to leave this morning—to take Charity and get out of town, but my car wouldn't start."

"Oh, Daughter. Please do not go away again. I could not bear it." Tears ran down her cheeks.

"What choice do I have, Mother? What about Charity? I

can't allow anyone to take her away, and I can't leave her here." I hesitated, not wanting to hurt my mother. Unfortunately, I had no choice. This was the time for honesty. "I won't let you keep her. I'm sorry, but I won't allow Father to treat my daughter the way he treated me."

Mother nodded slowly as she wiped her face with her sleeve. "I understand. I really do. But would she really be better with strangers?"

I locked eyes with her. "Yes, she would be better with strangers."

Mother made a strangling sound and stood up. "I . . . I am sorry," she stammered. "I must go."

I watched in shock as she turned to leave. "Mother, I didn't mean . . ."

She turned and looked back at me, sadness in her face. "Yes, you did. You meant every word." She tied her cape at the neck. "I will come back tomorrow, Lizzie. Please forgive me for being hurt by your comment. I am certain I deserve it, but these are not easy words to hear from your daughter." With that she hurried out the front door.

I felt even worse than I had earlier. Besides Charity, my mother was the one person who really loved me, and I'd just caused her pain.

The rest of the day I worked quietly, shifting back and forth between fear and guilt. I kept my eyes on the front door and the street, but the man never came back. By four o'clock, I was beginning to believe he wasn't really the stalker from Kansas City. A lot of people have orange cars and wear red baseball caps. And besides, it had been dark outside, the only illumination coming from the porch light outside the restaurant. Maybe my eyes had tricked me. Even though it made me feel better to consider that possibility, I knew in my heart that since strangers were rare in Kingdom, the chances were astronomical that the man I'd seen wasn't the one who'd been following me.

By five thirty there were only a few customers left in the restaurant, so Cora told me to go. Since my car wasn't running, she let me use her vehicle to drive to Ruth's. Cora lived close by, so she told me to drive the car back to the restaurant and she'd walk in the morning unless the weather was bad. If that happened she'd call so I could pick her up. Cora's car was much newer than mine and drove beautifully. Before turning off on the road to Ruth's, I took a quick tour around the town, looking for the orange car. I didn't see it anywhere. Charity and I pulled up to Ruth's around six thirty.

"Where is this lady's potty, Mama?" Charity asked, casting a suspicious eye toward Ruth's small white house.

"I don't know," I said truthfully. Ruth used to have an outhouse, but I had no idea if she still did. "But even if it's like Grandma's, I want you to show good manners."

Charity crossed her chubby little arms and scowled at me. "If it's outside, I'm not goin'."

"I guess that's up to you. We'll just have to see how long you can hold it, huh?"

She nodded solemnly. "I guess we will."

Before we made it to the porch, Ruth opened the door and held out her arms. "My two beautiful girls are here!"

When we reached her, she hugged both of us. "Let us go inside, where it is warmer, *ja?*"

Charity and I followed her into her living room, where a fire blazed in the large fireplace. It was toasty in the cozy room.

135

"Let me take your coats," she said with a smile. "Supper is ready. Are you hungry?"

Charity frowned as she slipped off her coat. "Are we having cheeseburgers?"

"Charity Lynn!" I said sharply. "That's not good manners."

Ruth laughed. "Charity, you have it right. I have made you a German cheeseburger."

"What's a Ger . . . Ger . . . man cheeseburger?" my daughter asked skeptically.

"I bet I know," I said with a smile.

"*Ach,* I am certain you do," Ruth said, grinning. "If you two ladies will follow me, we will start our supper."

"Can I ask one question?" Charity's feet were planted firmly in one place, and it was obvious she wasn't moving until her qualms were put to rest.

"Yes, you may." Ruth faced her, trying to match her serious expression. Even with everything weighing on my mind, I had to stifle a laugh. The sight of the silver-haired elderly Mennonite woman, dressed in black, bending down until she was almost nose to nose with my dark-haired little girl was funny and precious.

Charity put her little hands on her hips. "Just where do you keep your potty?"

Ruth straightened up, the deep laugh lines around her eyes creased with humor. "Perhaps it would be best if I showed you."

"I think that *would* be best," Charity said with a frown.

Ruth took her hand and led her to the hallway off the kitchen. Then she opened a door. Inside was a bathroom with a regular toilet.

"Does this meet with your approval?" she asked my subdued daughter.

Charity smiled up at her as if she'd just given her a new doll. "Oh yes. Thank you very much. We can eat cheeseburgers now."

"*Ach*, I am so glad." Ruth winked at me. "I hope you will follow me to the dinner table."

"Yes, thank you." Charity trotted past us, headed down the hall toward the kitchen, the source of the wonderful aromas that filled the house.

I started to follow her, but Ruth grabbed my arm. "My son and his wife put it in for me this spring," she whispered. "They told me they would not allow me to use the outhouse any longer, since I fell on the ice last January."

"Oh, Ruth. Are you okay?"

"*Ja*, I am fine." She wrinkled her nose like a little girl. "But I am so glad they forced this new room upon me. I do not miss trips outside when the temperatures dip below zero."

I smiled. "I understand."

"Good. Now we eat, *ja*?"

"I'd love it. And thanks again for inviting us over."

Ruth put her arm around me. "*Ach, liebling.* It is I who rejoice that God my Savior has brought you back to me. I have prayed for you every day since you left and have missed you more than I can say."

I hugged her. "Thank you, Ruth. I've missed you too."

"Are you two ever gonna come in here?" Charity called from the kitchen. "This stuff is smellin' pretty good."

Ruth chuckled. "I think our presence is being requested for supper."

"I agree."

We spent the next hour reminiscing while we ate warm *bierocks* straight from Ruth's oven. Ruth sliced Charity's meat pie open and put a slice of cheese inside along with a dab of mustard. Charity loved it and asked for another. We also had homemade applesauce and apple plum streusel for dessert. For a while I forgot about the man in the red baseball cap.

"The next time you come over, I will make you the white cookies you loved so much," she said as she poured me a cup of coffee. "Do you remember them?"

"Of course I do. And I also remember all the wonderful Sunday afternoons we spent in this room. I can't tell you how much they meant to me."

Ruth opened her mouth to respond but was interrupted by a loud, insistent knock on the door. "Excuse me," she said. "I am not expecting anyone and cannot imagine who would visit me now."

I felt my heart drop to my feet as Ruth left the kitchen. Had the man in the red cap tracked me here? I got up and grabbed Charity out of her chair, scooping her up in my arms.

"Mama, what are you doing?" she yelped. "You're hurting me."

"Be quiet," I hissed. "We need to leave." I hurried over to Ruth's back door and grabbed the knob. Even as I said the words, I realized how futile my actions were. We wouldn't get far in the snow. We were trapped, and I was frightening Charity. I took her back to her chair while trying to soothe her confusion. I'd just taken my own seat when I heard a male voice thunder from the next room. I held my breath as heavy footsteps headed toward Ruth's kitchen. I could only stare at the doorway until the owner of the voice stood inside it, glowering at me.

I looked up into the angry face of my father.

CHAPTER 11

Father and I stared at each other for what seemed like an eternity. A familiar fear coursed through my body, but when I saw it mirrored in my daughter's face, something rose up inside me.

"Hello, Father," I said, my voice quivering. I took a deep breath and gathered up my courage. "It's good to see you." I sounded strong and self-assured, even though I didn't actually feel that way.

His eyes took in my jeans and sweatshirt. I'm certain he also noticed that I wore a little makeup. The look on his face spoke volumes.

"I would have appreciated hearing you were back in Kingdom from your own lips," he snarled, his bushy black eyebrows knit together in a tight frown. "Instead, I find out from your mother."

I sat up straight in my chair and smiled at Charity, who looked at me with wide, frightened eyes. The tension in the room was obvious to her, and I needed to reassure her that everything was all right. When she saw me smile, her face relaxed some, but she gazed at my father's furious expression with alarm.

"I wasn't sure you would welcome the news, Father. That's why I spoke to Mother first."

"So you crept into town like a thief?"

That did it. I stood up, pushing my chair back. "No, Father. You see, I'm not a thief, so there's no reason for me to act like one—or feel like one. I'm more than willing to talk to you and to let you see Charity while I'm here, but only if you can refrain from threats and intimidation. I won't put up with it anymore. The choice is yours."

Ruth, who'd been standing off to the side, walked up next to me and took my hand. "I will not have anger or violence in my home, Elder Engel," she said, addressing my father. "I do not mean to be disrespectful, but I will determine what is allowed in my house, not you."

Father swung his menacing eyes toward the small woman who held my hand. Expecting him to unleash his full fury on her, I squeezed her hand tighter. But to my surprise, her words seemed to ease his rage.

"There will be no such actions today, Sister," he said. "And I am no longer your elder, so you do not need to address me as such."

Ruth bobbed her head slightly. "I understand the church procedures, but I will still show you the respect due your previous appointment until I deem it is no longer appropriate."

His features softened further. "Thank you, Sister Ruth. I appreciate that."

His eyes locked on mine. "Your mother informed me that a stranger has come into town who has ill intentions toward you. This matter has been turned over to the elder board, and the man will be dealt with. You have no more reason to fear him. I came here to tell you this. Now I will take my leave."

I'd asked my mother to wait on approaching the elder board. Obviously she'd gone against my wishes. Apprehension filled me. I wasn't convinced this was the way to handle things. Instead of helping me, the action could actually lead the man in the red cap right to my doorstep.

"Have they talked to him yet? I . . . I'm not sure this is what I want."

He shrugged. "I have no idea, but the situation is now out of your hands. We have a responsibility to protect this town. It is distressing that one of our own put us in an unsafe position. I hope your rebellion against God will not cause further peril to our good citizens."

I opened my mouth to fire back a sharp retort when suddenly Charity spoke up.

"Mama," she said softly, "who is this man?"

I had a choice to make, and I had to make it quickly. Taking a deep breath, I said, "This is your grandfather, Cherry Bear."

The uneasiness on her face melted. "My grandfather?"

I nodded.

She got down from her chair and scurried up to my startled father, wrapping her arms around his legs. "Do you know my grandma?" she asked him. "She's a very nice lady who makes good cookies."

I cocked my head to the side and stared at my father, challenging him to respond to his granddaughter. He stood there like a statue, his mouth quivering as if he wanted to speak but couldn't find the words. Finally Charity let him go and eased back toward her chair, looking quizzically at my father's face. Then she turned toward me.

"Is Grandpa mad at us?" she asked.

I shrugged. Let him deal with his own attitude.

"I have said what I came to say," he said in a low voice. "Now I will leave. Thank you for your hospitality, Sister Ruth." With that, he whirled around and stomped out of the house.

Charity watched him walk out, confusion on her little face. I went to her and wrapped my arms around her. "Honey, Grandpa is mad at Mama, not you. You're a wonderful little girl, and I don't want you to feel bad. It's not your fault. It's mine."

She squeezed my neck. "Why would anyone be mad at you, Mama? You're the nicest person I know."

I chuckled and hugged her tighter. Then I helped her back into her chair and slumped down in mine. I felt completely drained. Ruth silently warmed up my coffee. I could tell the confrontation with my father had disturbed her.

"I'm sorry, Ruth," I said. "I had no idea he was coming over tonight."

She shook her head. "It is not your fault, Lizzie. I must confess that I do not understand Matthew." She put the coffee-pot back on the stove and slowly took her seat. "He has not seen you in all these years, yet his heart appears to be just as hard as when you left." She let out a long, slow sigh. "He has been instrumental in bringing strife into our church, and it worries me. I believe in being submissive to authority, but I cannot disagree with those who say change must occur. It is not an easy time for any of us."

I took a sip of coffee and put my cup down. "It would be unfair for me to comment since I'm no longer a member of the church. But I could never understand why the Jesus in the Bible was so different from the Jesus my father presented to me. Jesus loved people, spent time with sinners, and forgave. My father used to tell me that Jesus was disappointed in me—and that He would punish my sin." I shrugged and picked up my cup again. "I couldn't live up to that kind of expectation, so I finally gave up. If Jesus is only looking for perfect people, I'm not his gal."

Ruth reached over and put her age-spotted hand on mine. "Our Lord is not looking for perfection. He loves us with grace and mercy. These are not qualities you found in your father, I am afraid. Your father's love has been conditional, based on your actions, but God's love is not so. His love never changes. He accepts you unconditionally."

I shook my head. "But He's a holy God. Father says He cannot abide sin, and won't commune with those who have sin in their hearts."

"My dear girl, is Charity perfect? If she does something wrong, will you reject her?"

I felt tears spring to my eyes. "Of course not. I would never do that."

"Why do you think your heavenly Father's love is less than your own? He *is* love, *liebling*. Without Him, you would not know love at all. You are His beloved child, and He will never turn a deaf ear to you. Many people before us have fallen short of the mark. Adam, Eve, Cain, King David, even the apostle Peter. Where does it say in His word that He could no longer hear them? Where does it say He would not speak to them?"

I stared at her. "But . . . but I've always heard . . ."

Ruth chuckled softly. "I am afraid that we hear many things that are not true. You must learn to hear from God yourself, my Lizzie. Through His Word and through His Spirit. Then man will not be able to twist the truth and cause you pain."

Ruth's words struck deep in my heart as I thought about

my love for Charity. Why was it hard for me to believe God could love me the way I loved my own child?

Charity, who'd been concentrating on eating the last of her dessert, noticed me looking at her. "Are you okay, Mama?" she asked.

"Yes, I'm fine, Cherry Bear. I'm sorry about Grandpa. Did he scare you?"

She shook her head. "No, but I have a question."

"And what is that?"

"Mama, is Grandpa your daddy?" Her frown made it clear she was still bewildered by the confrontation with my father.

"Yes, Cherry Bear. He's my daddy."

She pondered this for a moment. "Does he love you, Mama?" she asked slowly.

I wasn't sure how to answer this question and hesitated. "I don't know. I hope he does, but I'm not sure."

"So some daddies don't love their children?"

Oh boy. Where was this going? "I guess some of them don't. But most of them do, sweetie."

She blinked several times as she stared at The Princess, who sat on the table next to her. "My daddy doesn't love me, does he?"

I looked at Ruth, whose eyes flushed with tears. I scooted up my chair next to Charity and put my arm around her. "If your daddy knew you, he would love you, honey. I'm sure of it."

I wasn't the least bit confident of that, but I couldn't allow Clay's selfishness to hurt my daughter. My half-truth seemed to work.

"He would?" she responded, a small smile causing the corners of her small mouth to turn up.

I hugged her tightly. "Yes, he would."

This seemed to mollify her. "Mama, I'm very tired. When are we going home?"

"We'll leave in a few minutes. Why don't you take The Princess into the living room and play with her there. I'll say good-bye to Ruth, and then we'll go . . . home." It still felt odd to call our makeshift apartment over the restaurant "home," but it was the closest thing to a home we had.

"Okay, Mama." Charity grabbed her doll and skipped into the other room.

"*Ach, liebling,*" Ruth said, "I am so moved by your strength and courage. You have done such a wonderful job raising Charity. She is very blessed to have you for a mother."

"I'm afraid I'm the one who's blessed. But I dread the day I have to explain the truth to her about her father. What will she think of me?"

"She will know that in a world where babies are so casually torn out of their mother's womb, a place that should be the safest place in the world for them, her mother bore her, took care of her, and loved her with a great and godly love." Ruth's voice caught, and she sobbed into her napkin.

I reached over and put my hand on her arm. "Ruth, that means more to me than I can say."

She took a deep breath and tried to steady her voice. "I know that boy and his family tried to get you to take the life of that precious baby, but you stood your ground, even though your father rejected you both." She put her other hand over mine. "I am so proud of you, Lizzie. So very proud. I want you to know that. If you ever need anything, anything at all, I want you to come to me. Perhaps I can help to take the place of a father who should know better. Who should love better."

Now it was my turn to get weepy. "Thank you, Ruth. You've

always been such a good friend. I'm so grateful to have you in my life."

"I wish I could ask you to live here with me," the elderly woman continued, "but my small house only has one bedroom, and I am afraid you would not be comfortable. Nevertheless, anytime you need a place to go, you are always welcome. I have a couch and a cot that can be used as a bed."

I smiled at her. "Thank you so much. For now, we're quite comfortable at the restaurant. We have nice rooms, and Avery Menninger gave us some very fine furniture. Please don't worry about us."

"All right. But never forget my offer, *liebling*. It is good as long as I am alive."

I thanked her again, and we went into the living room, where Charity was playing quietly on the couch.

"Are we going now, Mama?" she asked when we entered.

"Yes, Cherry Bear. Let's get your coat on."

She walked over to the chair where we'd put our outerwear when we came in, picking up her small coat and handing it to me. She held out her arms, and I helped her wiggle into it. Then I pulled her stocking cap over her dark curls and wrapped her scarf around her neck.

"You put your mittens on while I say good-bye to Ruth," I said.

She nodded but grabbed my sleeve. "I hafta say good-bye to Ruth too. You go first, Mama."

Ruth chuckled. "I am blessed to get two good-byes."

I put my coat on and then hugged my old friend. "Thank you so much for the wonderful meal. Maybe next time you can come to our place."

"*Ach*, I would love that, *liebling*. Thank you."

Charity, now with her mittens on, waited patiently for me to finish with Ruth. Then she went up to the old Mennonite woman who bent down as far as her aged body allowed. My daughter wrapped her arms around Ruth's waist. "Thank you very much for the good cheeseburgers," she said solemnly. "And thank you for having a very nice potty."

Ruth laughed jovially as she gave Charity a hug. "You are quite welcome, *liebling*. And I, too, am happy for a very nice potty."

We left Ruth's house with a promise to see her again soon. On the drive back to the restaurant, I turned the events of the evening over in my mind. I was thrilled to reestablish a relationship with Ruth, whose acceptance of me and my daughter meant more than words could express. And I'd made it past Charity's questions about her father—for now. But the most significant incident was that I had confronted my father and refused to be bullied. And I had every intention of keeping it that way. For my sake and for my daughter's.

However, I was still bothered about Father's revelation concerning the man in the red cap. What would happen if the elders actually confronted him? Would he accuse me of thievery? Would the elders abandon me and Charity? One part of me felt angry with my mother for going against my wishes. Another part was hopeful that confrontation would drive the man away for good.

But the loudest voice in my head warned me that circumstances could be combining together to create an inescapable avalanche of disaster that could end up burying me alive.

CHAPTER / 12

Cora was right about Fridays being the busiest day in the restaurant. Weekends were seen as family time by the citizens of Kingdom, so Friday was the last chance to eat out for almost everyone except the single folks who liked to gather together on Saturday mornings. The day started off busy, and the pace kept up all the way through lunch. Cora warned me more than once that dinner would be a challenge, and I'd begun to worry. Would I be able to keep up? The last thing I wanted to do was to let Cora down.

Because of the increased business, she offered only four dinners on Fridays, which made things a little easier. The menu consisted of her famous meatloaf, roast beef with oven-browned potatoes, chicken-fried steak and mashed potatoes, and of course her wonderful fried chicken dinner. The meatloaf and roast beef were cooked ahead of time and kept warm, but Cora had to fry the chicken and steak as it was being ordered. That meant she wouldn't be able to help wait tables. I'd be on my own. By three o'clock I was already tired and fairly confident that by the time the restaurant closed, I'd be thoroughly exhausted.

Keeping up on orders and taking care of folks in the restaurant helped to keep my mind occupied, yet a cloak of fear enveloped me the entire time. Where was the man in the red cap? Would he suddenly burst in and have me arrested? Accuse me of stealing money from my employer while all our customers looked on? Would he bring the elders with him, all of them convinced I was guilty?

Besides the apprehension that clutched at my heart, I was also filled with an overwhelming sadness. Though we'd been in Kingdom less than a week, it was beginning to feel like home. Strange, because when I'd left five years ago, it hadn't felt like that at all. To say I was surprised by my reaction was an understatement. If given the chance, could we actually be happy here? Even with my father's rejection?

Ebbie Miller came in for a late lunch, and we talked some. He was as concerned as everyone else about the church, but he was convinced that prayer was the most important tool in bringing peace.

"I'm uncomfortable with the resentment I see building between brothers and sisters in the Lord," he said softly. "How can Christ be honored through it?" I could see the pain in his dark brown eyes. "I appreciate the mediators who are trying to establish a dialogue and work this out, but I'm convinced my place is one of prayer. God can do what man cannot."

Although I wasn't sure I agreed with him, I walked away thinking what a nice man he was. Maybe an arranged marriage with Hope would work after all. I certainly wasn't any expert on wedded bliss, so I intended to keep my opinion to myself. Watching their relationship evolve should prove to be very interesting. For Hope and Ebbie's sakes, I prayed it would work. However, it would take something a step beyond an orchestrated marriage to bring me a husband. Especially in Kingdom. No man in this town would ever be interested in damaged goods. Noah's face floated unbidden into my mind, and I pushed it quickly away.

A little after three thirty, Mother walked in the door. I motioned toward an empty table, where she took a seat. I went to get a pot of coffee and to warm up some leftover coffeecake from breakfast. Mother loved the desserts at Cora's, and it tickled me to share them with her. Partially because of the knowledge that my father would be upset to learn she was enjoying something he didn't allow.

"Are you angry with me?" Mother asked as I put our food on the table.

"I'm not really angry," I said, "but I wish you'd held off until I was sure that was the right thing to do." I poured coffee into both our cups and sat down.

She sighed as she reached for her cup. "I did not mean to speak to your father about your situation, but he could tell I was upset and insisted that I explain why."

"Just because he *insists* doesn't mean he always has to get his way, you know."

She gazed at me, a frown deepening the fine lines around her eyes. "I know that, Daughter. But I felt he would do the right thing. And I believe he did."

As I reached for my napkin, I could see my hand shake. "So . . . did the elders find the guy? Did they speak to him?"

She shrugged her thin shoulders. "I do not know, but they did go to look for him. Your father was gone for quite a while last night. I believe he may have driven to Washington to see if the man was staying in a local motel."

"He rode there in this weather? In the snow?"

151

Mother silently prayed over her food while I waited for her answer. I couldn't see my father putting out much effort for me. Especially when the roads were so bad.

"Yes," she said when she lifted her head. "He came back very late, and I did not have a chance to ask him about his journey before he left this morning. He had to shoe two of Aaron Metcalf's horses. I stopped by the shop before coming here, but he was not there."

I quietly sipped my coffee, trying to quell the queasy feeling in my stomach. Had Father confronted my stalker? What would happen now?

"Grandma!" Charity's voice rang out in the restaurant. She came running from the kitchen up to my mother. "Miss Cora and I made roast beef and meatloaf." She took my mother's hand and smiled at her. "And it looks good, Grandma. Do you want some?"

Mother laughed and hugged her granddaughter. "Not right now, Charity, but thank you. I am sure it will be delicious. Which one will you have for dinner?"

She gazed gravely at Cora, who had followed her to our table. "I don't know. There will be fried chicken tonight too." She sighed. "There are too many good things to eat here. It's quite a problem."

Cora guffawed. "Well, that's the first time anyone ever called my food a problem." She knelt down next to Charity. "Tell you what. How 'bout we fix you a plate with a little bit of everything? That way you can try them all. Wouldn't be right for you to miss the roast beef and meatloaf, since you helped to prepare it."

Charity turned to stare at me, her eyes wide with amazement. "Mama, can I have some of all the dinners? That would be wonderful."

I grinned at her. "Yes, as long as you only have a little bit of each one. I don't want to have to roll you upstairs."

She giggled. "I won't eat too much. I promise." She slid her hands down the front of her purple corduroy overalls. "I don't think I'm too fat. So it's okay."

Mother chuckled. "You are not fat, Cherry Bear. You are just perfect."

I was touched to hear my mother use my nickname for Charity, who wrapped her arms around her grandmother.

"Thank you, Grandma. And I think you're just perfect too." She hesitated a moment. "Well, except for . . ."

"I know, I know," my mother said. "The potty."

Charity let go of her. "Yes, but I'm pretty sure it's not your fault. I think it's the fault of my grandpa. Why is he such a mean man, Grandma?"

Cora put her hands on Charity's shoulders. "I gotta start gettin' our steaks and chicken ready to fry," she said quickly. "Are you gonna help me?"

"Oh yes, please. I like the noise it makes when the food goes in the fryer."

"I like it too," Cora said. "Say good-bye to Grandma and Mama for now."

She waved her little hand. "Bye. I'll be cookin' if you need me." With that she skipped away, headed toward the kitchen.

"Anna, I've never said anything negative about your husband in front of Charity," Cora said, her tone serious. "I want you to know that. I'd never, ever do that."

Mother reached out and put her hand on Cora's arm. "I believe you, Cora. You are not the person who painted that negative picture in the child's mind. Her grandfather did that all by himself. Please do not worry. I am so grateful to God for your intervention in the lives of my daughter and granddaughter. I cannot thank you enough for your generosity and care."

Cora patted Mother's hand with her other one. "I'm the one who's been blessed, Anna. Havin' these two in my life . . . well, I don't feel so lonely anymore." She looked at me with tears shining in her eyes. "You'd think bein' surrounded by folks all day would keep an old lady like me from feelin' alone, wouldn't you? But it's not true. At the end of the day, everyone goes home, and the silence is deafening. But with you and Charity here? Well, there's always someone waitin' for me. I haven't experienced that since Edgar died." She let go of Mother's hand and dabbed at her eyes with her apron, leaving a spot of flour on each cheek. "Well, guess I better get into the kitchen before Charity tries fryin' up the chicken by herself." She smiled. "And she could probably do it too."

As Cora walked away, my mother shook her head. "I wonder sometimes how well I could cope without your father. Cora has business sense and skills, but I have no talent or abilities that would support me."

"Mother, that's not true. "You're as good a cook as Cora, and you're a wonderful seamstress. Trust me, you'd have no trouble taking care of yourself."

I couldn't help but wonder why she'd brought the subject up. Was it really because she was afraid of being a widow, or was there another reason she was thinking about life without my father? In my wildest imagination, I couldn't see her ever leaving him. It just wasn't done. Not in Kingdom anyway.

We finished our coffeecake, and Mother headed home,

promising to let me know if she heard anything more about the man in the red ball cap.

Around four thirty, the café began to fill up in anticipation of a menu that wouldn't be served until five o'clock. As Cora promised, I was so busy I barely had enough time to catch my breath. Hope came in with her father. I was surprised to see Samuel in the restaurant, but though a little stiff, he was friendly toward me. I wondered how the meeting with the pastor and the elders had gone, but I didn't have the time or opportunity to ask Hope about it.

A little after seven thirty, Cora came out of the kitchen and pulled me aside. "We're pretty well caught up. I've got plenty of chicken and steak cooked and ready. Why don't you take a break? I'll serve the customers for a bit."

I couldn't argue with her. My legs were so sore I could barely stand. Sitting down for a few minutes sounded like heaven. I handed her my order pad and went into the kitchen, where Charity was sitting at the small table Cora had put up for her. Paper was spread out all over the tabletop, and a large box of colorful crayons lay opened, a bright red one clutched in her hand.

"Looks like you've been drawing some wonderful pictures," I said, sinking down into the chair across from her. If I didn't know better, I'd have thought my legs sighed with relief.

"I'm drawing stuff for you, and for Grandma, and for Miss Cora." She pushed one of the pages toward me. "And I drawed this one for Grandpa. Can we give it to him?"

Her crude picture clearly showed a tall man with dark hair and a beard, dressed in black clothing, bent over with his arms out, hugging a little girl and a woman. It was obvious the child was Charity, and I was the other figure.

"Miss Cora said that God wants to answer our prayers, Mama," she said softly. "So I drew my prayer. I want my Grandpa to love us. I asked God for it, and He told me He would do it."

"G-God told you, Cherry Bear? What do you mean?"

"He told me." She smiled. "He's workin' on it. God said to tell you not to be afraid anymore, Mama."

Pain and exhaustion forgotten, I stared at my daughter with dismay. I knew Cora had been talking to her about God, but now Charity actually imagined He'd talked to her? What in the world could I say? How could I tell her that God doesn't have conversations with regular people? Before I could figure out how to respond, the door to the kitchen burst open and Cora came in. The look on her face struck fear into my heart. Was the man in the red ball cap in the café? Had I finally been exposed?

"Lizzie," Cora said, her voice shaking. "There's someone here to see you. I didn't know what to tell him."

I got up from the table and ran to the door, pushing it open. I looked out at the full tables, trying to spot a red cap, but there wasn't one. Even though I didn't see him at first, it really wasn't hard to spot the person Cora had been so concerned about. He was the only man sitting at a table by himself. We locked eyes at the same time, and a cold chill ran through me.

Staring back at me was Clay Troyer, Charity's father.

CHAPTER / 13

I pleaded with Cora to keep Charity in the kitchen and then headed out into the dining room. After checking up on the customers, I walked slowly toward Clay's table, feeling as if I could barely control my body. My legs felt like gelatin, and the cold terror that seemed to hold my heart in its icy grip made it hard to breathe.

I quickly sat down across from him, only because I was worried about passing out. Why was he here? What could he want? He looked even more handsome than I remembered. His brown hair was combed back from his face, making his widow's peak visible. And although his eyes were hazel and Charity's were dark brown, the shape of his eyes and his turned-up nose were mirror images of my daughter's. The similarities were striking. Even more than I'd imagined. Not being able to find my voice, I simply waited.

"Hello, Lizzie," he said finally. "Sorry to just drop in like this. I don't mean to upset you."

"What do you want, Clay?" My voice was weak and shaky, but I didn't care.

He looked around the packed room. Several people stared

at us. Although most Kingdom residents had never met Clay because he'd lived in Washington, it probably wasn't hard to put two and two together. Especially since he looked so much like Charity. "This might not be a good time to talk," he said. "I know you're busy."

"What do you want?" I asked again. "I'm not getting up from this table until you tell me why you're here."

He cleared his throat. He was nervous, and it caught me by surprise. He'd always been so confident, so sure of himself.

"I've been looking for you for a long time, Lizzie," he said, his voice low. "But no one here would tell me where you were."

"That's interesting," I said. "You knew where I was when I was pregnant. And you knew where I was for quite a while after Charity was born. Maybe I'm just forgetful, but I don't remember hearing anything from you. Of course, I was approached by your parents, offering me money for an abortion."

"I-I know," he stammered. "And I'm sorry. That wasn't my idea—it was my father's. He moved us from Washington, Lizzie, even though I didn't want to go." He stared down at the table for a moment, as if trying to gather his thoughts. When he looked up, I was startled to see tears in his eyes. "You probably won't believe this, but I wanted to marry you. My father freaked out, sold our house, and took Mom and me to Seattle."

"I was still in Kingdom then, Clay," I snapped. "Again, I don't remember receiving a proposal. Or anything else."

He nodded. "I know, and you're right; I should have come for you sooner. I'm sorry. I was confused and a little afraid of my father. But I really did try to find you." He shook his head. "If you can't forgive me, I'll understand. But if you would only talk to me, I—"

"Are you okay, Lizzie?"

I jumped at the sound of a male voice from behind me. Noah stood next to my chair, staring fiercely at Clay.

"I-I'm fine, Noah. But thanks for—"

"What are you doing here, Clay?" Noah said, cutting me off. "Seems like you're running about five or six years behind schedule."

"Sorry," Clay said darkly, "but I'm not sure what business this is of yours." He looked back and forth between us. "Are you two—"

"No," I said, quickly. "We're not anything." I grabbed Noah's arm. "Thank you, Noah, but I'm okay. Really."

He nodded slowly, still glaring at Clay. "If you need me . . . for any reason, just let me know."

"I will. I promise. But for now, it might be best if you would go back and finish your pie."

Noah finally stopped scowling at Clay and peered into my eyes. "All right. But I intend to hang around for a while. Until this guy leaves."

Clay started to say something, but I held my hand up, and he shut his mouth.

"Thank you," I said, "but that won't be necessary. Clay will be leaving shortly. Trust me."

With one last withering look aimed at Clay, Noah turned and left.

"Wow, what's up with that guy?" Clay asked. "He always seemed to have a chip on his shoulder. Especially when it came to you."

"Maybe so," I said. "But he's trustworthy and honest. Unlike some people."

Clay's face fell. "I guess I deserve that, Lizzie. But all I'm asking for is thirty minutes of your time. I just want a chance to explain."

"I really couldn't care less. Your explanation isn't the least bit important to me anymore."

"Thirty minutes, and I'll never bother you again. I promise." He blinked nervously several times. "And . . . maybe I could see Charity? Just once before I go?"

That same frozen hand of fear tightened around my heart again. "Why, Clay?"

He leaned closer to me, and I could smell the scent of his cologne. It was the same one he'd worn the night Charity was conceived. Just that brief whiff made me feel a little faint. "Lizzie, I'm not here to hurt you. Please believe me. I just came to apologize and offer you some help. Financially, I mean. You should have had my support all along, and I want to make it up to you. There's a check for five thousand dollars in my pocket. I know it's not enough, but at least it's a start. And if you decide you don't want me to see Charity, I'll accept that. I'll still help you both with whatever you need."

"What I *needed* was *you*. In person. Not your money, although that certainly would have made things easier." I noticed Cora taking an order from a nearby table. "I've got to get back to work," I said, standing to my feet. "Cora needs me."

"Will you let me wait for you until the restaurant closes?" he pleaded. "Please, Lizzie."

I wanted to tell him no. Wanted to order him to get out, but the man in the red ball cap was still out there. If I suddenly had to leave Kingdom, that five thousand dollars could be the difference between losing Charity or keeping us together. How could I afford to send him away?

"I guess you can stay, but I have no intention of letting

you hurt my daughter. You've caused all the damage you're going to."

"I understand."

I started to walk away when I thought of something and came back. "How did you know I was here? Did Roger Carson tell you?"

Clay didn't say anything, just looked at me.

"You can tell me the truth. He's the only person I've seen who would contact you." I shook my head. "He acted like he cared about me, even gave me his number and told me to call him if I needed help. I threw his card away because I knew he couldn't be trusted. Boy, I was right about that."

"Roger called me because he *does* care, Lizzie. He knew I'd been looking for you and was trying to help the both of us."

I snorted. "Yeah, sure. Well, thank him for me the next time you talk to him. 'Cause I'll never speak to him again as long as I live."

As I worked to serve the last of our customers, anger fueled me with new energy. Then, as the hour grew later, I began to wonder just who I was mad at. Roger? He barely knew me. Most likely, he really was trying to help his friend, although it would have been nice if he'd asked me what I wanted. Clay? Because he was trying to make things right? In the end, I was probably just angry at myself. I'd caused my own problems from start to finish. If I'd said no to Clay, I wouldn't be in this mess. Of course, every time I thought that, I also had to face the fact that if I'd said no, I wouldn't have Charity. And I wasn't sorry about that. Not at all.

Mother's words about beauty for ashes floated into my mind. Maybe all the bad things that had happened to me weren't God's punishment after all. Ruth's words, which echoed my grandmother's, came back to me. *"Your father's love has been conditional, based on your actions. But God's love is not so. His love never changes. He accepts you unconditionally."* Two fathers. Two different reactions. Or were they? I felt so confused I wasn't certain about anything anymore. After writing down Avery Menninger's order wrong, I forced myself to quit thinking about my troubles. I owed it to Cora to concentrate on the job at hand.

It was almost nine thirty when the last family headed out and Cora locked the door behind them. I was cleaning the dishes off their table when she came up next to me. She cast a quick glance at Clay, who had waited patiently for almost two hours.

"Never thought I'd see Clay Troyer again," she said quietly.

"I didn't either."

"I used to buy almost all my supplies from his daddy when he ran that wholesale grocery business in Washington. As soon he was old enough to drive, Clay started delivering them." She shook her head. "Didn't like Art Troyer. Mean cuss. His wife always looked so beat down." She shrugged. "Clay was always nice to me, though. A lot nicer than his father."

"Yeah, that's what I thought once. That he was nice, I mean. But I found out the hard way that there's more to him than meets the eye."

"It's that way with most folks," she said. "I don't like people who show me one face but are busy hidin' behind another one." She smiled at me. "That's one of the reasons I like you so much, Lizzie. You're exactly who you say you are. One of the most honest people I've ever known."

I felt shamed by her words. If she knew the real reason I'd

come to Kingdom, she'd probably be disappointed in me. Just like everyone else.

"What do you want me to do with Charity?" She cocked her head toward the kitchen.

I stepped a little closer to her to ensure that Clay couldn't hear us. "Would you please take her upstairs for a while? I know you're tired, and it's asking a lot, but I won't be long. I intend to get him out of here as quickly as possible."

"Of course I will," she said. "I'd rather spend time with Charity than go home alone. No need to hurry." She reached out and grabbed my shoulder. "Be careful, Lizzie Lynn. The devil can appear as an angel of light."

I hugged her. "Clay's not the devil, Cora. But I'll be on my guard."

She nodded. "Okay. I'll be prayin' for you, if you don't mind."

"No, I don't mind. I'll come and get you as soon as—"

Before I could finish my sentence, someone began banging on the front door with so much force the windows rattled.

"What in the world?" Cora said. She hurried up to the front door as the knocking grew louder. "Avery, stop poundin' on my door like that," she yelled. "You're gonna break somethin'."

I followed her to the front of the room and waited as she unlocked the entrance. Avery Menninger stepped inside, his eyes wild, his hat missing, and his hair standing on end.

"We've got to call the sheriff, Cora," he shouted. "Right away."

"Avery, calm down," Cora said. "What in heaven's name has you in such a tizzy?"

He collapsed into a nearby chair. "I was on my way home, almost to the main road, when I saw an orange car parked on the side of the road. Seemed odd, like some stranger made a wrong turn, so I stopped to see if I could help. Thought the driver had plowed into a tree, 'cause his front bumper was messed up. But there weren't no tree anywhere close to him. Checked inside the car, but it was empty, so I hitched Glory up to the bumper of the car and went lookin' for the driver with my flashlight."

He gulped and ran his hand over his face. "And I found him all right. Lyin' in the ravine off the side of the road, his head all bashed in." His eyes moved quickly between the three of us. "Stone-cold dead, he is. Stone-cold dead."

CHAPTER 14

Sheriff Saul Ford sat at a table with Avery, grilling him about the dead man found on the road to Kingdom. Sheriff Ford, an imposing man over six feet tall and built like a football player, scowled at Avery as if he were purposely holding back information. And Avery seemed to wither under the sheriff's displeasure.

"There just ain't anything else I can tell you," Avery said, the pitch of his voice getting higher each time he spoke. "Like I said, I just got out to check on the car 'cause I thought someone might be in trouble. That's all there is to it."

"I pass lots of cars parked on the side of the road," the sheriff growled, "but I don't get out and look at 'em. Doesn't make sense."

"He's told you over and over that we don't get many cars on that road," Cora interjected, obviously getting impatient with Ford's interrogation of her friend. "Why do you keep askin' the same questions? We don't know the man. He's a stranger. Avery did the right thing by notifyin' you. Why don't you leave him alone?"

"I don't remember askin' you for your opinion, ma'am,"

he snapped. "When I'm ready to talk to you, I'll tell you. Now, hush up."

"Wait a minute, Sheriff," Clay said. "That's no way to talk to Mrs. Menlo. These people aren't suspects. There's no need to be rude."

Ford stood to his feet. "Oh, there's not? Well, maybe I oughta take you in for questioning, young man. Seems to me you're the only person here that don't belong."

Clay gave the sheriff a slow smile, but his eyes simmered with anger. "I think that's a fine idea. But first let me make a call to our family lawyer and see what he thinks about that idea. My guess is that he'd have a problem with it since you have no evidence that this poor man's death wasn't accidental. And no evidence that I ever knew him. What do you suppose our high-priced Seattle lawyer will have to say?"

I half expected the sheriff to come unglued at Clay's confrontational attitude, but instead he grimaced like he was in pain and sat back down. My guess was that the bad-mannered lawman had gone up against lawyers in the past and wasn't willing to go down that road again.

"Well, I guess he coulda gotten out of his car for some particular reason," he said in a subdued voice. "Maybe to relieve himself." He tipped his hat toward Cora and me. "Sorry to be blunt, ladies. Then he slipped and fell down the ravine, hittin' his head on the rocks below."

Clay sighed audibly. "So if you're convinced it's an accident, why are you grilling Mr. Menninger? It's after midnight, and everyone's tired."

The sheriff glared at him. "Gotta cover all the angles, boy. That's the least the dead man deserves, don't you think?"

Clay shrugged. "Of course. But before you spend any more

time bothering innocent people, why don't you apply your efforts toward determining how the man actually died? Doesn't that make more sense?"

I could barely comprehend the back-and-forth patter between Clay and the sheriff. It was as if I were underwater, trying to understand them but not quite able to make out their words. I didn't know the dead man's identity, but I certainly knew why he was in Kingdom.

Try as I might, though, I couldn't find the courage to speak up. Couldn't say the words that would reveal the truth. All I could do was sit and watch the bizarre scene unfolding in the dining room. Thankfully, except for asking my name, the sheriff didn't question me. He probably equated my silence and spacey demeanor with shock. And maybe he was right. Questions kept bouncing back and forth in my head like out-of-control Ping-Pong balls.

Was the man's death really an accident? If so, would anyone ever trace him to me? And if it wasn't an accident, who killed him? I found the possible answer to that question more frightening than anything else. Only a few people knew about the stranger who'd been tormenting me. And there was only one person I could think of who might be capable of killing him—my father. Even though he claimed to be part of a religion that believed in peace toward your fellowman, I'd seen his rage up close and personal. I knew what he was capable of. But would he actually kill someone? I found that extremely hard to accept.

"Guess that's it for now," Sheriff Ford said. "We'll be back tomorrow, lookin' around. We need to find out more about this guy. Contact his family. That kinda stuff. Then we'll have the doc in Washington take a shot at him. If he don't think there's anything hinky about the way this man met his Maker, we'll pack 'im up and send 'im on home. Otherwise, I gotta call in the KBI and ship the body to the coroner's office. Hate havin' those Bureau boys around. Snooty bunch of college boys that think they know everything. Couldn't find their—" He stopped and looked at Cora and me. "Well, you get my drift."

He put his hat back on his balding pate. "I expect this won't be the last time you'll see me." He shook his head. "This is one weird place." He pointed his finger at Avery and then swung it around the room at the rest of us. "You religious people act all holy, but you got your skeletons just like everyone else. Hidin' out from the rest of the world don't keep you from payin' for your sins, you know."

With that, he walked out the front door, slamming it behind him. There was silence in the room for a few seconds.

"Well, I better head on home," Avery finally said. He shook his head. "That man makes me wish I'd just minded my own business. He's one of the reasons we try to solve our own problems in Kingdom. Sheriff Ford's never made a secret of his dislike for this town and everyone in it. I don't trust him. I really don't."

Although I didn't say anything, I agreed wholeheartedly with Avery. When Clay brought up an out-of-town attorney, the sheriff seemed to jump from suspecting foul play to assuming the death was accidental so fast it almost made my head spin. Was he planning to search for the truth or sweep the incident under the rug so it would make his life easier? That would certainly keep the "Bureau boys" he detested out of his hair.

"Pshaw," Cora said, rising from her chair. "You did the

right thing callin' the sheriff, Avery. Don't you let that ornery man rattle you. Go on home, but come back tomorrow for breakfast. My treat."

Avery smiled for the first time since finding the body. His wife, Emily, had passed away almost five years ago, and with Berlene married and gone, Cora's Café was a second home to him. He said his good-byes and left.

"You want me to stay for a while?" Cora asked, looking straight at Clay.

I shook my head. "No, thanks. Clay and I still need to talk. You go on home."

"Well, at least let me go upstairs and check on Charity once before I leave."

I nodded at her, and she climbed the stairs, leaving Clay and me alone. Cora had put Charity to bed shortly after Avery arrived. I was thankful my daughter slept so peacefully. Once she went to bed, she was out like a light. The last thing I wanted her to know was that someone had been killed in Kingdom. She was so happy here. I had to wonder if the sheriff's investigation would endanger our future in this small town. If he uncovered too much, it could lead back to me.

I turned my attention to Clay. "You said you wanted to tell me something. Please make it fast. I'm exhausted."

He got up from where he'd been sitting and came over to my table, pulling up a chair next to me and sitting down. His eyes looked tired. "Any coffee in the kitchen?" he asked. "I've still got to drive back to Belleville tonight. Got a room at a motel there."

"I figured you were staying with Roger and Mary."

He shook his head. "Came here to see you, and I didn't

want to feel obligated to visit old friends. Too many people know me in Washington."

"So Roger isn't aware that you're here?"

"Not for certain, though he might suspect it. And I'd rather he not find out, if you don't mind."

I shrugged. "Like I said, I have no intention of talking to him anyway."

He smiled. "Good. Now about that coffee?"

"I'll get some."

"No. I'll get it. You rest. You worked a lot harder than I did tonight."

"Okay. There's some in the large pot on the stove. Should still be hot. Clean cups are drying next to the sink."

"No coffeemaker, huh?"

"You remember where you are, right?"

He chuckled. "Yes. I guess it could be worse. I could be grinding the beans."

I gave him a small smile. "You've got that right."

He stood up. "I'd almost forgotten how beautiful you are when you smile."

"Please, don't . . ."

"I know. I'm sorry." He turned and headed toward the kitchen just as Cora came down the stairs.

"Where is he?" she asked as she came into the room.

I explained that he was getting coffee.

"My goodness," she huffed. "I don't want him messin' around in my kitchen."

Before I could stop her, she hurried toward the kitchen door. I thought about calling her back, but it *was* her kitchen. If she didn't want him in there, that was her business. I didn't care. A few seconds later the kitchen door opened and Clay came out.

"Cora's getting the coffee," he said, coming back over to the table. "Guess I'm not welcome in her kitchen."

"Clay, I'm really tired. Please say what you came here to say and then go. Don't drag this out."

"Okay, okay." He leaned closer to me. "Look, Lizzie. I know what you must think of me, but I just want one chance to explain. That's all." He tried to take my hand, but I pulled it away.

He sat up straight and folded his arms across his chest. "Well, here it is. I cared deeply for you back then—when we were together. But my hormones were out of control. If I had to do it over again, I never would have . . . I mean, I talked you into something you weren't ready for, and it was wrong. You can hate me for it, but there are a lot of boys out there who are just too dumb to realize the consequences of their actions until they're older. It doesn't make them bad. It makes them immature and stupid. And that was me."

He uncrossed his arms and ran a hand through his thick hair. "When I found out about the baby, I went to my parents. I told them I loved you and wanted to marry you. My father came unglued. Threatened to disown me. I guess it was a couple days later when he drove to Kingdom and attempted to buy you off."

"You mean tried to get me to kill our child?"

He nodded slowly. "You've got to believe me; I didn't know anything about it. Not until after we moved. I was furious."

"But you still didn't come after me."

"No. No, I didn't. Not then."

"Why?" I asked, trying to keep from crying. "It was terrible here. My father . . . Well, he made my life a living hell."

Clay took a deep breath and let it out slowly. "I'm so sorry. But I couldn't leave."

I started to ask him why again, but then Cora came into the room with a pot of coffee and two cups. She set them on the table. "I'm goin' now," she said to me. "You need anything else?"

"No, this is great. Thanks, Cora."

She hesitated a moment. I could tell she was worried.

"I'm fine. Really. You go home. I'll see you in the morning."

"Okay, but sleep in. I can handle the Saturday morning crowd. They're not in a hurry anyway. Only reason they gather here is to gab."

I smiled at her. "Thanks, but you wake me up. I want to help."

Cora glared at Clay. "You be nice to this girl. You hear me? Don't you confuse her."

Clay nodded at her. "It's not my intention, Cora. I promise."

She stared at him a few more seconds and then went to get her coat and hat. I said good-bye to her once more as she went out the front door. A few seconds later I heard her car start up.

"She cares a great deal about you," Clay said. "I'm glad."

"Answer my question," I said in clipped tones. "Why didn't you come for me?"

He sighed deeply. "My father had a major heart attack only days after we got to Seattle. He was very sick for a long time and died later that year." He swiped at his eyes with his hand. "I should have contacted you, Lizzie. But I was worried about him—and my mother. She had a breakdown, and I had to care for her. Even though I wanted to be with you, I couldn't find a way to leave."

I clasped my hand to my chest. "Oh, my goodness, Clay. I had no idea. If only I'd known...."

He waved his hand at me. "Don't even go there. It's not your fault. If my head had been clearer, I would have found a way to get word to you sooner. Unfortunately, by the time I tried to let you know what was going on, you were gone."

"You tried to find me?"

"Yes. Some old friends from school told me you'd left Kingdom, but no one knew where you were. I sent several letters to your parents but never got a response."

My head was spinning. Had I made a terrible mistake? Had Clay actually loved me all along? The possibility was too much for me to handle right now. I suddenly felt faint and put my head in my hands, feeling as if I were on a train speeding out of control. Too much was happening at one time, and all my emotions seemed to be on a collision course.

Clay reached for me. This time I let him take my hand. "I'm sorry. I didn't come here to make things worse for you, but I had to explain. To let you know that I didn't desert you on purpose."

I gazed into his eyes. "What do you want now, Clay? Where do we go from here?"

He stared past me, sadness evident in his expression. "I'm not here to ask anything of you, Lizzie. Really. All I want is for you to take the check I brought and let me help you in any other way I can." His eyes bored into mine. "Someday, if possible, I'd like to meet my daughter. And I'd like to be a part of your lives. In any way you'll let me in."

I felt a tear slide down my face, but I quickly wiped it away. "You've got to give me time to think."

"That's no problem." He let go of my hand, reached into his pocket, and pulled out an envelope, which he pushed toward me. "Here, take this. Like I said, it's not a lot. Certainly not all the child support I should have been paying all these years, but it's all I've got right now. I'll get more. Eventually, I'll make it up to you."

I took the envelope and slid it into the pocket of my apron. "Are you working? I mean, your family always had so much money."

"Yes, there's money, but it's not mine yet. I chose to start at the bottom in my father's company so I could make my own way. Earn a place in our family business instead of having it handed to me on a silver platter." He smiled. "I'm making a decent living, but I'm certainly not rich. Someday, when I deserve it, I'll run Troyer Enterprises, but I intend to handle things differently than my father. I want our employees to respect me in a way they didn't respect him."

"Does your mother know you're here?"

He nodded. "Yes, and with her blessing. My father was the one who wanted nothing to do with you. My mother would love to see her granddaughter. I'm afraid my father's hatred has cost all of us too much."

"I can certainly understand that," I said softly.

"I know you can." Clay stood up and went to get his coat that was flung over the back of a chair in the corner of the room. "You get to bed." He took a small notepad out of his wallet and a pen from his pocket. Then he scribbled something on it. "Here," he said, handing it to me. "That's the number of the motel in Belleville. If you want to see me again, call me.

I won't call you, and I won't come back." He smiled sadly at me. "If I don't hear from you by Sunday evening, I'll check out Monday morning and go back where I came from. You won't hear from me again, except for further checks to help you raise our daughter."

Without another word, he walked out the front door. I watched as he started his car, turned around, and drove out of town. Snow had started falling again, and the flakes danced in the light from the front porch like little white ballerinas. I felt more bewildered than I ever had in my entire life. One man was dead, and another man I used to love with my whole heart had come back into my life. Finally, because there was nothing else I could do, I bowed my head and prayed, tears dripping on the tabletop.

"God, I need wisdom. Do I stay or do I go? And what about Clay? Is this why you brought me here? So that Charity could have a father? Could you please make my pathway clear so I don't make a mistake? Maybe you do love me the way Ruth says. I understand the love of a parent for a child. If you really do love me like that . . ." I sobbed, unable to control my emotions. After a few seconds I tried again. "If . . . if you really do love me like that, it would be so wonderful. Please forgive me if I've misjudged you. I'm really sorry. Maybe we could start over. If . . . if that would be okay with you." I opened my eyes and looked toward the ceiling. "Please help me, Father. Please deliver me. If you do, I'll serve you the rest of my life. I promise."

As the last syllables faded from my voice, a quiet peace invaded my entire being. And I wept again.

CHAPTER / 15

The next morning dawned cold and raw. The wind whipped the barren trees outside like stalks of wheat, but the Saturday morning regulars filed in anyway. Just as Cora had said, almost every customer was single. Most of them widowed. Most of them male. Other than church events, this weekly ritual had become their primary social connection.

I'd crawled out of bed when I heard Cora come in, even though she tried to be extra quiet so as not to wake me. Hearing her stirring around downstairs was easy, since I'd never fallen asleep in the first place. As tired as I was, I'd spent the night lying in bed wondering what to do. Wondering about the dead man. Wondering if I should say anything or just be quiet. In the end, I decided to keep my mouth shut and wait. I'd asked God to guide me, and I didn't feel the urge to leave Kingdom. If the doctor in Washington ruled the death an accident, maybe this would all go away on its own, and I wouldn't have to tell the sheriff anything.

Several questions continued to haunt me, though. Perhaps his death put an end to his stalking, but I still had no idea why he'd started following me in the first place. And I wasn't sure if he'd actually sent the notes. If he was connected to Reba, then perhaps her vendetta was at an end. It was possible that Charity and I were finally safe. But just in case, the first chance I got next week, I'd drive into Washington and open a bank account. The sooner that check from Clay cleared, the quicker I could draw the money out if we needed to leave Kingdom. While it was possible the death of the man in the red cap meant we wouldn't have to run anymore, it could just as easily mean I was one step closer to being jailed. There was no way for me to know. All I could do was try to trust God to help me make the right decision.

The other thoughts that had rambled around in my mind, chasing away sleep, had to do with Clay. I'd been angry for many years, and now I'd found out that he'd really cared about me all along. That he'd wanted to be part of my life. As usual, I'd assumed the worst, never thinking that he might be dealing with his own problems. One thing for sure, I intended to take it slow in that area. My daughter's feelings were of utmost importance. Telling her he was her daddy and then having him leave again would be too hurtful. I couldn't allow that to happen.

During the night as I'd lain in the dark, I realized one other truth had to be faced. I had deep feelings for Noah Housler, and they weren't just feelings of friendship. Noah had been raised Mennonite, just like I had. Well, not quite the same. His parents were very loving people. Yet no matter how understanding his mother might be, I was pretty certain she wouldn't be thrilled about her son marrying a woman with an illegitimate child. I sincerely doubted that was Noah's desire either. I decided that my affection for Noah wasn't going anywhere, and forgetting about him was the only choice open for me.

I stumbled through the morning so tired I kept making mistakes. After the main breakfast rush died down, Cora sent me back upstairs to take a nap. This time it didn't take long for me to drift off. I dreamt that I stood alone on the bank of a large river. On the other side I could see the town of Kingdom. Several people stood there, bidding me to come to them. At first I only recognized my mother and Cora. But then I realized Clay was there, too, holding Charity's hand. There was a small boat fastened to a dock in front of me, so I untied it and got in. As I rowed to the other side, the waves became choppier, threatening to toss me into the water. I called out for help and finally saw another boat coming my way. A rescuer.

At first I couldn't see his face, though I tried desperately to make it out. Just before he reached me, I realized it was Noah. He kept telling me to row toward him, but my oars were so heavy, I couldn't move them in the water. Even though I tried to hold on, they slipped from my grasp.

I woke with a start, my breathing quick and heavy. I thought I'd been asleep only a few minutes, but when I looked at the clock, two hours had gone by. In spite of the disturbing dream, I definitely felt better. I got up, brushed my hair, and headed back downstairs to find only two customers in the restaurant.

"Hey, did you get some rest?" Cora asked when she saw me.

"Yes, thank you so much. It's just what I needed."

"Well, you may get a lot more. The weather's gettin' really bad. I'm sendin' everyone home. As soon as these two finish up, I'm headin' outta here before it gets any worse." As if confirming Cora's declaration, a gust of wind shook the old building, and our two stragglers gathered their jackets and hats. Cora checked them out and grabbed her own coat.

"Honey, I'm gettin' out of here while I still can," she said. "You lock up the place and batten down the hatches. We may be in for a pretty bad storm." She frowned at me. "I checked the generator. You should be fine."

I smiled at the kind woman who had given Charity and me a safe harbor. "You take care going home."

"Won't take me but a couple of minutes. I'll be fine. Charity's drawin' in the kitchen. Tell her I said good-bye, okay?"

I nodded as she went out the front door and down the steps to her car. She had to hold on to the handrail to stay on her feet. But her trusty car started right up, and she pulled away seconds later. I flipped the Open sign to Closed and watched her until I could no longer see her taillights.

I glanced over at the clock. It was only a little after three. As soon as I finished cleaning up the breakfast dishes, I'd have the rest of the day to myself. I'd just started to gather the dirty plates when someone knocked on the door. I looked up to see Hope standing there, the wind whipping her cape around. She reminded me of a big black bird, its wings beating furiously. She had one hand on the doorknob, the other hand trying desperately to keep her bonnet on her head. I hurried toward the entrance so I could let her in.

"Who's at the door, Mama?" Charity had come out to see what was going on.

"It's Hope, honey. You go back and start cleaning up your papers. We'll go upstairs pretty soon and watch some videos. Okay?"

She smiled and nodded. As she headed into the kitchen, I opened the front door and Hope practically fell into the room.

"It's not locked," I told her. "In fact, I almost always forget to lock that door. One example of the difference between Kingdom and Kansas City."

Hope chuckled. "And an example of my automatic obedience to signs. I didn't even try to open it."

"You'd better head home soon," I said, fighting the wind as I tried to shut the door.

"We're on our way now," she said breathlessly. "But I had to tell you something. It's about the meeting Monday. I couldn't talk to you about it last night because I was with Papa."

"I wondered what happened." I pointed at a nearby table. "Do you want to sit down?"

"No. Papa is locking up the shop, and we will leave right away." She sighed. "Oh, Lizzie, it was a disaster. They made no progress at all. Papa tried his best to bring some kind of peace between the dismissed elders, their followers who still attend the church, and Pastor Mendenhall, but he couldn't. Your father and the men on his side wouldn't budge. They insisted that our pastor resign. They want to bring new leadership to the church. They want your father to be the new pastor."

"My . . . my father? That just can't happen. He's not . . . I mean, he wouldn't be . . ."

"Yes, I know," she said simply.

"So what happens now?"

"Pastor Mendenhall is calling for a vote this Sunday, after Communion."

"Of course." The tradition in the church required that male members vote for all new ministers. "But how will that help my father and his supporters who have left the church? They have no vote."

Hope shook her head. "My father has never heard of such

a thing occurring, but in hopes of fostering unity, Pastor Mendenhall insisted that all those who left the church be allowed to attend the meeting and cast their vote."

"That had to give my father hope that he'll get his way."

"Yes, but Pastor Mendenhall insists that the women vote as well. Your father was pleased with Pastor's decision to bring those who left back in for the vote, but he is furious with the suggestion that women be included."

I stared at her openmouthed for a moment, but then I smiled. "Boy, Pastor Mendenhall is getting pretty gutsy. I like that."

"I do too," Hope said, "but I'm wondering if his suggestion might backfire on him. How will the men in our congregation react? The women have never been given the opportunity to vote before."

I snorted. "I hate to inform my father and his followers, but women have had the vote for a while now."

Hope tried to suppress a grin but couldn't. "So I hear."

A knock on the door revealed Hope's father, Samuel, standing on the porch, motioning for her to come with him. She waved at him.

"I must go," she said, "but I thought you should know about this. We all need to pray very hard. Our church, even our town, may be at stake." She leaned over and kissed me on the cheek, and then she left.

I watched her and her father climb into their buggy and head home. Thankfully, they didn't live far, because their buggy swayed and rocked in the strong gusts. Daisy lowered her head and fought the wind's fury, as if determined to get her masters to safety.

I finished cleaning up while Charity picked out a video.

With cups of hot chocolate, we settled in to watch our favorite movie, *Sleeping Beauty*, while the storm outside grew more intense. True to Cora's word, our electricity stayed on. The generator was housed in a strong ventilated shed in back of the building. It would take a pretty strong wind to bring it down. But if that happened, the fire I built in our stove would keep us plenty warm.

I forced myself to think about the movie and block out all the other images that tried to capture my thoughts. Today was a day for Charity and me. Besides, I needed the mental break. Suddenly, Charity called out.

"Mama, Mama! Stop the movie! Stop the movie!"

I grabbed the remote control and pressed Pause. "What's the matter, honey? Is something wrong?"

She pointed at the screen. "See? Prince Phillip looks just like that man who came to see us."

I looked at the cartoon character carefully. "Well, I guess they do look a little alike, Cherry Bear. But trust me, Noah isn't Prince Phillip. Besides, Noah's hair is a little lighter, and he has green eyes, not brown."

Charity shook her head, her curls bouncing with the action. "You're not looking with the right eyes, Mama. You better look again."

I sighed. When Charity was convinced of something, it was almost impossible to change her mind. "Okay, maybe Noah looks a little like the prince. But he isn't, and I don't want to talk about it anymore. Let's finish our movie. Okay? We need to be thinking about dinner before long."

She started to say something when we heard the door downstairs open and Cora shout my name.

"You stay here, honey. I'll be right back." I hurried down

the stairs wondering why Cora would risk getting out in the storm.

"Lizzie?" she called again. She sounded upset.

"I'm here, Cora. What in heaven's name . . ."

She stood near the front door, clutching her keys in her hand. The panic on her face frightened me. "Lizzie, I . . . I've got to leave. Right now. My sister's taken a turn for the worse, and I have to go to Oregon to be with her. I booked a flight from Topeka that leaves in three hours. With the weather so bad, I'm not sure I can make it there in time, but I have to try."

"But . . . but what about . . ."

She took some keys off her chain and handed them to me. "Here are the keys to the restaurant and to my house. We have enough food to get through the next week." Then she gave me a large envelope. "If I'm gone longer than that, there's a check in here from the bank in Washington. You cash it. It will give you some money to buy what you need. Before you go to town, call Maybelle Miller at Maybelle's Restaurant. Her number's in there. Except for what I buy from local farmers, I have my supplies sent to her. Maybelle will sell you some of what she has if she's got any extra, and she'll help you put in an order for whatever else you need.

"I also made a list of the farmers I buy food from. Most of my vegetables and fruits are in canning jars downstairs. I'm sure you saw them on the shelves when you were down there, but if you need more, you can contact any of the farmers. They put up extra every year just in case I run out." She sighed and shook her head. "I keep hopin' someone will open a store here in Kingdom so my restaurant supplies aren't so hard to come by, but for now, this is what you have to do to keep us stocked."

I nodded.

"I'll call you after I get to Oregon and get my sister settled. Just write down any questions you have, and I'll answer them then." She hugged me tightly. "Please keep the restaurant goin' for me, Lizzie. I can't afford to have it shut down." She let me go and put her hand on my cheek. "I'm sorry to do this to you, honey, but I have no other choice. My sister has no one else."

She turned to leave as I stood there with the keys and the envelope in my hand. I was flabbergasted. I couldn't refuse her after her kindness to me, but how could I run the restaurant alone?

I heard myself say, "Everything will be all right, Cora. Don't worry." It was as if someone else was moving my lips and saying those words. How would everything be all right? I'd never run a restaurant by myself. Even when Betty was on a bender, I'd left all the important matters for her to take care of when she got back. Besides, I had my own problems and couldn't be sure how much longer I'd be around.

As she headed for the front door Cora turned and said, "Oh, and get in touch with Callie Hoffman. She inquired about a job a while back, before I hired you. She's trustworthy and a good worker. She'll help you get through. You settle on a wage for her, and I'll pay it. God bless you, Lizzie. I'll be praying for you. Please do the same for my sister and me."

She suddenly stopped and hurried over toward the corner of the room. Then she bent over. When she stood up she had an envelope in her hand. She glanced at it quickly and then came back toward me. "Here," she said. "Someone must have left this for you. No tellin' how long it's been here. I didn't notice it earlier, but that doesn't mean much."

I took it from her and watched as she closed the door behind her, got in her car, and drove away. I stood staring at the front door, wondering if there was any way in the world I could keep Cora's Corner Café from going under before she returned. As I turned to go back upstairs, I suddenly remembered the envelope and carried it over to a nearby light. Someone had written my name on the outside. An old fear raced through me. I tore the blue envelope open and pulled out the paper inside.

> *I'm still watching you and Charity, Lizzie. I told you you'd never get away from me. Running away has only put more people in danger.*

I slumped to the floor with the note clutched in my hand and began to cry.

CHAPTER / 16

I spent the next two hours in automatic mode, finishing our movie and getting Charity to bed. Although I tried to act as if nothing was wrong, she kept watching my face, her expression one of concern. I couldn't completely hide the terror that caused my heart to pound in my chest.

Once she was in bed, I went back downstairs to get a cup of coffee and think. How could there be another note? The man who wrote them was dead, wasn't he? Would I never be free from him? Eventually my fears narrowed down to one unanswerable question. When had it arrived? There was no postmark. The envelopes in Kansas City had all been postmarked in Kansas City, although there was never a return address. This envelope had obviously been hand delivered.

I quickly checked the front door of the restaurant. It certainly wasn't airtight. I could easily slide an envelope under it. Someone had brought it to the restaurant and left it for me. But when? Last night I'd quickly swept the floor before going to bed, but I was so tired, I only concentrated on the areas under the tables. I could have easily overlooked it. It had been pushed between a large decorative cupboard and the corner. It was a miracle Cora even noticed it.

After heating up some coffee and pouring myself a cup, I slumped down into a chair in the dining room and turned the note over in my hands. It was definitely written by the same person. Same blue paper. Same blue envelope. Same threats—except that this one wasn't just targeted at me or my daughter. What did the writer mean by saying I'd put even more people in danger? Who was he talking about?

I noticed that the envelope was a little worse for wear. It could have been on the floor for a couple of days. Perhaps it had been pushed under the door, either kicked into the corner unnoticed by a customer or blown there by the wind once the door was opened. I'd been at Ruth's Thursday night and Cora had swept up. She probably would have noticed it. So that meant the note had been left sometime between late Thursday night and this afternoon. The man in the red cap had been found late last night. He could have brought it Thursday night or Friday before he died. It had to be from him. I couldn't accept the alternative—that the writer was still a danger to me and those I loved.

I finished my cup of coffee and watched the storm outside gather in intensity as questions inside me raged as well. The man in the red cap was dead. He couldn't hurt me anymore. Surely this note was the last one I'd ever receive. I suddenly remembered Charity's words after her prayer. *"God said to tell you not to be afraid anymore, Mama."* It sounded so simple. Of course, Charity didn't understand how complicated life really was. All of the sudden something my grandmother used to say popped into my mind.

"God spent a lot of time in His Word telling us to 'fear

not,' Lizzie. I truly don't think He was just trying to fill up pages. Do you?"

"That sounds good, God," I whispered into the darkened room, "but so far my life has been crammed full of things to be afraid of. How do I ignore them?" I shook my head. "I'm trying to trust you. I really am. Help me. Please."

Then I remembered Cora's visit. I'd forgotten it with the discovery of the note. She had gone to be with her sister and had turned the restaurant over to me! How in the world could I run it alone? Was there anyone else who could do a better job? There was Cora's previous helper, Julie, but she wouldn't be much help, since she and her husband were expecting a baby any day now. Maybe it would be better to close until Cora got back, but I'd promised her I'd keep the things going. Could I possibly pull it off now that I'd found the note? How would I ever be able to keep my mind on the restaurant?

I finished my coffee, made sure the front door was locked, and trudged upstairs. Sitting in our living room by the window, I pushed the note out of my thoughts and ran several scenarios for running the restaurant through my head. Shortly before midnight, I came to the surprising conclusion that I might actually have the expertise to make it work. My father had spent his life telling me I couldn't accomplish anything, that I had no talents or gifts, but even though I tried to find a reason for failure, I could only see success.

There really wasn't any aspect of the business I didn't know. Besides waiting tables, I'd helped in the kitchen and knew almost all of Cora's recipes. And those I wasn't sure about were in a notebook kept in the kitchen. Cora had written them down for Julie, so she'd have them when Cora was away. By one o'clock in the morning, I had it worked out in my mind. Cora's Corner Café would open Monday morning as scheduled, and I would keep it running until Cora came back.

After getting ready for bed, I searched for a place to hide the note, trying to push its dark threats out of my thoughts. If I could prove that the man in the red cap had written it, I might be able to dismiss it. Unfortunately, there was no way to be absolutely sure. Even more frightening was the thought that maybe his death wasn't an accident. Was I missing something? Or someone? Who could possibly want the man dead, and why? Was my father involved, or someone else? Someone with a completely different motive?

Along with that mind-numbing possibility, I still wondered about the man and his hateful threats coming right before I'd lost my job. Could all these circumstances be related in some strange way? Try as I might, I couldn't figure out how. It did seem extremely odd, though. The man finding me in Kingdom was another one of those *coincidences* that seemed to be questionable. I couldn't make sense out of it and could feel the beginnings of a stress headache gripping my temples. Thinking about it wasn't going to accomplish anything, so I tried to direct my thoughts toward the restaurant and my new responsibilities. However, an uneasy fear seemed to have burrowed its way into the pit of my stomach, and I was certain it had no plans to vacate anytime soon.

Sunday morning dawned frosty but bright. The sun was out, shining on a fresh layer of snow. I began to wonder if I'd ever see grass or dirt again. Since I'd arrived, Kingdom had been covered with snow. I fixed breakfast for Charity and me while wondering what was happening at the church. This was the morning of the big vote. I watched the street from the restaurant as I made notes for the upcoming week.

Mother had mentioned a few days ago that she would try to come by today, since the restaurant was closed, and we could spend some time together undisturbed. Leaving the house on Sundays, other than for church, was frowned upon, so I wasn't sure if her declaration was just false bravado. However, I hoped she'd come because she would know how to reach Callie about helping at the café. Besides, I wanted to learn the outcome of the voting.

It was almost two o'clock when the buggies began rattling down the street, the congregants heading home. It was much later than the normal dismissal time. I saw my parents ride past, my father urging Blackie faster than usual, but I wasn't sure what that meant. I waited in the dining room, still praying Mother would come.

Finally, at almost three thirty, our buggy came up the street with Mother driving. I stepped out onto the porch and waited for her to tie up Blackie and come inside. As she got closer I could clearly see the unhappiness on her face.

"Come on in, Mother," I said, holding the door open for her.

She walked into the closed restaurant and glanced around the room. "Where is Charity?" she asked in hushed tones.

"She's down for a nap."

Mother pulled me over to a table and sat down. "Today I experienced something in church I never want to go through again, Daughter. It was so distasteful." She put her hand on her chest as if she were experiencing pain. "Perhaps you could pour me a cup of coffee before I tell you more? I need something to calm my nerves."

My mother loved her coffee, and even though I'd told her more than once that coffee couldn't actually produce a calming influence on the body, she wouldn't abandon her insistence that it brought her peace when she was disturbed. I'd given up arguing with her.

I hurried into the kitchen. The coffee was still hot, since I'd been drinking it as I waited for her to arrive. It only took me a couple of minutes to return with her cup and a small container of cream.

She poured the cream into her coffee and then grabbed it like a lifeline. After a couple of sips, she put the cup down and sighed. "Pastor Mendenhall addressed the church after Communion and told them about the vote to remove him. He said that he only wanted God's will and assured us that if he had betrayed our trust in any way, he was willing to step down without any further unpleasantness. He stated his view very simply but eloquently. He believes that in the past we have been too strict with one another. He reminded us that God is a loving God, full of grace and compassion, yet during the past several years there have been too many people pushed out of the church because they broke the rules we imposed on them. Instead, he said, we should have extended love and forgiveness toward our hurting brothers and sisters."

She blinked rapidly and her voice broke. "He looked right at me, Elizabeth Lynn. I believe you are one of the people he was thinking about."

"I appreciate that. Pastor Mendenhall was always kind to me. After I got pregnant he went out of his way to tell me if I needed anything I could come to him. I guess he meant it."

"Yes," she said, nodding. "I truly believe he did." She wrung her hands together several times before picking up her cup once more. Instead of taking a drink, she just held it. "After that he called for a vote. Slips of paper were passed out, and we were told to write *Stay* or *Go*. Pastor asked that the slips be given to the men *and* the women.

"Your father stood up and asked for a chance to speak first. Pastor Mendenhall agreed and gave him the pulpit. Matthew announced that the women's votes would not count, as far as he was concerned, and then he went on for about twenty minutes, expounding his view that righteousness is produced by our stringent adherence to the regulations handed down by the elders. He lambasted our pastor, saying that he had been infected by the world, and that he was opposing the founders of Kingdom. That the purpose of our town was being corrupted. He accused Pastor Mendenhall of seeking members but not holding to sound doctrine."

She shook her head. "You may not realize it, but many people have left our congregation with your father's sanction. Pastor has worked hard to bring them back. Some have come. Some have not. Your father would turn his back on all who have left, choosing to see them as apostate. He faults the pastor for seeking their hearts."

She sighed deeply. "All I could think about was the passage in Luke where the Lord says he came to seek and save the lost." Mother reached up and removed her bonnet, smoothing her salt-and-pepper hair with trembling hands. "How can seeking the restoration of our brothers and sisters be wrong? As your father spoke, it became clearer and clearer to me how wrong he is."

She cast her eyes up toward me. "I hate to say this, Daughter, but I was . . . embarrassed by him. I have never said that about my husband before, but I must speak the truth."

"It's all right, Mother. You have the right to your feelings. I like hearing what you think."

She took another deep breath and let it out slowly. "Well, your father does not share your opinion. He would rather I stay quiet."

"Go on. What happened next?"

"After your father finished, the vote was taken." Her smile was tremulous. "The people voted overwhelmingly in favor of keeping Pastor Mendenhall. Women and men both. Only five voted against him."

I frowned at her. "But what about Father's supporters? Surely there were more than that. At the very least, there are two other elders besides Father who left their positions. If all of their wives voted . . ." I stopped and stared at her. "You voted for Pastor to stay, didn't you?"

Mother raised her chin. "Yes, I did. And it felt good, Lizzie. Someone wanted my opinion, and I gave it."

"Does Father know?"

"I have no idea, but I am sure he suspects." She stared into her coffee cup. "He did not speak to me all the way home. I have never seen him so angry. He went straight into the bedroom and shut the door without even asking for lunch. After waiting a while, I left and did not tell him where I was going."

"I'm sorry he's upset, Mother, but he brought this on himself. His attitude is finally having consequences. It's very difficult for me to feel sorry for him."

"I know, and I would not expect you to. But you know, even though I must stand against his views in this, I do feel compassion for him. His father molded him into the man he is. When we courted and were first married, Matthew was a very different person. Loving and sweet. And very thoughtful. But the seeds of anger sown in his heart by your grandfather could not hold back an evil crop, and eventually your father became what he is today." She shook her head slowly. "I so miss the man he used to be. His tender touches and the sweet things he did for me." She blinked back tears that resisted her efforts. "He would bring me flowers, Lizzie. He would gather wildflowers and bring them home to me, just like you used to. If only he could find that man inside him again. It would change everything."

I reached over and put my hand on her arm. "How long can we blame Father's choices on someone else?" I asked gently.

She turned her grief-stricken face to me. "How long will you blame your father for yours, Elizabeth?"

I dropped my hand. "That's not fair, Mother."

"Yes, it is, Daughter. I think it is very fair."

I leaned back in my chair. "Wow, when you start speaking your mind, you go full steam ahead, don't you? Couldn't you ease into this a little slower?"

A burst of laughter bubbled up out of her. "Oh, Lizzie. You have a way of making me laugh when I have no plans to do so."

I smiled at her. "And of course you're right, Mother. I'll have to work on my attitude, I guess." I felt as if I'd turned a corner the other night when I'd prayed, but my mother was correct in her assessment. I still had a deep and abiding bitterness toward my father. Forgiving him would be difficult, but I knew it was necessary before I could heal completely.

"It makes me happy to hear you to say this, Lizzie. I hope our church members will join me in praying for your father. He needs all the help heaven can give him. Even with everything he has done, I feel the man I married is still somewhere inside him. Trapped, but wanting to come back to me. I've seen it in his eyes."

She pushed her cup toward me. "Now, I would like another cup of coffee, if you don't mind. And I believe I would like to have a rather late lunch with my daughter and granddaughter."

"That sounds wonderful," I said "but first I need to talk to you about something."

"Of course. What is troubling you?"

"Have you heard about the man they found dead on the road to Kingdom?"

She nodded. "Terrible. I understand he pulled his car off the road and then tumbled down the ravine. It is such a dangerous place. Our citizens know how treacherous it is. But this stranger did not and paid dearly for his mistake." Her forehead furrowed. "But what does this have to do with you?"

"Mother, that was the man who was following me. The man who stalked me in Kansas City."

Her eyebrows shot up with surprise. "I had no idea. But what does this mean, Daughter?"

"I wish I knew. The sheriff was here. At first he acted as if there might be some kind of foul play. Then suddenly he seemed to change his mind and said that the man likely slipped down the ravine and struck his head on the rocks. That his death was accidental. But I don't know . . ."

"Any man's death is a tragedy," Mother said, a strange look on her face. "But you are concerned that something untoward occurred in this instance?"

"Maybe. I . . . I don't trust the sheriff. I got the feeling he wasn't really interested in finding out the truth."

Mother nodded. "He does not have a good reputation among our citizens. We try to involve him as little as possible in our affairs." She frowned at me. "Is there any other reason you have to doubt his conclusion?"

I hesitated a moment before blurting out my concerns. "That man died not long after the elders were informed about his pursuit of me."

Her eyes widened, but she didn't respond.

I hesitated a moment before shaking my head. "I'm sorry, Mother. Now that I say it out loud, I realize how ridiculous it sounds. I know there are some in the church who may think differently than others about certain things, but all Mennonites are committed to peace. And the Ten Commandments are followed without exception. I was foolish for allowing something so silly into my thoughts. I guess I was just concerned by the timing."

Mother was silent as she stared at her coffee cup. I couldn't shake the feeling that she was keeping something from me. But what was it?

"So now what will you do?" she asked finally.

"Nothing. I've thought about taking Charity and leaving town. Afraid this man will be linked to me in some way and that his death will lead the police in Kansas City here to Kingdom. But the truth is, I have no way of knowing if they're even looking for me. Or if this incident will turn up on their radar. As awful as is sounds—"

"This unfortunate event may be your way out? Because of this terrible situation you may be able to stay here?"

Even though Mother said the words softly, they still sounded dreadful. Yet they were exactly what I'd been thinking. I nodded slightly. "I hate to think I might profit from the death of another human being, but the truth is, it's entirely possible. His harassment of me is definitely over." The newest note popped into my mind, but I decided not to mention it to my mother. She didn't need anything else to worry about.

"But he could have reported your whereabouts to someone else. Is that not correct?"

"Yes, but no one's shown up. It's been days since I first saw him here. Why hasn't anyone come?"

Mother shook her head. "Is there no way you can find out what is going on in Kansas City, Lizzie? No one you can call? No one you can trust?"

"I . . . I thought so, but since that man showed up, I have to admit that I'm not sure anymore. How did he know I was here?" I took a deep breath and let it out slowly. "I don't think it's smart to contact Meghan. She may have said something that led him here. I can't take any chances. The only other person I trust is recovering from a heart attack, and I won't bother her about this. It might impede her recovery."

Mother sighed. "Then all we can do is pray that this is finally at an end, and I will certainly do so. I do not want you to leave me ever again, Daughter." Her voice broke. "I could not bear losing you and Charity a second time."

I wanted to promise her we would stay, but I couldn't. Not yet. "Well, we're here for now, Mother. Let's enjoy our time together. All right?"

She nodded, but the look on her face made me ache inside. When I'd left Kingdom five years ago, my concerns had been for myself and my child. I knew my mother would be hurt, but I hadn't fully counted the cost of her loss. I felt a strong desire to see joy on her face again. With God's help, I hoped I'd get that chance.

"Was there anything else you wanted to talk about?" Mother asked as she took another sip of coffee.

"Yes." I tried to gather the courage to tell her something she wouldn't be happy to hear. "Clay came to see me, Mother."

She almost dropped her cup. It hit the table with a thud, spilling coffee over the side. "Cl-Clay Troyer? He . . . he's back?"

I quickly told her about his visit while I wiped up the spilled coffee. "I haven't called him yet. He said if he didn't hear from me by tonight, he'd leave and never come back."

"Oh, Lizzie. His parents . . . I mean, they actually asked you to destroy your child. For money. The evil that resides behind a request like that . . . I cannot advise you to let these people back in your life."

"You don't have to worry about that. Clay's father is dead, and even though his mother wants to see Charity, I have no intention of allowing it. Clay seems to want to do the right thing, Mother. How can I deny him the chance to prove himself?"

She shook her head. "I was very disappointed in him when he deserted you, Lizzie. Yet deep in my heart, I rejoiced that he and his family were out of our lives. I can't advise you here. You need to seek God's wisdom in this matter."

"I have."

My mother's eyes widened. "You are praying again, Daughter?"

I smiled at her. "I am praying again, Mother."

Tears filled her eyes, already reddened by weeping. "This is the best news anyone on this earth will ever give me," she sobbed. She reached out and took my hands. "God is so faithful. Please do not judge Him by the mistakes your parents have made. I could not bear the guilt in my soul for your decision to turn away from Him. A mother's heart cannot bear this responsibility."

"You were never responsible for that," I said softly. "Quite the opposite. You and Grandmother planted the seeds in my heart that whispered to me in the night. If you both hadn't laid a good foundation, I may not have ever found my way back to God. Please never doubt that for a moment."

She scooted her chair closer and put her arms around me, crying quietly. Finally she straightened up. "My soul exceedingly rejoices."

I smiled at her. "I'm glad."

She finally let me go, a look of happiness on her face. I cleared my throat and hesitated, not wanting to chase away the moment, but I had to know the truth. "Clay told me that he wrote to me, Mother, not knowing I wasn't here anymore. Is that true?"

She didn't answer right away. I hoped against hope that Clay hadn't lied. If he really had sent letters, it would be the proof I needed to believe he was sincere.

Finally she nodded. "Yes, he wrote to you. I never actually read the letters, Lizzie. Your father took them. As far as I know, he did not read them either."

"So Clay was telling the truth," I said slowly, letting this new revelation sink in.

"This does not mean it is God's will for you to take up with this man again," Mother warned. "You must turn this over to God and ask His counsel. Do not jump into anything without His wisdom. Please, Daughter. I worry about your happiness as well as Charity's."

"I understand," I said, although I truly believed my mother had just delivered the answer I'd been seeking. Clay cared about me. He'd always wanted to be with me. Maybe Charity would finally get the father she wanted. I stood to my feet.

"I'll get lunch ready right away. Charity has already eaten, so we'll let her sleep a little longer. If she's not up soon, I'll wake her so you can spend time with her before you leave."

"Can I help you?"

"No, it will only take me a minute." I was on the way to the kitchen before I remembered my other news. I stopped and turned back to look at her, catching her distressed expression. Obviously, my news about Clay was as unwelcome as I'd suspected it would be. "Mother, I almost forgot to tell you. Cora's left town. Her sister is ill, and she's gone to be with her. I have no idea when she'll be back. She suggested I ask Callie Hoffman to help out in the restaurant until she returns. Do you know where the Hoffmans live? Can you contact Callie for me?"

"Oh, Lizzie," Mother said. "Will you be all right? Can you keep the restaurant going without Cora?"

I shrugged. "I don't have much choice. Cora can't lose the income, and I need a place to live and food to feed Charity. So for as long as it takes, I'll be running things."

"I wish I could help you," she said.

I chuckled. "Yeah, Father would really like that. Might be all it takes to really make him blow his top."

"Well, perhaps I can help you indirectly in some way."

Her offer touched me, but she was already defying my father by stepping foot in the restaurant. "Let's wait and see what happens. I don't want to do anything that would cause further strife between you and Father."

The look of disappointment on her face distressed me. "How about this? When you come to visit, you can watch Charity. Keep her occupied. I can't tell you how much that would help."

"I would be happy to do that, Daughter, and on the way home I will stop by the Hoffmans and inform Callie that you need her assistance."

"Thank you, Mother. I'll have lunch ready in a jiffy."

"Lizzie," she said, drawing out my name slowly.

"Yes?"

"That man. The one who died?"

I waited for her to finish, but as I stood there, I realized that my mother was afraid of something. I'd seen it in her eyes ever since I'd told her that the dead man had turned out to be my stalker.

"Wh-when did the man die?" she asked.

"I don't know. The sheriff didn't say. Why?"

She shook her head and wouldn't look at me.

A cold chill ran through my body. "Mother, I must know why you're asking."

"I do not want you to jump to conclusions."

I walked back toward the table where she sat. "You're scaring me. Tell me what you're thinking."

"The other night when your father drove to Washington to see if the man who was following you might be staying there . . ."

"Yes? What about it?"

She clasped her hands together and leaned her forehead against them. "When I washed the clothes your father wore that night I found . . . something." She put one hand loosely over her mouth and stared at me, fear in her eyes. "Oh, Elizabeth. There was blood on his clothes. I am so afraid. Could your father's anger have led him to actually take a life?"

CHAPTER / 17

My mother's question shocked me. I'd determined my own suspicions to be ridiculous only minutes earlier. But now my mother was expressing her own misgivings, and no one knew my father better than she did. Was it possible? Could he be involved?

"Did you ask him about it?" I asked, trying to keep my voice steady.

She nodded, her eyes still wide with panic. "He told me he found a dead deer in the middle of the road when he drove back from Washington. And that when he moved it, his clothing was stained."

"Well, that certainly sounds reasonable. Deer get hit by cars a lot around here. Is there any reason for you to doubt him?"

She sighed, her body shaking. "I don't know. When I told him about the man from Kansas City, he was so upset. He said something about putting a stop to the situation."

I smiled at her, my chest feeling tight. "That doesn't sound too ominous. Father didn't say he was going to put a stop to the *man*—just to the situation."

Her mother's eyes narrowed as she turned this thought

over in her mind. "But if you could have seen his face. It was so . . . dark. I have seen his anger many times, but this was something beyond that. It was . . ." She shook her head. "I do not know how to describe it."

I patted her hand. "I can't believe Father is capable of murder." Even as I said the words, the constriction inside me tightened. Although I didn't think my father cared enough about me to take a life, rejecting the core belief of his Mennonite faith, I felt uncertain. I'd seen his anger. Was it possible? Feeling protective of my mother, I tried to push the fear away. If I suspected him of something so heinous, it would certainly frighten her.

"You do not understand the depth of his feelings for you, Daughter. You have always mistaken his harshness for a lack of affection for you, but the opposite is true. I think he is afraid of how much he loves you."

"So what are you saying?" My tone was sharper than I intended, but her insistence that my father had some kind of deep devotion toward me made me angry. It just wasn't true. My mother flinched at the harshness in my voice, and I immediately felt bad.

"I see I have upset you," she said gently. "That was not my intention."

I waved her comment away. "I'm the one who's sorry. I know I'm sensitive when it comes to Father. In many ways I've allowed my bitterness to twist my past experiences.

"On the way to Kingdom, I began to remember some of the good things that happened here. And the wonderful people who were in my life. For some reason, I'd shoved all those memories into a closet in my mind, refusing to acknowledge them."

I frowned at her. "But when it comes to Father, my memory is sharp and precise. The spankings for no reason, the cruel punishments, the unkind comments. They're not embellished by my imagination. They're very real."

She was silent for a moment. Then she nodded. "You are right, Daughter. There is no excuse for his treatment of you— or for my acquiescence to his behavior. All I can pray is that you will one day forgive us."

"I've already forgiven you, Mother. Maybe you were wrong in allowing Father's behavior, but you were afraid. And your intention was to be a submissive wife. I may not agree with your choices, but at least I understand them." I sighed. "I know I must forgive Father, and I'll work on it. Understanding his actions will be hard, though. As a parent, I just can't excuse his behavior."

"Forgiveness is a decision, Daughter, and is not based on our ability to excuse it. However, I will pray that one day you will see your father through eyes of compassion. Perhaps then you will be able to understand him too, but I see it will take the grace and help of the Almighty to accomplish it." She held up her hand when I began to protest. "What is the popular phrase people in the world use? I guess we will have to 'agree to disagree'?"

"Yes, that's it," I said, my displeasure at her statement dissipating at her use of such a "modern" phrase. "But wherever did you hear that?"

She chuckled. "I have a friend who goes to Washington and buys the newspaper once a month. She hides it from her husband and children, but the ladies and I look at it when we quilt. You will understand if I do not reveal her identity. We are . . . flying under the radar."

Even though I was frustrated with my mother's attempt to downplay my father's abusive behavior, her revelation made me laugh. The idea of a group of old-fashioned Mennonite women giggling over a newspaper while they quilted was just too funny. The tension between us broke, and we spent the rest of the afternoon and early evening enjoying each other's company and playing games with Charity. My mother had never seen a manufactured child's game before, so explaining Candy Land to her was not only challenging but extremely comical. Charity and I giggled at her obvious confusion, but no one was more amused than Mother. Even funnier was Charity taking Mother by the hand and leading her to see the bathroom in the restaurant, accompanied by my daughter's patient instruction as to what a proper potty should be.

By the time my mother left, she seemed much more relaxed, but I suspected she was still bothered about the blood on Father's clothes. As was I. The coincidence was troubling, but I had no real reason to suspect anything else. I tried to put it out of my mind, but for some reason the thought seemed to sit in my psyche, refusing to be banished.

Charity went to bed early, worn out after our fun but busy afternoon. As I said good-bye to Mother, I checked the time. If I was going to call Clay, I'd have to do it soon. I went upstairs, plopped down on the couch, and thought about my choice. Clay and I hadn't been together in years. Was it too late for us? Even if we could never be a couple, was it fair for me to keep him out of Charity's life? Didn't I owe my daughter the chance to get to know her father? I found the piece of paper with his number on it and hurried downstairs to the wall phone in the kitchen. As I dialed the number on the old rotary phone, I prayed I wasn't making a mistake. When the phone rang, for some reason the sound made me jump. The front desk put me through to Clay's room.

"Lizzie?" he said after I said his name. "It's late. I was beginning to worry."

"Listen, Clay," I said. "I can only do this one day at a time. And I don't want to tell Charity who you are until I'm sure this will work out. But if you could stay awhile . . ."

His warm, gentle laughter drifted through the phone. "I can stay. Until you tell me to go."

"Okay, if you're certain you really want to."

"I am. I definitely am." He cleared his throat. "When can I see you?"

I explained the situation with Cora and told him I would be really busy all day tomorrow. "I'm pretty sure I'll be wiped out by tomorrow night. Would you mind waiting until Tuesday? You could come in around six. I'll close early, make you dinner, and you can spend the evening with Charity and me."

"That sounds perfect. I have some business to take care of, so I'll spend tomorrow getting that done. See you Tuesday. And Lizzie?"

"Yes?"

"Thank you. Thank you very much."

"You're welcome." I hung up the phone, feeling cautiously positive about having Clay back in my life. For Charity's sake. But I couldn't help thinking about Noah. As I stood there, I chided myself for even allowing him into my thoughts. We had no future together. For now I just needed to concentrate on building my relationship with Clay. Perhaps I could finally give my daughter the one thing she needed most. A family. If that was ever going to happen, it would probably only happen with Clay.

I tried to feel happy about the possibility, but for some reason, there was an odd sadness stirring deep inside my heart.

CHAPTER / 18

I crawled out of bed early the next morning to start the scrambled eggs and mix up the pancake batter. Around five thirty I got Charity up and dressed, and then I brought her downstairs and set her up at her little table in the kitchen. She'd wanted to stay in bed, but until I was certain she could get herself dressed and ready in the morning, I couldn't risk having her show up in her pajamas during the morning rush. She grumbled a bit, but I made her a couple of pancakes, put warm syrup and butter on them, and added a squirt of whipped cream right in the middle. That put a smile on her face, and her grumpiness evaporated.

A little before six, I went out to flip over the Open sign. Avery Menninger was already waiting outside, along with several others. I let them in and had just started to close the door when my mother pushed it open.

"Mother," I said, surprised to see her. "What are you doing here?"

"I thought you might need some help with Charity this morning."

I looked outside but didn't see our buggy. "What's going on? Where's the buggy?"

She closed the door behind her and took off her heavy cape. "Your father forbade me to use it, so I walked."

I grabbed her arm and pulled her toward the back of the room. "Mother," I said when we were far enough away so that the people in the restaurant couldn't hear us, "it's freezing outside. You shouldn't have walked all the way here. I can't believe Father allowed you to do this. What's wrong with him?"

"I do not care anymore." Her blue eyes flashed with emotion. "I have had all I can take, Lizzie. Last night your father issued an ultimatum. He plans for us to leave Kingdom and move farther into the country. Away from this town. Away from people in general. I told him I would do no such thing." She put her hand on my cheek. "I will not leave you and Charity. I simply will not."

I opened my mouth to say something, but she shushed me.

"We will talk about this later. Now you must concentrate on your customers. Tell me where my granddaughter is."

I silently pointed toward the kitchen. Without saying another word, she walked away. I'd never seen her act like that, not in all the years I'd known her. I wanted to cheer her on, yet the idea of my parents separating weighed heavily on my heart. Looking back toward the dining room, I found Avery and the other customers staring at me. It was time to concentrate on the task at hand.

I began to put my plans into action, and by ten o'clock everything was running like clockwork, albeit a little slower than normal. Some of my time was spent explaining to everyone what had happened to Cora. It didn't take long to see how much she meant to the people of Kingdom. Cora was more than the owner of the town's only restaurant—she was a friend, confidante, and helper. I had to wonder if I could fill her shoes, not only in my handling of the restaurant, but in her personal touch with people. I was certain everyone would be relieved when she returned. Especially me.

Around ten thirty, during a short lull, I pulled Mother aside and told her about my call to Clay.

"So you are standing by your decision to stay in town for now?" she asked.

"For now. But if I get any idea that the sheriff can link me to the man in the red cap, I'll cash Clay's check and leave."

"Will you let me know where you go?" she asked, her eyes searching my face.

"Not for a while, Mother. I can't take the risk, and I won't put you in a situation where you have to lie."

She nodded and looked away. "It seems wrong to run away when you are innocent, Elizabeth Lynn," she said. "But I understand being willing to do anything to keep your daughter in your life." She went back into the kitchen to check on Charity. I'd seen the pain on her face, but I couldn't make promises right now, even though I wanted to.

Mother informed me that Callie Hoffman would be in after lunch. She'd promised to cover for Leah at the school in the morning, while she went to Washington for needed supplies. I welcomed the help, but I was actually happy to have the morning to myself. A little time on my own would show me just how I wanted to use Callie. Sure enough, by the time the lunch menu was being served, I'd decided I'd have her take over the same duties I'd been doing. Cora had it right. Cooking was a full-time job. Serving customers, except when we were behind, was impossible if I was going to keep up with all the orders and get food out as quickly as I wanted to.

Mother kept Charity occupied all morning. I thought she'd leave after lunch, but she stayed, seemingly unconcerned about my father. At one point, when I was running behind, she took plates out to the tables. I'm sure my customers were shocked at being served breakfast by the wife of Matthew Engel. But Mother took it in stride, as if she'd been doing it all her life. I was proud of her.

True to her word, Callie Hoffman came into the restaurant a little after one o'clock, looking much as she had when I left town. She was a small, delicate young woman with curly red hair and big, beautiful eyes. She had such a slight build I worried that she wouldn't be strong enough to do the job. But she followed my instructions to the letter, and the customers seemed to like her very much. She wore a white prayer covering over her hair, and her dress was a lovely pink with small white flowers. I noticed that several of the women who came in on Monday had traded their black prayer coverings for white. And the black and dark blue dresses were in the minority for once. The meeting on Sunday seemed to be having an effect that Father would not appreciate.

I took a break at three and ate a late lunch while Callie checked on the few remaining customers. Everyone's needs seemed to be met, and the atmosphere was relaxed and jovial. While sipping a well-deserved cup of coffee, I looked up when the front door opened and Noah walked in. I smiled at him as he strolled over to my table.

"I heard about Cora," he said. "Looks like you're making it through your first day with flying colors."

"I did okay, but not without some help." I tipped my head toward Callie, who was filling Abel Bennett's iced tea glass. Abel wasn't much older than Callie, and it was obvious he found the young Mennonite girl to his liking. I chuckled and lowered my voice so they wouldn't hear me. "Been a long time since anyone stared at me with that sappy hangdog look."

Noah laughed and sat down at the table. "Are you talking about me?"

I was so surprised I almost spit out my coffee. Instead, I swallowed too quickly and choked. It took a while for me to stop coughing.

"Sorry," he said, his forehead wrinkled in concern. "You seem to choke up a lot around me."

I shot him a dirty look. "What . . . what did you mean?" I managed to get out. My voice was weak and raspy.

He grinned. "You knew how much I liked you, didn't you? For crying out loud, I used to follow you around like a lost puppy."

I shook my head in amazement. "We were best friends. Of course, I knew you liked me. I liked you too."

He turned his head sideways and raised one eyebrow. "I'm afraid it was more than that, Lizzie. I can't believe you didn't know it. Surely you could read between the lines."

"Read between what lines? I never suspected . . . Why didn't you say something?"

"I guess I was too shy."

I snorted. "Noah Housler, you were never shy a day in your life."

His startling green eyes bore into mine. "Only when it came to expressing my feelings for you."

I felt as if I couldn't catch my breath and didn't want to launch into another coughing spasm. I took a moment to calm myself and picked up my coffee cup, staring at him over the rim. Was he teasing me? He seemed serious. How could

I have missed his interest? Finally I lowered my cup to the table. It wasn't big enough to hide behind anyway.

"I think you're kidding," I said with a smile, "because I had the biggest crush on *you*. If you liked me, I would have known it."

His jovial expression turned serious. "Sometimes when we don't value ourselves enough, we can miss seeing how other people really feel about us, Lizzie."

I stood up, determined to get away before he could see how flustered I was. "C-can I get you . . . I mean, do you want to order something?"

He smiled again, but this time it seemed a little forced. "Sure."

"Apple pie?"

"You know what? Think I'll actually order an entire meal. What's on the menu today?"

I ran over the specials with him, stumbling over my words.

"That hot roast beef sandwich sounds perfect. And coffee, please." The twinkle came back into eyes. "But don't sell the last piece of apple pie. I doubt I'll be able to pass it up."

I nodded quickly and fled from the room. When I reached the kitchen, I pushed the swinging door open and leaned against the wall next to it. I thought back to the time Noah had consoled me after my father's whipping. He'd been so sweet to me, promising that everything would be all right. But in all the time we'd spent together, there was never a moment when I'd thought his feelings for me were more than friendship. If only I'd realized . . .

I pushed myself away from the wall. If I'd known he liked me I probably wouldn't have gotten involved with Clay. Why hadn't Noah said something before he left for school? I would have waited for him. For as long as it took. I shook my head, angry with myself for even thinking that way. It wouldn't do any good to wonder what might have happened. The past was behind me, and thinking about it now was a waste of time.

I prepared his hot beef sandwich, making sure to give him extra mashed potatoes and beef. I was just finishing up when Callie came into the kitchen.

"Is that Noah's?" she asked. "Do you want me to carry it out to him?"

"That's okay," I said quickly. "You make sure everyone else has what they need. I'll take care of Noah."

She nodded. "Am I doing all right? Sorry if I'm a little slow."

I turned and smiled at her. "A little slow? You're putting me to shame. You're twice as fast as I was when I started working in my first restaurant. I hope you'll stay on, Callie. Of course, when Cora gets back, I can't promise anything."

"I understand," she said softly. She put her hand on my arm. "Thank you so much for giving me this job, Lizzie. Even if it only lasts a short time. I'm very grateful for the chance to save up some money."

"Plans?"

She blushed. "No. Well, maybe. I hope to be married some-day, and I want to make certain we'll have enough money to buy a house."

"Oh?" I chuckled. "Abel Bennett can't keep his eyes off you. Is that your future intended?"

Her eyebrows shot up. "Abel Bennett? Oh my, no. It's Levi Housler."

"Levi? Noah's brother?"

"Yes, that's right."

I cleared my throat. "Isn't he . . ."

"A little old for me?"

I put Noah's plate down on the counter and nodded. "He's almost thirty, isn't he?"

Callie stuck her chin out, and her eyes flashed with defiance. "He is twenty-eight years old, and I am twenty. That is only eight years' difference. My parents were ten years apart."

"I'm sorry if I sounded judgmental. I didn't mean to."

A smile chased the bravado from her face. "I apologize too. I guess I'm feeling somewhat defensive."

"Totally understandable. How do your parents feel about your relationship?"

She looked at me with a confused expression. "There is no relationship. Levi doesn't even know I like him." She grinned. "I'm working on him gradually."

I couldn't help but burst out laughing. Callie seemed to understand my reaction and put her hand over her mouth as she giggled. At that moment she looked exactly as she had when we'd been in school. Although I was only a few years older than her, I felt almost ancient.

"Well, this will be interesting. I intend to keep an eye on you and Levi. My money's on you."

She cocked her head to the side. "I'm sorry, I don't understand. Why would you spend money on me?"

For all of Callie's boldness, she was still a Kingdom girl. It took great effort for me to keep a straight face while I explained the worldly expression to her. But she nodded happily once I cleared up the confusion, and she thanked me for having confidence in her ability to attract Levi's attention.

"I'd better get this food out to Noah before it gets cold."

"You can't tell Noah that I'm planning to marry his brother," she said.

"I won't. I promise."

She smiled and turned to fill the coffee and tea pitchers. I grabbed Noah's plate and pushed against the kitchen door, amused by her refreshing honesty and naïveté. She wasn't being sneaky, just straightforward about her plans to marry the man she loved. I wondered if Levi suspected anything. However, even with my limited experience with men, I'd come to the conclusion that most of them had no clue what women were thinking.

As I walked toward Noah's table with his plate, I wondered if he knew how deep my feelings ran for him. I prayed silently that this wasn't the case. I tried to look as indifferent to his presence as I could. Unfortunately, I forgot about a slight bulge in the rug that I'd been avoiding all day. My toe hit it, and I almost fell. Noah's plate went flying out of my hands and slid across his table. He desperately tried to catch it but was only partially successful. The plate flipped and most of his lunch plopped into his lap. I stood there with my mouth hanging open, horrified by what I'd just done.

Abel Bennett began to snicker, and my mother stood up from the table where she'd been eating with Charity. Except for Abel's snorting, there wasn't another sound in the room until Noah looked at me innocently and said, "Could I have some extra gravy with that?"

I was so embarrassed I turned and ran back toward the kitchen, past Callie, who was holding a carafe of coffee and a pitcher of tea. I sat down at Charity's small table and buried my face in my hands. Why did I keep doing such ridiculous things around Noah? A few moments later Callie came in without the tea and coffee.

"Are you all right?" she asked.

I nodded, not trusting my voice.

"It was just an accident," she said gently. "Noah took it very well. You should—"

"Why don't you let me talk to her?"

I glanced up in dismay. Noah stood in the doorway, mashed potatoes sliding down his pant leg, and a big wet stain on his dark slacks.

Callie nodded at him and left the room smiling.

"I-I'm s-sorry," I said, my voice shaking. "You m-must think I'm an idiot."

He didn't say anything for a moment. Then he came over to the small table, where I crouched on the child-sized chair. "I would never think that about you," he said gently. He grabbed my hand and pulled me to my feet. "What I think is that you're the most intelligent, entertaining, and surprising girl I've ever known. And I thought that even before you served supper in my lap."

I started to protest, to apologize for being such a klutz, but he put his fingers on my lips and his eyes sought mine. I knew beyond a shadow of a doubt that he was getting ready to kiss me, but before he could finish what he'd started, a voice bellowed from behind us.

"I might have known I would find you in a compromising position. You haven't changed at all. Have you, Daughter?"

I pushed Noah away and looked past him. There at the door stood my father, the self-righteous expression on his face all too familiar.

CHAPTER/19

"Elder Engel, this isn't Lizzie's fault." Noah turned to face my outraged father while I just stood there like my feet were glued to the floor.

"I am not interested in hearing from you, boy," Father growled. "And I am no longer an elder in the church. Surely you remember that, seeing as you have usurped my position?"

Noah started to say something, but my father waved his response away. "I am certain the church board will be interested in how their new elder conducts himself. I may not be a part of Kingdom Church any longer, but I will surely warn them about your behavior." With that, he stormed out of the kitchen.

"Noah, I'm so sorry . . ." Before I could finish my sentence, Noah turned around and planted a kiss firmly on my lips.

"That's what I intended to do before your father burst in. I hope it doesn't offend you in any way."

My thoughts were so jumbled, I muttered something nonsensical. Then I gathered up my wits and gently pushed him away. "Now my father thinks I'm a . . . a . . ."

"Lady of loose morals?" he said with a cockeyed grin. He

grabbed me by the shoulders and gazed into my eyes. "And are you, Lizzie? Are you who your father says you are?"

I stared back at him as a fire began to burn somewhere in the pit of my stomach. I shook his hands off. "I most certainly am not!" I said it so loudly I actually startled myself.

"Then why don't you stop acting like it? Quit allowing your father to define you. He's wrong, you know. He's been wrong your whole life."

"How can you possibly say that?" My voice shook with emotion, but I didn't seem to be able to control it.

"Because I know *you*," he replied, his eyes flashing with emotion. "The problem is that you don't. Maybe it's time you had some faith in yourself."

Before I could respond, raised voices from the restaurant drew my attention. I hurried past Noah, pushed open the kitchen door, and found my father standing in the middle of the dining room, shouting. The only customer left was Abel Bennett, who got up, handed some money to Callie, and quickly left. Callie prudently turned our Open sign over and pulled down the shade on the front door.

"I will not go with you, Matthew." My mother sat at a table with Charity, whose eyes were wide with alarm as she watched my father's tirade.

I went over and whispered to Callie, asking her to take Charity upstairs. She quickly gathered up my daughter and led her away. Before they left, I assured Charity that everything would be all right, but the anxiety on her face stoked my own indignation. After I heard the door upstairs close, I whirled around and looked my father in the eye.

"How dare you come in here and frighten my daughter," I said. "And how dare you try to bully my mother . . . and me."

He took a menacing step toward me, but someone stepped in between us. Noah.

"This is over," Noah said in a low voice.

With Noah standing between us, I couldn't see all of father's face, but his eyebrows rose, and I saw something in his eyes I'd never seen before. Was it fear?

"When I was younger, I couldn't stand up to you the way I wanted to. But I'm not a child now, and neither is Lizzie. I won't allow you to intimidate her. And I'll certainly never allow you to lay a hand on her again, Matthew. Never. Do you understand me?"

Father's expression turned toxic, and he shook with anger. I began to worry for Noah's safety. "Why, you little pretender. You claim a position on the board of elders, yet I find you in a sinful situation with my daughter. And then you threaten violence against me? The foundation of our religion is a rejection of violence. But you do not seem to understand this, do you?"

"Funny," Noah said, his voice calm yet strong, "I thought the foundation of our religion was Christ, His sacrifice, our redemption, and His grace to live the life He's called us to. Perhaps it is *you* who doesn't understand. And I would certainly question your view of nonviolence. It appears it doesn't apply to your treatment of your daughter."

Father took another step toward Noah, his hand raised, but Noah stood his ground, and I was afraid he would allow Father to strike him. I stepped in front of him.

"That's enough, Father. I want you to leave. Now. You've frightened Charity, and I won't have it. You will not terrorize my daughter the way you did me. And you will not run roughshod over anyone else I care about. It stops right now."

"What right do you have to talk to me like that?" he thundered.

"All the right in the world." I sounded confident, but my knees were shaking so hard I was convinced everyone could hear them knocking together. "As Noah said, I'm an adult now, not a frightened little girl. I will make my own decisions, and I will live my own life. You will stay away from Charity—do you hear me? And as far as my mother, if she's told you she doesn't want to go with you, then she'll not go. And that's the last of it."

He stood there, trembling. I saw uncontrolled wrath in his face, and I began to wonder if that expression was what the man in the red ball cap had seen just before he died.

"I believe Lizzie asked you to leave," Noah said quietly. "It's time for you to go, Matthew."

They stared at each other for several seconds, but it felt like hours to me. Finally my father turned toward my mother. "I am telling you for the last time to come with me, Anna. And I forbid you to come here ever again. Or to see Elizabeth Lynn and that illegitimate child of hers. I will not give you another chance to defy me. Do you understand?"

My mother stood up slowly. "I will not go, Matthew. I will continue to visit my daughter and my grandchild. And you do not need to give me another chance. I do not seek one. I have made my choice."

My father's face turned pale, and he sputtered incomprehensibly. Finally he gathered himself together and said, "You are not welcome in my house, woman. If you come home, you will find the door locked."

My mother smiled slowly. "If you remember, Matthew, that is not your house. It was my mother's and was passed down to me. I am afraid you are the one who will have to leave if you choose to do so. You may certainly keep me out for a while, but I am confident the board of elders will side with me if we must appear before them."

"As one of the elders, I can assure you that's exactly what will happen," Noah said. "I don't wish to see a marriage dissolved, Brother Matthew. Even yours. We'll be available to you both for counseling. Of course, you'll have to decide if you want restoration before we can help you. For now, however, I think it's wise for you to move out of Sister Anna's house."

Father's eyes swept over all of us, finally settling on Mother, who refused to back down from his angry gaze. "Is this what you want, Anna? For me to leave our home? If your answer is yes, please do not think for a moment that I will ever return."

Mother's eyes flushed with tears. "Even with everything you have done, Matthew, I still love you. I may be the only person in the world who does. But I will not turn away from Lizzie and Charity. I cannot. If I did, my heart would surely break in two. Do not misunderstand me. I am not putting my child and grandchild before my husband, but I know that our marriage is . . . wrong. Even though you say you will reject me for my decision, I want you to know that my door will always be open to you. However, for you to come back, you must agree to counseling through our church. And you must accept Lizzie and Charity into your life."

My father took a deep breath and let it out slowly. "I will never do that."

"Then I am sorry for you, Husband. And ashamed. Ashamed that you call yourself a follower of Christ, yet you do not understand even the basics of love."

"Is that all?" Father's eyes seemed to sweep over my mother's face as if trying to capture it one last time. I realized that tears were streaming down my cheeks. Quickly wiping them off with the back of my hand, I took a step closer to my father.

"Before you go, Father, I have a question, and I would like an answer. The man who was found dead on the road, the stranger—did you have anything to do with his death? I must know."

He paused for a moment and then shook his head slowly, looking down toward the floor. "I will not answer your question, Elizabeth," he said finally. "You may suspect me if you wish; that is not my concern." He turned and walked toward the front door. Before turning the knob he looked back at me. "I will tell you one thing, but that is all. If this man *was* killed, you are asking your question to the wrong person." He stared at Noah for a moment and then looked at Mother once more. With that he unlocked the door, stepped outside, and was gone.

My mother instantly collapsed into her chair. "Oh, Lizzie," she said softly. "What have I done? What have I done?"

I went over to the table, pulled up a chair, and put my arms around her. "It will be all right," I said gently. "You did what had to be done. I'm proud of you, Mother."

"Proud of me?" she said, sobbing. "I have turned my husband out of my house. I am not sure God would approve of it. Not at all."

"Sister Anna," Noah said, sitting down with us at the table, "you didn't turn him out. He turned himself out. Remember that he ordered you out of your own home. You only did what had to be done. The church will back you fully. You have my word."

She shook her head. "I cannot go home now," she said,

her voice breaking. "Will you let me stay with you, Lizzie? At least tonight? I won't be any trouble. I promise."

"Of course, Mother. You can stay here as long as you like. Charity and I would love to have you."

"Thank you, Daughter. Thank you so much." She raised her wet face to mine. "Elizabeth Lynn, I want you to know how proud I am of you. So blessed that you are my daughter. And even though you may find this hard to believe, I have always been proud of you. That has never changed. I fear the reason you sought the love of a man when you were younger was because you could not find any compassion in your father. But you have proven to be a strong woman, raising a child alone and overcoming adversity with character and dignity. I want only to be more like you."

I hugged her tighter. "I'm not someone to emulate, Mother. I've been very foolish about a lot of things. I can see that now. I shouldn't have run away from Kingdom in the first place. Not everyone was against me, as I thought. And I probably should have stood my ground in Kansas City. I ran away again, hoping my problems would go away instead of facing them."

"Does this mean you will go back there?" Mother asked, her voice slightly muffled by my shoulder.

"I don't know. I'm going to have to think things out, but if I do decide to return and face the music, I know I can leave my daughter here with you—and that she'll be safe."

"Thank you, Lizzie. You cannot know how much that means to me." She let go of me and wiped her face with a napkin on the table. "I will go check on Charity and send Callie downstairs. I believe you two need to prepare for your evening customers?"

I looked at the clock on the wall and gasped. "Yes. Yes, I do. Thank you, Mother."

She rose from her chair and walked slowly toward the stairs. I knew the gravity of what had happened between her and my father weighed heavily on her shoulders. She'd been taught that a good Christian wife obeys her husband at all times. I was certain standing up to him had taken more out of her than I could even imagine.

"She'll be okay, Lizzie," Noah said. "Your mother is much stronger than you realize. I can't imagine how difficult it's been, living with your father all these years. Yet she's endured."

"Yes, she has. And now it seems as if their lives together are over."

He smiled at me. "I guess these situations are what faith is for. How about we pray for them and ask God to intervene?"

"That sounds good, but if my father isn't willing to change, how can God fix their marriage?"

He reached over and took hold of my hand. "Well, He's the only one who can get inside Matthew's heart. You can't do it, nor can your mother. Why don't we pray that God will soften him? I have no doubt that God can do anything."

"You're an odd man, Noah Housler," I said. "You steal a kiss in the kitchen, and now you talk as if you and God are best friends."

He smiled and squeezed my hand. "He *is* my best friend, Lizzie. And He's yours too." Noah let go of my hand and stood up. "I need to get home. My mother will be frantic wondering where I am." He pulled on his thick black coat and wide-brimmed hat. "I don't mean to be nosy, but you mentioned trouble in Kansas City. I knew about the man who followed you here, since the church elders were informed of his presence, but I don't know anything else about your situation. Is there something I can do to help you? Would you like to talk about it?"

"Not right now, but thank you for caring."

"Well, I'm here if you need me. I'm a pretty good listener."

"I appreciate your offer, Noah. I'll keep it in mind."

He glanced around the dining room. "Do you need some help in the restaurant? I can clean off tables with the best of them."

I chuckled and shook my head. "Elder Noah Housler busing tables? I'm afraid I'd never live it down. But thanks anyway."

"Okay." Before walking out, he paused to stare at me. I felt as if his eyes were looking straight into my soul. "Just remember that if you need anything, Lizzie, all you have to do is ask. I promised once to take care of you, didn't I? I meant it, you know."

With that he left. His parting comment should have made me feel safer, but for some reason it didn't. I tried to shake off a sense of apprehension as I worked on the evening meals, but it dogged me the rest of the day. And before I fell asleep that night, Noah's words kept echoing through my mind. It took a while before I was able to fall into an uneasy sleep.

CHAPTER / 20

Tuesday started off slowly, and I welcomed the chance to decelerate a bit. Mother had stayed the night, sleeping in my bed while I took the couch. It felt odd to have her there, but I liked it.

She suggested that Charity and I could move into her house once Father had cleared out, but I put her off. Noah was right. As impossible as it sounded, I had to pray that God would touch Father's heart and bring him home. I would also pray that the man who returned would be the husband my mother had once loved. A man I couldn't remember at all. And even though I appreciated her offer, I'd grown to love our apartment and didn't want to leave. Of course, Charity would be horrified if we moved into the house with the "bad potty," so for now, we would stay put.

Things picked up around lunch. A little after two o'clock, Hope came in, and she brought Leah Burkholder with her. It was wonderful to see her after all these years. I would have known her in an instant. She had been a plain little girl and had grown into a plain young woman. But the intelligence in her eyes and the way she spoke made her the kind of person people felt drawn to. I had no doubt she was a wonderful teacher, and could see immediately why the children loved her. I told her I planned to enroll Charity after the Christmas break if we were still in town. Leah had a cup of coffee and then left, needing to get back to the school.

"She's so much more confident than she was as a child," I told Hope when Leah had gone.

Hope nodded. "Leah came into her own when she began teaching. I believe it is because she discovered the gifts God placed inside her. When we find our destiny, it gives us confidence. . . . But not in ourselves—it is in God, who puts us where we are supposed to be and gives us what we need to succeed." She sighed. "I must admit that I'm still looking for my special place, but I have put my desire in the Father's hands. I'm waiting for His leading."

I could relate to that. Once again I remembered the voice that had told me to come to Kingdom. I was convinced that Clay hadn't shown up here by accident. Surely it was part of God's greater plan to bring us back together. Only time would tell if I was right.

"Besides bringing Leah to talk to you about the school, I wanted to tell you that the elders went to your father last night in an attempt to heal the wounds caused by our recent vote. When they got to the house, your father refused to talk to them. He told them he was leaving in the morning and asked them to let your mother know he'd purchased a horse and buggy from Avery Menninger. He's leaving Blackie and their buggy behind so she won't be without transportation."

"Wow. It's hard to believe he thought enough about Mother to do that," I said. "But it will certainly make life easier for her."

"I'm sorry he's leaving, Lizzie. I pray he'll be all right. He seems to be a man who needs a wife to care for him."

I could have told her it was my mother who'd asked him to go, but I decided that wouldn't be wise. There might be people in the church who would give her a hard time about it, and she didn't need that kind of pressure. "He did have a wife who cared for him, Hope. Problem was, he couldn't do the same for her."

She was silent for a moment before asking, "Do you know where he'll go?"

"I have no idea. He said something about moving farther out into the country, where he wouldn't have to be around people. That should suit him just fine. He has a hard time getting along with other human beings, you know."

"What a lonely life. I feel so sorry for him." The sincerity in her eyes made me feel a little ashamed. She seemed to have more sympathy for my father than I did.

"He brought all this on himself, don't you think?" I asked a little defensively. "I mean, my mother did everything she could to make him happy, but he refused to show her even the slightest kindness."

She looked surprised. "I'm sure you know more about your parents than I do. But I used to watch him help her out of their carriage before and after church services. He seemed so . . . solicitous. Every time there was a church dinner, he would insist on getting her plate so she wouldn't have to wait in line. And when it rained, he would bring the buggy as close to the building as possible to save her from getting wet."

"Of course he did all those things in front of church people, Hope. After all, he valued his position as an elder. But at home he ruled like a tyrant, and if I repeated the things he's said to me and my mother . . . Well, you wouldn't believe them."

She reached over and rested her hand on my arm. "I'm really sorry, Lizzie. I know it wasn't easy. But people are rarely one-sided. Your father must have good traits. Every child of God has a part of His Spirit inside him, pulling him toward goodness. Anyway, that's what I've observed." She laughed lightly and removed her hand. "Of course, here I am in Kingdom, seeing little of the outside world. Forgive me for speaking foolishly, will you?"

"I'm sure there's truth in what you say, it's just that . . . I don't know. I guess it's hard for me to see any good traits in my father." I sighed. "My mother says his life was very hard growing up. My grandfather may have been even harsher than Father."

She nodded. "I imagine it has made relationships difficult for him."

I felt myself flush with irritation. "Well, he made my life hard, but you don't see me mistreating my family and trying to toss Pastor Mendenhall out of the church."

Hope's light complexion paled. "I've upset you. Again, I apologize. Perhaps I should go."

"Please, Hope, don't leave. I'm the one who should be apologizing. My emotions are very raw when it comes to Father. I'm trying hard to forgive him, and it's taking a toll on me. I don't mean to take it out on you. Your friendship is extremely valuable to me, and I have no intention of letting anything come between us. Especially my father. I'll think about what you said. I really will. It means more than I can say to have a friend who will speak candidly with me. Thank you." I smiled at her. "Now, I insist you try a piece of the banana bread I made this morning. It's so good it will put color in your cheeks."

She laughed. "I'm told I could use some roses in my cheeks, so I will gladly try a slice. Perhaps with a cup of your wonderful coffee?"

"You got it."

Before I could get up, a young man came in through the front door. He was tall and dark haired, with bright blue eyes and a walk that commanded attention. He strode over to our table and stuck his hand out.

"Hello, I'm Jonathon Wiese," he said without taking his eyes off Hope. "My family moved to Kingdom a couple of years ago. I heard Matthew and Anna's daughter was back in town." He finally shifted his gaze to me. "I wanted to meet you and tell you how pleased I am that you're back."

"Well, thank you, Jonathon. I had no idea there were new families in town."

His smile revealed perfectly even teeth that were so white they gleamed. "Believe it or not, there are several of us. I hope our influence will be felt in the church. I'm glad to see we're moving toward change, although I regret your father felt the need to leave. I'm sure he's convinced he's doing the right thing, but we have no choice except to move forward. We must alter the things that separate us from the grace of God. Don't you agree?"

Hope smiled at me. "Jonathon is a revisionist, Lizzie. He believes our church must adjust its stodgy ways if we are to keep our relevance. I must say that I agree with most of what he says."

Jonathon flashed his flawless teeth at Hope. "So there are some points you don't agree with, Sister Hope? Perhaps we could spend some time discussing them. I value your opinion."

It would have been obvious to a blind man that Jonathon was interested in much more than just Hope's view of church doctrine. Feeling like a third wheel, I excused myself. The two of them barely noticed I'd left. I had to wonder if their relationship was a threat to Hope's arranged marriage with Ebbie. Jonathon seemed so self-assured and dynamic, whereas Ebbie was quiet and shy. But since it wasn't any of my business, I cut some banana bread for Hope, asked Callie to make sure she had coffee, and got back to work.

Mother watched Charity all afternoon. I told her more than once that she could leave whenever she wanted to, but I sensed she was afraid to run into Father, even though I shared with her what Hope had said.

I was in the kitchen preparing the evening special, chicken and noodles, when Callie came rushing into the kitchen.

"Lizzie, it's the sheriff. He wants to see you."

Mother cried out, and my heart felt as if it would burst. Was this it? Had he come for me? In that moment, I realized I may have been terribly foolish to remain in Kingdom. With Clay's money, Charity and I could have already been far away. But the voice that drew me to Kingdom had promised me everything would be okay. If that voice truly belonged to God, I could be secure in His promise. I squared my shoulders and followed Callie into the dining room, trying to look confident even though I didn't feel that way. Sheriff Ford sat at a table in the corner. Except for a man I didn't know who was drinking coffee and reading a book, the room was empty.

"You wanted to see me, Sheriff?" I asked, trying to keep the apprehension out of my voice.

"Yes, Miss Engel. The autopsy came back on that dead man in the ditch."

"I don't understand, Sheriff. Why tell me about it?"

He shrugged. "I heard the owner of this place was outta town, and you were in charge. Seemed like the best way to spread the word would be through a public joint like this. I mean, most of the town's people come through here, don't they?" He scowled at me. "Any reason not to tell you?"

"No. Sorry, Sheriff. That makes perfect sense." I heard my mother come out of the kitchen and stand behind me. I felt her hand on my shoulder. "Please, go on."

He leaned against the nearest table and crossed his arms. "Well, the doc in Washington ruled the death an accident, mostly because he couldn't prove it was anything else. Seems the wound to the dead guy's head coulda been caused by fallin' down that ravine and landin' on the rocks. So we're through with our inquiry into this matter." He reached into his coat pocket and pulled out a small notebook.

"Do . . . do you have any idea what he was doing out here?" I tried to keep my voice steady, but my nervousness was obvious.

The sheriff frowned at me. "Could be anything. Maybe he came here to hunt. We get all kinds of yahoos out here this time of year." He scribbled something in his notebook. "I don't got time to figure out why this guy was in the area. We're callin' it an accident, so my part in this is done. That's all I care about."

"Did you at least find out who he was?"

The sheriff nodded and scanned his notes. "His name was Dave Parsons. Retired from the water company. A real loner who fancied himself a part-time private eye." Ford snorted. "Lotsa nuts out there think they know how to do the job of a professional. 'Course all they usually end up investigatin' is cheatin' spouses and crud like that. Could be that's why he was out this way, but we'll never know, I guess.

"Police went through his apartment, but there wasn't nothin' there. No notes, no computer, nothin' helpful. No way for anyone to know why he was so far from home." He closed the notebook and stuck it back in his pocket. "Only livin' relative is a sister in Florida who hasn't seen him in years. We're releasin' the body to her. She wasn't too happy about bein' responsible for him, but that's her problem."

He pushed away from the table and stood with his hands on his hips. "You folks got any questions?"

I shook my head. "Thank you for coming by, Sheriff. And we'll make sure everyone knows that Mr. Parsons' death was an accident. I'm sure it will help folks to feel safer."

"That's my intention. Mind you, I still think you're all a little wacky out here, but you deserve to know there ain't no crazed killer runnin' around knockin' people off."

I almost burst out laughing at his comment. The sheriff had to get in one last word about the town even when he was trying to apologize. What a character. "Thanks, again. And have a good day."

"You too." With that he was gone. Did the doctor's ruling mean my worries about the man in the red cap were over? I wanted to feel relief that his death had been deemed accidental, but it was clear that the sheriff's main interest was getting the case off his hands. What about the truth? There was no way I could believe with certainty that Dave Parsons wasn't killed by someone else. And if his death wasn't an accident, what did that mean? Discovering that Parsons was a part-time detective confirmed my suspicion that he'd been following me. That seemed to point directly to Reba.

Unfortunately, I still couldn't be sure, and I couldn't assume that I was actually in the clear. At least knowing the police hadn't found anything to connect Parsons to me made me feel a little more secure. For now, anyway.

"Can I talk to you?" Mother asked.

"Sure."

I started to follow her to the kitchen when I realized that Callie hadn't been working when the sheriff first visited. She looked upset.

"Had you heard about the man who died?" I asked her.

She nodded. "News spreads through Kingdom pretty fast. I just can't help feeling bad for him. The dead man, I mean. Sounds like he didn't have anyone. No one to mourn his passing." Her eyes were shiny with tears.

I was touched by her tender heart. "It is sad. But *you're* mourning his death, Callie. I'm sure he'd appreciate it."

"I guess you're right. I hope so." She turned away to check on our only customer, who looked somewhat stunned by the drama from the sheriff's visit.

While Callie warmed up the man's coffee, I joined my mother in the kitchen.

"So what does this mean?" she asked when the door closed behind me.

"I honestly don't know, Mother." I kept my voice low, so Charity wouldn't overhear us. "At least I don't have to worry about him anymore. However, it now seems even more likely that someone hired him to tail me." I shook my head. "I feel like I'm trying to put a puzzle together that's missing several of the pieces. Something's wrong with this whole picture, but I can't put my finger on what it is."

Mother took my hands in hers. "I truly believe God brought

you here, Daughter. If you can trust Him to work it out, you will be at peace. I know in my heart that somehow everything will be all right."

I looked into my mother's eyes and saw the love she had for me. She was speaking from the deepest part of her soul, and it brought me a feeling of assurance. "I'm doing my best to trust Him, Mother. I've been mad at God for a long time, but I've had to confront the reality that I alone caused all my problems. Through it all, He just kept loving me. The least I can do is to have a little faith in Him now."

"We are both clinging to the Rock, Lizzie," she said in hushed tones. "And each other." She kissed me on the cheek and went out into the dining room.

I stood next to the sink, trying to gather my thoughts. I'd been trying to figure out what to do to protect me and my daughter ever since Kansas City. As I'd told my mother, I had the distinct feeling my life had become a giant picture puzzle with several vital pieces missing. I certainly wasn't omniscient, and the truth was that only God knew what was going on. He was the only one who could add the missing parts. I had no idea what to do now. Stay? Go? Wait? I didn't have the answers.

I took a deep breath. "God," I whispered, "you know me better than anyone. You know how wrong I've been, and it seems you've forgiven me, even though I certainly didn't deserve it. I thank you for that. I have no idea what my next step should be. All I know to do is to trust you to lead me. If you tell me to go back to Kansas City and face Reba's lies, I'll go. If I'm supposed to just stay here, I'll stay. But until I hear from you, I'm not moving.

"Since Clay came back, I've been wondering if he's here

so Charity can finally have a father. If this is what you want, God, then I'll do it. You know I have feelings for Noah, but he's not Charity's father. More than anything, I want my daughter to be happy. If that means moving forward with Clay, then that's what I'll do. I'm counting on you to show me your will and to protect Charity and me. My future is in your hands, Lord. It's all I have to give you. In Jesus' name, amen."

Already feeling my load was lighter, I hurried to begin meal preparations. The Tuesday night special was fried catfish, and I needed to get it breaded and ready for the fryer. I'd almost forgotten that Clay was coming that evening, so when Callie announced his arrival, it took me by surprise. I'd promised to close early so we could spend the evening together. I hadn't realized then that my mother would be staying with me, but as I was lowering the first fish into the bubbling oil, she announced that she was going home after we closed.

"I love being here," she said, "but I must confess that I miss my home. And I must make certain Blackie has been fed."

"I think that's wise," I told her. "But any time you feel lonely, you come back and spend time with Charity and me. Our door is always open."

She smiled. "As is mine, Daughter."

I gave her a big hug, and then she went to round up Charity, who was visiting with Callie in the dining room. Mother and Charity came back into the kitchen, and Mother informed me that Callie had offered to drive her home in her buggy after work. I was relieved to know she wouldn't be walking. The temperatures were still extremely frigid.

I stopped by Clay's table and found a bouquet of red roses

waiting for me. "Oh my. I've never gotten roses before. Thank you so much."

He chuckled. "You're blushing, Lizzie. I'd like to buy you roses every day just so I could see you look like that."

He was so handsome, wearing a white sweater that highlighted his hair and eyes. "Let me get you something to drink," I said, smiling. "We're not that busy tonight, so I should be able to close soon."

"Thanks. Coffee would be fine."

I nodded and was headed for the kitchen when I saw Ruth and her daughter giving Callie their supper order. I hurried over to say hello.

"*Liebling,*" Ruth said, smiling, "I so hoped I would see you this evening. I heard about Cora. There is no one I know who is more capable of keeping the restaurant going than you."

I laughed. "Well, it's only my second day, so I don't think I can brag on myself yet. But so far so good. I'm just praying that her sister recovers quickly. Unfortunately, her condition sounds very serious."

"Yes, I am afraid you are right. But we know our God is a God of healing, *ja*? So I will keep praying for His very best."

I leaned over and gave her a quick hug. "If I'm ever sick, you're the person I want praying for me."

"That's the way I feel too," Myra said with a smile. She looked past me and frowned. "Lizzie, who is that handsome young man you were talking to? He doesn't look familiar."

"Why, that's Clay Troyer. He used to live in Washington."

Ruth's eyes grew big. "Lizzie, is this not the man who . . . I mean . . ."

"Yes, he's Charity's father," I said quietly. "He came to town the other day looking for me, offering to help support his daughter." Those feelings of rejection and the fear of people's censure I'd felt after Charity was born came rushing back, even though I knew Ruth loved me.

"Why, he looks like a very nice man," Myra said, giving her mother a quick look.

Ruth smiled. "I am sorry, *liebling*. Perhaps my surprise at seeing him here caused me to act inappropriately. He certainly does look like a pleasant fellow."

I wasn't sure how Clay would feel about being called a "pleasant fellow," but at least the awkward moment had passed. It was silly of me to fear Ruth's disapproval. She was the one person who had always believed in me. "He really is," I said. "He brought me roses. No one ever gave me roses before."

Myra clapped her hands together with glee. "They're beautiful, Lizzie. You're a lucky girl."

Ruth just smiled and nodded but didn't say anything.

"I've got to run," I said, "but why don't we all get together for dinner soon? Hopefully Cora will be back before long."

"That would be lovely," Myra said. "Just let us know when your schedule eases up."

"Yes, *liebling*," Ruth said. "I will bake those white coconut cookies for you. And for Charity."

Myra opened her purse and grabbed a piece of paper. "Here's my phone number, Lizzie. You can call me anytime, and I'll get a message to Mom."

"You have a phone?" I asked, although I wasn't completely surprised. Myra and her husband, Charles, were rather free spirits. Although Myra dressed modestly, she didn't wear a prayer covering unless she was going to church. And on the farm she wore overalls while she worked. I'd always admired her ability to be her own person.

241

She laughed warmly. "Yes, we have a phone and a truck. There's no way I'm driving a buggy all the way from the farm to pick up Mom. It would take me forever to get back and forth."

"Ruth, you ride in Myra's truck?" I was stunned. My father wouldn't get into a gas-powered vehicle if God himself came down and ordered him to.

She nodded. "*Ja*. Seeing my daughter is more important to me than our mode of transportation. You will notice a few motor vehicles around Kingdom now. They are vital to many of our people. Especially our farmers. The Houslers own two of them, and Noah and Levi are now elders in the church."

"Wow. And you approve of an elder owning a motor vehicle?"

She laughed. "*Ach*, Lizzie. Have they not driven tractors all along? Is this so different? I do not think so." She smiled at the expression on my face. "See, I am not as conventional as you imagined."

I chuckled. "I guess not."

"Myra is trying to talk me into a telephone," she said. "She believes it will provide me more protection if I should need help." She grinned mischievously. "We will see. So far, the Great Protector has done a pretty good job caring for me." She reached over and patted my arm. "I can hardly wait until we can get together again."

"Me either." I said good-bye to her and Myra and rushed back to the kitchen.

Except for Friday nights, most of the folks in Kingdom liked to eat early, so by six thirty most of our customers were already filing out. I flipped the Open sign over and prepared to close. While Callie took care of the people who were still eating, I got to work on my own dinner. Within a short time I had three plates of chicken-fried steak, mashed potatoes with gravy, and green beans with bacon ready to go.

I took Charity to the bathroom downstairs because I didn't want Clay to see her before I cleaned her up some. I washed her face and hands and carefully brushed her hair. She looked adorable in her dark blue pinafore and white blouse. It was a small miracle that she'd managed to stay tidy.

I checked myself out in the mirror. The hot steam from the kitchen had given my shoulder-length hair even more curl than usual, as well as added some color to my cheeks. As I stared at my image, I worried that Charity might notice the similarity between herself and Clay. But I consoled myself with the knowledge that, at her age, it would probably never occur to her. I certainly didn't want to tell her the truth. Not yet, anyway.

By the time I reached the top of the stairs, Mother and Callie were waiting for me. I hugged Mother good-bye and thanked Callie for taking her home. After they left, I took our plates out of the oven, where I'd put them to keep them warm, and transferred them to a large tray designed for carrying more than one meal at a time. I intended to be very careful to avoid the bump in the rug. There was no way I was going to repeat my shameful performance from yesterday.

"Mama, who is that man out there?" Charity asked after peeking around the corner and looking out into the dining room.

"He's a friend of mine. From a long, long time ago, Cherry Bear. He wants to meet you, and I want you to be very nice to him. Can you do that for Mama?"

She nodded solemnly. "Is he a good man or a bad man?"

I smiled at her. "He's a good man, honey. You don't need to worry about him."

"He won't yell like Grandpa?"

"No, he won't yell like Grandpa." I knelt down in front of her. "Cherry Bear, Grandpa is a very sad man. Sometimes when people are sad, they get angry, like Grandpa did. But that just means we need to pray really hard for him."

She looked at me quizzically. "Will you pray with me sometime, Mama?"

Shame rolled through me. Because of my bad attitude toward God, I'd never prayed with my little girl. "Yes, I will. Tonight before we go to bed. But now let's have dinner with Mr. Troyer."

"Toyer?" she repeated.

"No, it's *Troyer.*"

A couple more attempts made it clear the first *r* in Clay's last name wasn't going to make an appearance that evening. "Well, maybe you can just call him Clay."

Charity screwed up her face as if thinking this over. "If I call him Clay, will I still be ladylike?"

"Ladylike? Where did you hear that word?"

She shook her head, causing her dark curls to bounce. Then she bent closer, as if she was telling me a secret. "Grandma told me that when I wear a dress I have to be careful not to show my underwear. It's not *ladylike.*"

I tried to suppress a grin. "And did you show your underwear?"

She sighed and threw her arms up in a sign of surrender. "Well, I guess I did. But my back itched really bad, and I had to do something about it, didn't I?"

"Yes, I think that was probably an emergency. Maybe the

next time your back itches you can tell me, and I'll scratch it for you. And Grandma's right, it's probably best if you don't show your underwear."

She rolled her eyes. "Well, I know that *now.*"

I laughed and hugged her close. "Cherry Bear, you are the most wonderful person I've ever known. Do you realize how much I love you?"

"Yes, Mama. I do."

I let her go and smiled. "Good. I want you to always be sure I love you. And I always will, you know."

"Forever and ever?" she asked, grinning.

"Yes, forever and ever." I stood up. "Now, are you ready to have dinner with Mr . . . I mean, Clay?"

She nodded. "Yes, let's go!"

I took her by the hand and led her out to the dining room. Clay may have gotten a quick glance once, when my mother was ushering her upstairs, but as far as I knew, this would be his first good look at Charity. As we approached the table where he sat, I noticed his eyes focused on her as if there weren't anyone else in the room. When we got closer I realized they were wet with tears.

"Clay, I'd like you to meet Charity," I said, trying to keep my voice level. "And Charity, this is Mr. Troyer." I smiled at Clay. "We have a little trouble with the letter *r*, so if you don't mind, can she call you Clay?"

"I would be absolutely honored," he said. "Charity, you're very beautiful, just like your mama."

My daughter seemed to suddenly turn shy. "Thank you," she whispered. She hung back, half hiding behind me.

"Why don't you sit down with Clay while I get our food?" I said, pulling her around, lifting her up to a chair, and getting her settled. "I'll be right back. Why don't you tell Clay about the pictures you drew today?"

I turned and left, hoping her shyness would disappear. It was important to me that Clay see how bright she was. I needn't have worried. It only took a couple of questions from Clay to get her wound up. I could hear her beginning to jabber as I went into the kitchen to fetch the tray with our plates. While carrying it to the table, I cautiously avoided the dangerous bump in the rug. By the time I got back, Clay was laughing heartily at something Charity had said. It felt strange to see them together, even beginning to bond.

"Chicken-fried steak?" Clay said when I put the plates down. "Wow, I haven't had chicken-fried steak in a long, long time. One of my very favorite foods in the whole world."

"Me too," Charity said, never taking her eyes from his face.

I could have pointed out that she'd only had chicken-fried steak one other time, but I kept my mouth shut.

I gave in to Charity's plea for pop and also brought a coffee-pot to the table for Clay and me. Dinner went by quickly as Charity gave Clay the rundown about everything that had happened since she'd come to town. He got an earful. From my mother's "bad potty" to meeting a man who looked just like Prince Phillip from *Sleeping Beauty*. Clay glanced over at me during this particular part of Charity's recitation, and I tried to look innocent, but I could feel my cheeks burn. Thankfully, he didn't ask any questions, and we soon moved past the uncomfortable topic and on to something safer. Charity began to regale him with all the foods she'd helped Miss Cora prepare.

"You'll be running the restaurant by yourself before long," Clay said, his eyes crinkled with humor.

Charity considered this idea. "I think I might be able to," she said after a brief pause. "It's really not too hard. Alls you gotta do is drop stuff into grease or flip things over on the grill. But I'd hafta get a tall chair. I can't reach most things in the kitchen, you know."

Clay shook his head. "No, I didn't know that. You look pretty big to me."

She grinned at him. "Thank you. I'm really much taller than I look."

Clay laughed. "You know, I've always felt the same way."

I brought out cherry cobbler for dessert. After we finished, I told Charity it was time for bed. She could barely keep her eyes open.

"But I don't wanna go to bed, Mama," she whined. "We have company, and I wanna stay downstairs."

"You should mind your mother," Clay said sharply. "Bad little girls don't get presents from Santa, you know."

I frowned at him as Charity's eyes grew large, and her small bottom lip stuck out in a pout. "I'm not a bad little girl," she said, hurt in her voice.

"No, you're certainly not," I said. I stood up and took her hand. "Come on, we're going upstairs." I could feel anger rising inside me, though I tried to keep myself composed.

Clay cleared his throat. "I . . . I'm sorry, Charity," he said, stumbling over his words. "I know you're not a bad girl. Will you forgive me for saying that? I just wasn't thinking."

She stared at him for a moment. Finally she smiled. "It's okay. Sometimes I don't think either. We all make mistakes. Mama says that all the time."

"Yes, I do," I said quickly, attempting to keep my temper in check. "Now let's go, young lady."

I made her say good-night to Clay and took her upstairs to bed, still stinging over Clay's words. He had no right to say something like that to Charity. Perhaps she was his child too, but he wasn't raising her. I was. I intended to confront him when I went back downstairs.

After tucking Charity into bed, I said, "Honey, Clay hasn't been around many little girls. He didn't mean what he said. Some adults just don't know how to talk to children."

She sighed, as if dealing with grown-ups were the bane of her existence. "I know that, Mama. Grown-ups say really silly things sometimes. Like Grandpa."

I smiled at her. "Yes, just like Grandpa. Do you still want to pray for him?"

She nodded solemnly. "Yes, and for Clay too."

I found it ironic that we were praying for my father as well as for her father, even though Charity had no idea who Clay really was. Charity's prayer was sweet and childlike. She simply asked God to help her grandpa to "not be sad anymore," and to teach Clay "all about little girls." By the time I returned to the dining room, Clay had cleared our table.

"You didn't have to do that," I said.

"Yes, I did." He shook his head. "I'm so sorry, Lizzie. Guess I was channeling my dad. He used to talk to me that way all the time. It just popped out." He gazed into my eyes. "Please forgive me. It won't happen again."

"All right, Clay. As long as you never make another comment like that to Charity. Even when she's acting badly, I never call her bad."

"You're totally right. I wasn't raised in a home that was very affirming or supportive. I'm so glad Charity is being brought up differently. You're a wonderful mother, Lizzie."

I shook my head. "I'm not sure about that, but I try. I love Charity with all my heart."

"Am I forgiven?"

"Yes. As long as we understand each other about Charity."

He held up his hands in a gesture of surrender. "You're the boss. I'll work at keeping my dad's voice out of my head and his words out of my mouth."

"Thanks." The remnants of my previous anger melted away. If anyone understood the echoes of a parent's disapproving words, it was me. "And thank you again for clearing the table. It was very thoughtful."

He grinned. "After that great dinner? It was my pleasure." He patted his flat stomach. "That's the best meal I've had in a long, long time. I don't cook, and neither does my mother. After Dad died, she decided she'd fixed all the meals she was going to."

"Well, I can't blame her. I guess when you're alone it's a relief not having to cook anymore."

"I guess so, but sometimes I wish she'd venture into the kitchen again for me. Even on holidays we go out to restaurants. I miss the family dinners we used to have."

"You still have other family, don't you, Clay? I remember that there were some aunts and uncles."

He sighed and shook his head. "After my father died, Mom cut everyone off. She's become something of a hermit. It's obvious she's really hurting, Lizzie. She keeps it all inside, but she's different than she used to be. Kinder but sadder. I've tried my best to make her happy. Unfortunately, I've come to the conclusion that I'm just not enough. As hard a man as my dad was, she loved him. And I think she counted on him too." He shrugged. "Maybe having security was even more important to her than love. I don't know."

I reached over and touched his arm. "I'm sorry, Clay. I really am."

He put his hand over mine. "Thank you. I really appreciate that. My parents weren't kind to you, Lizzie. Wish I'd known what was going on at the time. When my mother finally told me about their *offer,* I was absolutely horrified."

"I . . . I assumed they were acting for you," I said softly. "I had no idea. . . ."

He let go of my hand and picked up his coffee cup. "I know I didn't handle things the right way, but I must say I'm still surprised you could believe that. I thought you knew me better. In fact, I thought you loved me. Was I wrong?"

I shook my head. "No, you weren't wrong. But after your parents tried to pay me to have an abortion and I didn't hear a word from you, I assumed it had all been an act."

"So I could get what I wanted?"

I stared down at the table, too embarrassed to look at him. I could only nod.

Clay let out a deep breath. "I guess I can see why you came to that conclusion. After you got pregnant, I disappeared. I sure wish you would have had more faith in me, though."

"I do too, Clay. I wasn't a very secure person. My father—"

"I know. He didn't treat you very well, did he?"

"No. Maybe I judged you by his standards. I can see now what a big mistake that was."

He waved a hand in the air. "Don't apologize to me. The truth is, none of it was your fault. I took advantage of you and caused the entire mess. It shouldn't have happened."

"You're right. It shouldn't have happened, but I'm certainly glad to have Charity. So something good came out of it."

He smiled. "She's beautiful, Lizzie. You've done a wonderful job with her. I'm sure it hasn't been easy raising her alone."

"It hasn't, but being her mother is the most important thing in my life. She's given me so much joy. I don't know what I'd do without her."

He sipped his coffee and then put the cup down. "You never did tell me why you came back to Kingdom. I was certainly surprised to find out you were here."

I hesitated. Should I tell him the truth? I looked into his face and saw something there that made me remember how I used to feel about him. How much I'd loved him. Slowly but surely the entire story tumbled out. About the threatening notes, the man in the red cap, Reba, running from Kansas City to Kingdom. Everything. Even things I hadn't told my mother. When I finished, I felt better, as if sharing my burden had cleansed me, but I was also a little terrified of having made myself so vulnerable.

"Oh, Lizzie," Clay said, reaching out for my hand. "I hate to think of you going through all of this by yourself. What can I do?"

"There's nothing anyone can do. I've put it in God's hands. I didn't take that money, and I had nothing to do with that man's death. God will have to defend me, I guess. I plan to raise my daughter and not worry about what might happen next."

He smiled and squeezed my hand. "I think that's the best thing you can do. I'm proud of you." He frowned as he stared at our hands, fingers intertwined. "My father had business partners in Kansas City. Some of them have good connections into the political goings-on there. Would you let me ask them to find out what's happening in regard to these trumped-up charges?"

"I want to know what's going on, Clay, I really do. But what if their inquiry leads back here? I haven't decided what I want to do about this situation yet."

"Nothing will go wrong, Lizzie. Trust me. These are the kind of people who wouldn't do anything to put you in danger. They're very discreet. Long-term friends of the family."

I mulled it over. Not knowing was almost worse than the original threat. If the charges had been dropped, Charity and I would be free. I decided the chance was worth taking. "Okay," I said slowly. "But please tell them to be very careful."

"I will. Don't worry."

Clay pulled my hand up and kissed it lightly. "If I'd been with you, none of this would have happened. You wouldn't have had to run away. I'm to blame for everything."

"No," I said firmly. "You're not. I see that now." I shook my head. "Since coming back here, I've realized a lot of things. My father planted a seed of insecurity in me that gave me a wrong view of my life, and of so many people. Maybe I had no way to know what was going on with you, but I immediately jumped to the wrong conclusion when you moved away. If I'd been a little more self-confident, I probably would have tried to contact you for an explanation. Instead, I just assumed the worst. That you didn't care."

He stroked my arm lightly, causing goose bumps to pop out all over my skin. "You made a very logical conclusion, Lizzie. Frankly, we both made mistakes. After we buried my father, I should have come back here in person, not relied on letters as a way of contact. My mother might have wanted me by her side, but she would have been all right for a week or two. I put her above us. Above you. Above my daughter. And that was wrong." He blinked back tears. "I've missed out on so much. I'll never get those years back."

"Maybe we both need to stop blaming ourselves," I said gently. "Isn't it time to move on?"

He took both my hands in his. As I looked into his eyes, I had the strange sensation of falling off a cliff. The emotions I once felt for him flooded back.

"Lizzie, I know this will seem sudden, but it isn't. Not really. I want what we should have had all this time. I want you to marry me and come back to Seattle. I'm serious about Dad's business. In a few years I'll be in charge, and we'll have everything we could ever want. Charity will be able to go to the best schools. The best college. And you'll both be safe. No more running. No more worrying about money. Let me take care of you, Lizzie. Let me love you the way I should have six years ago. I'll make you happy. You have my word."

The sincerity in his face made me believe it was possible, but I was so taken aback by his proposal, I couldn't come up with an answer. This is what I'd always wanted. To give Charity her father. Wasn't this the reason God brought me back to Kingdom? I wanted to say yes, but feelings for Noah gripped my heart and stopped me from being able to give Clay the answer he wanted.

"I . . . I don't know, Clay. It sounds so amazing, but will you let me think about it?"

He kissed my hand again. "Of course. Maybe my offer took you by surprise, but it really shouldn't. Haven't we both always known that we were meant to be together? We're simply righting a long-standing wrong. Doesn't that make sense to you?"

I nodded. "It makes complete sense. I feel the same way. I'm just confused . . ."

"I understand. There's no pressure. I want you to be sure. Sure of us. Sure of me."

I smiled at him. "I never stopped loving you."

He grinned. "I fell in love with you the first time I saw you. Did I ever tell you that? When your father pulled you out of school, I was heartbroken. That's why I begged to take over the delivery route to Kingdom back when Cora was buying her supplies through our family store."

I laughed. "When I found out you were delivering on Thursdays, I always found a way to be in town so I could see you. Thursdays were my favorite days. I couldn't wait until that old delivery van drove into town."

"You know what? You're even more beautiful now, Lizzie. I still see the girl in you, but there's a woman in your eyes as well. And I love them both."

I could feel that same pull that had led me down the wrong path years ago, so I gently dislodged my hands from his. "It's getting late, Clay. I've got to get some sleep. Tomorrow morning will be here very early."

He looked at his watch. "Yikes. You're right. Sorry."

"That's okay. When Cora gets back, I'll take a few days off. Maybe you could spend some time with Charity and me? We could go into Washington for lunch."

He chuckled. "Manhattan's larger than Washington and only an hour and a half away. They have all kinds of restaurants and a very nice mall. I'll bet they're decorated for

Christmas. Maybe we could even take Charity to see Santa Claus."

"That would make her so happy, Clay."

"Then it's a date." He put on his coat and pulled on his hat and gloves. "Walk me to the door?"

I got up, linked my arm through his, and we strolled together to the front entrance.

"This has been a wonderful evening," I said.

"The best night of my life." He leaned down and kissed me softly. "I'll call you tomorrow."

"You have Cora's number?"

He nodded. "Got it the first day I came here. I had no intention of letting you get away from me again."

He kissed me once more and then walked out the door. I watched as he got in his car and drove away. Then I turned off the light and stood in the darkness. "Oh, God, this is all I ever wanted. To have a family. A father for Charity. Why can't I just jump in with both feet and take this wonderful gift you've given me? Am I afraid of being hurt again? Please help me. Show me what to do."

I picked up the vase of roses Clay had given me and began to climb the stairs. A face filled my mind. It should have been Clay's, but it wasn't. It was Noah's, and there was a sadness in his deep green eyes that echoed the ache in my heart.

CHAPTER / 21

Wednesday morning was busy. An odd-looking sky caused me to turn on the old battery-operated radio Cora kept in the kitchen. Another major storm was headed our way, and this one had the potential to be much more serious than the smaller storm that had passed through over the weekend. The predicted snow totals were significant. I couldn't be sure just why that brought so many people into the restaurant, but I suspected they were worried they'd be snowed in for a while. Getting one last chance to see their friends before the storm hit was too inviting to pass up.

A few customers asked about buying extra supplies from me. I had no idea what to do about their requests. Avery heard me talking to one old farmer who lived alone about a mile out of town and wanted to purchase some eggs and milk. Avery called me over to his table after we finished our conversation.

"Cora gives folks whatever they need during emergencies if she's got it," he said. "And they always pay her back. But don't put yourself at risk. Be sure you have what you need."

"I know we get a lot of storms out here," I said, "but snow doesn't necessarily mean everyone will be trapped inside."

"You lived in town when we had big storms. You'll find it's mostly the single farmers who need help. Most of 'em don't can fruits and vegetables for the hard winter months while lots of the womenfolk do. And gettin' stuck out in the country is a bit different than it is in town. We can all help each other get around, and our horses can be ridden without a buggy through pretty deep drifts. But living miles out of Kingdom with no one nearby can get pretty scary."

"Now that you mention it, I do recall Mother and Father taking food to folks who lived a ways out after particularly bad snowstorms. Can't imagine why I forgot about that."

"Your folks have always been right good about takin' care of their neighbors. Your mama puts up tomatoes, peaches, beans, and jams every summer and fall. A lot of them jars are for her neighbors. Not just for her and your pa."

I laughed. "Boy, I sure remember how hot the kitchen got when she was canning. I'd leave the house and walk to the creek, just trying to cool off."

"My wife did the same thing. The house was so steamy I never could figure out how she managed not to faint dead away." I could hear the sadness in his voice when he mentioned her.

"Hey, thanks for letting me know what to do about the supplies. You've been such a blessing to me and Charity. We love the furniture you gave us. If you ever want it back . . ."

He shook his head with vigor. "Ain't no reason for stuff to sit around gatherin' dust. Berlene has a new life far from here. She don't need it anymore. I'm grateful it's bein' used." His face, creased by years of working in the sun, wrinkled in a rare smile. "It does me good to see you and your little girl makin' a life here. Sometimes I kinda pretend you're my Berlene."

I smiled at him, touched by his heartfelt sentiment. "You know, I really haven't properly thanked you for that furniture. Why don't you come over for a late dinner one of these nights after the restaurant closes? I'll ask Ruth and Myra too. I know they'd love to spend some time with you, and I would too."

The old man nodded slowly. "I'd really like that, Elizabeth. I'd like that very much. Lately I've been spendin' way too much time alone. It would be real nice to sit down and share a meal with good people. Thank you."

"I look forward to it, Avery. I'll figure out a night that will work and get back to you."

He didn't respond, but I was happy my invitation pleased him. I just wished I'd thought of it sooner. On the way back to the kitchen, I began to understand that this restaurant really was more than just a place to eat. I thought back to something Cora had said when she'd petitioned my father all those years ago. She'd said the restaurant would be a ministry. A place that felt like home. And that's what it was. Although it had crept up on me slowly, I realized my job was starting to become important to me. And not just because it provided for Charity and me. It mattered. It gave people a place to belong. And no one knew more than I how vital that was.

I was filling up another pot of coffee when the sound of a bell startled me, almost causing me to drop the carafe on the floor. What in the world was that? I whirled around and realized it was Cora's phone. It was the first time I'd heard it ring. I grabbed the receiver.

"Hello?"

Cora's voice came over the line. "Is that you, Lizzie?"

"Yes, it's me, Cora. How are you? How's your sister?"

"Well, that's just it, honey," she said. "She's not good. Not good at all."

"I'm so sorry. I've been praying for her."

"Thank you, Lizzie. That's probably what's keepin' her goin'. How are things goin' back there?"

I gave her a quick rundown of the past several days, assuring her that everything was fine. Since I had her on the phone, I confirmed Avery's information about sharing kitchen supplies with Kingdom residents.

"Avery's got it right. You give folks what they need. Keep some notes so we'll know where everything went, but I've never known a one of 'em not to pay me back. Usually with more than they borrowed. And after the roads clear, if you run low on supplies, you go to Washington like I told you."

"Okay. Will do. When are you coming home?"

There was a long pause. Finally she said, "I just don't know, honey. It might be a while. And when I do come back, it will just be to get my stuff and sell my house. My sister needs me, Lizzie. I'll be movin' up here with her for good. Or for at least as long as she's alive. The doctor tells me that could be quite a while. MS patients can live long lives, but they need an awful lot of help."

I was stunned. "But what does that mean, Cora? What about the restaurant?"

"I been thinkin' a lot about that, Lizzie. Why don't you buy it from me?"

I snorted. "I don't have a dime to my name. How in the world could I do that?"

She laughed. "When I get back, we'll sit down and hash it out. We'll come up with a fair price, and you'll just send me what you can when you have it. My sister's well-to-do, so I

260

don't need much up here. You send me a little every month until it's paid off. I promise to make you a good deal."

"I don't know. I mean, I'll have to think about it. Is that all right?"

"Of course it is. You take all the time you need. I'll probably be here at least another three weeks. Will you be okay until then? Do you have enough money?"

"Yes, you left me quite a bit. Besides, there's also the money we're taking in. I'm sure there's enough for three weeks."

"Okay. Well, I gotta go, honey. I'll call you again soon. Oh, and if you need me, my sister's number is in my personal phone book in the little drawer to the left of the sink. Her name's Georgia Ballwin. Don't be afraid to call me. Sorry I didn't give you the number before I left. I was just so flustered I didn't think about it."

"It's okay. We miss you."

"And I miss you too, Lizzie. How's Charity?"

"She's doing just fine. I plan to start her in school after the Christmas break."

"Why, that's great news. Leah's a wonderful teacher, and she'll fall in love with Charity, just like I did."

I could hear someone talking in the background. "I gotta go, honey. But you take care. And think about what I said."

I promised I would and hung up the phone. Then I leaned against the wall and considered her offer. Actually, it appealed to me. But what about Seattle? Clay promised Charity would go to excellent schools and have everything a girl could want if we went with him. Didn't I owe my daughter the best I could give her? Why was I even considering the idea of staying in Kingdom to run a restaurant?

Thoughts tumbled around in my head like sightless birds

flying into each other. I wasn't doing myself any good thinking it over now. I had to find out what was happening in Kansas City before I could make any future plans.

Folks piled into the restaurant through lunch, but around one thirty the snow began in earnest and everyone headed for home. I'd hoped Clay would come in, but with the weather the way it was, I doubted he'd leave Belleville. My mother came into the kitchen, carrying dirty dishes.

"Mother, you need to head out. It's liable to get bad."

She was silent as she scraped off the plates.

"Mother? Did you hear me?"

"I . . . I wonder if I might be able to stay with you again, Daughter. I put some extra clothes and things in the buggy in case you would say yes." She smiled sadly at me. "I find the house so lonely since your father left. I would like to be with someone I love. Especially if the storm snows us in for a while."

I went over and put my arms around her. "Of course you can stay. You don't even need to ask. We love having you here."

She sighed. "Thank you, Elizabeth Lynn. But please, I will sleep on the couch. You do not need to give up your bed for me."

"Don't be silly. The couch is perfectly comfortable. And I must confess, when I put logs in the stove, I feel so comfortable and cozy that I've spent a couple of nights on the couch just because I love that room so much."

She gently pulled herself out of my embrace. "Then I will also confess that many nights I would tell your father I needed to stay up and sew just so I could nod off in my rocking chair in front of the fire."

"I remember Father chiding you for falling asleep in your chair. So you did it on purpose?"

She nodded. "There is something about a warm fire on a cold night that makes me feel so secure. Strange, is it not?"

"Well, if it is, I'm just as strange as you are."

She laughed lightly. "I will clean up the rest of the dishes, but then I must move Blackie to your father's shop. He will need to be protected from the storm."

I shook my head. "Why don't you do that now, before it gets any worse? I'll finish up the dishes."

She nodded. "Thank you, Daughter. That might be best."

I hadn't gotten the chance to tell her about Cora's offer, but that could wait for a more opportune moment. I was rinsing off the dishes when the phone rang again. As with the first time, I almost jumped out of my shoes. Twice in one day. Maybe it was Cora calling back. I picked up the phone. It was Clay.

"Lizzie, I wanted to come out there today, but with the storm moving in, it might be better if I stay put."

Disappointment flooded through me even though I was expecting the news. "I understand, Clay. I think it's wise. Sounds like it might be a pretty big storm."

There was silence for a moment. "Lizzie," Clay said finally, an odd tone in his voice, "one of the reasons I wanted to see you today is because I have some news. I'm afraid it will upset you."

My stomach turned over. "What is it?"

"I heard back from my contact in Kansas City, and it's not good."

My knees suddenly felt weak. I grabbed Charity's small chair, pulled it over near the phone, and slumped down. Thankfully, she was drawing in the dining room, since all our customers were gone.

"Just tell me, Clay. What did he say?"

I could hear him take a deep breath. "They're definitely looking for you. Harbor House has filed charges against you for embezzlement, and the story has hit the newspaper. So far, they're not naming you in the press. They're just calling you a 'former employee.' If there's any good news, it's that no one knows where you are. That guy, Parsons, if he was hired by someone at Harbor House, never got the chance to reveal your location. My source knows some guy named Webb on the city council who's dating that Reba woman who's running Harbor House, so I'm sure this information is accurate."

"Are you sure your source won't tell Commissioner Webb about me?"

He snorted. "I said he knows the guy. I didn't say he liked him. Seems Webb has a pretty rotten reputation. You can be assured my contact won't say anything that will lead to your location. But Lizzie, I think you can see how important it is that we get out of here as soon as possible. I'll take you and Charity to Seattle. No one will ever find you there. You'll both be safe."

My head swam, and I felt faint. "I thought about going back to face these charges, Clay. But how can I put Charity through that?"

"I understand," he said gently, "and I agree. I'll take care of you, Lizzie. I promise. You need to start packing. As soon as this storm moves out, we have to go. There's no time to lose."

"All right. We'll be ready."

"I love you, Lizzie. Everything will be all right. Trust me."

"I . . . I do. We'll see you soon."

We both said good-bye and hung up. I sat there, rocking

back and forth with my hands wrapped around my knees. So there it was. The decision had been made for me. I wanted to feel grateful that Charity and I had a place to go. But the idea of leaving Kingdom, my mother, and this wonderful restaurant, especially after Cora's offer, hurt me inside. Somewhere along the way, I'd fallen in love with this town and its people. A place I couldn't wait to get away from had become home. Now I'd have to leave. Again.

And though I didn't want to think about him, I couldn't get Noah out of my mind. How could I explain the situation to him? The idea of leaving him made it hard for me to catch my breath. Unfortunately, I had no other choice. I had to get Charity away from danger. Besides, Clay loved me. He would give us a good home.

I forced myself to stand up and finish the dishes. Mother came back after taking Blackie to shelter, and Charity, finding that she had both of us captive, used the situation to make us play Candy Land. I made hot chocolate and brought out a plate of cookies. Then I stoked the fire in the large fireplace and added several logs. We stayed downstairs so we could watch the storm through the large windows in the front of the restaurant.

Just as predicted, the wind picked up and heavy snow began to fall, blown sideways by huge gusts of wind. I was thankful we were inside, where it was safe and warm. Seeing it was almost six, I'd gotten up to make dinner when a pickup truck suddenly roared up outside the restaurant. Someone jumped out and ran up to the door. It was Noah. He had to fight the wind as he pushed the door open. His face was red from the cold, and he looked upset.

"Lizzie, Avery called me about thirty minutes ago. The

horse he sold to your father just found its way back to his stable. He's obviously broken free of his harness. Do you know where your father might be? We're concerned that there may have been an accident, and your father might be stranded out in this storm."

"No," I said. "I have no idea." I looked at my mother, who had gone pale, her hand covering her mouth. "Mother, do you have any idea where he's staying?"

She nodded slowly. "Yes. I am fairly certain he is at the old Strauss farm about two miles north of the main road."

"I thought that place was deserted. Why would he be there?"

"Mr. Strauss contacted your father about three months ago, asking him to oversee the sale of the property. It has not been lived in since their daughter, Ava, died over twenty years ago. So far no one has shown any interest because the house needs so much work. Your father thought perhaps he could do some repairs to make the property more desirable. Since he has the keys, it is the most logical place to look for him."

"I'll drive over and see if he's there," Noah said. "If not, I'll search the roads around that area." He turned to go.

"Wait a minute," I said. "I'm going with you."

Noah shook his head. "It's not a good idea, Lizzie. The weather—"

"He's my father," I said with determination, "and it's not open for debate. Wait here while I get my coat." I ran up the stairs, bundled up as much as I could, and hurried back down to the dining room. It seemed obvious that my father had met with an accident, but the words of that anonymous note echoed in my mind. *Running away has only put more people in danger.* Was this really an accident? Or was someone still

stalking me? Still stalking my family? I shook the thought
out of my head. Not every mishap was part of an evil plan
to harm me or the people I love. Besides, Dave Parsons was
dead. Dead men couldn't reach beyond the grave. Could they?
When I reached the bottom of the stairs, I found Charity and
my mother sitting together at the table while Noah stood
near the door. "Watch Charity for me, Mother. And don't
worry. We'll find him."

She nodded, not saying a word, but I could see the fear in
her eyes. It was echoed in my daughter's face.

"Everything will be okay, Cherry Bear. I'm just going to
get Grandpa. I'll be back in a little bit."

She smiled bravely, but I could still see the anxiety in her
expression.

"I'll take care of your mother, Charity. I promise," Noah
said, smiling.

"Okay, I guess," she said slowly. "If you promise."

"Anna," Noah said, "please lock this door behind us after
we leave." He frowned at me. "I know Kingdom is a small
town, but you should still lock your doors at night."

"I know," I said. "I just keep forgetting."

I'd started to follow him out the door when Charity called
out for me. I hurried back to her, hugged her tightly, and reassured her once more that I'd be back soon. She finally nodded, and I ran out the front door. As I came down the steps,
Noah was just getting into his truck. Although I thought it
odd that it had taken him so long to reach his vehicle since
he'd left the restaurant before me, I pushed the thought away
as unimportant.

We both got inside the cab, and he started the engine. He
was turning the truck around when Mother ran out the door

of the restaurant with something in her arms. Noah stopped, and I rolled down my window.

"Take this blanket," she said. "If Matthew has been out in the cold for long, he will need it to warm up."

"Good idea. Thanks," I said quickly. I took the blanket from her and held it in my arms as Noah started down the road.

"You can put that in the backseat," he said, nodding at the blanket.

I turned around, surprised to find another seat behind us. A quick look around the cab revealed that Noah had a rather new truck. I tossed the blanket in the back. "Nice truck," I said. "I thought an elder in the church would have something more humble."

He shrugged. "Got a great deal on it. I need something I can rely on for the farm. No one's complained."

A glance in the rearview mirror revealed my Mother standing in the street, watching us drive away while fighting the wind for all she was worth. Her long dress whipped around her, and she held on to her bonnet with both hands. It wasn't long before the snow made it impossible for me to see her any longer.

"She still loves him," Noah said.

"Yes. Yes, she does. If anything happens to him after she made him leave . . ."

"It won't, Lizzie. We'll find him." Noah reached over and popped open the glove compartment. He pulled out a flashlight and handed it to me. "When we get past the edge of town, use this to check this side of the road. Just in case. I'm going to the Strauss place first, but if he isn't there, we'll search the other side on the way back. If you see anything unusual, anything at all, let me know. Okay?"

"Okay." The snow almost blinded us as it covered the windshield. Noah drove slowly, out of necessity, and it gave me plenty of time to check the road for an overturned buggy. But even with the high-powered flashlight, it was hard to see much of anything. Noah was silent as he concentrated on the road. Although my concern was for my father, my mind drifted back to Clay's phone call. Was I doing the right thing? Was going away with Clay my only option?

"I heard Clay Troyer's still hanging around," Noah said suddenly, as if he'd been reading my mind. The coincidence startled me.

"Well, yes. I mean he isn't 'hanging around.' We've spent some time together. He's getting to know Charity."

"Nice of him to show up now. Where was he when she was born?"

I started to tell him that it really wasn't any of his business, but before I spouted off, I realized he'd only asked because he was concerned about me. I took a deep breath and calmed my ruffled emotions. "Look, Clay explained what happened." As I began to recount the story Clay told me about his father's death and his attempt to find me, Noah's expression grew even harder.

"Oh, come on," he said when I'd finished. "He's really plugged up all the holes, hasn't he? And how do you know any of this is true?"

"I asked my mother about the letters, and she confirmed that he really did send them. I never got to see them."

Noah didn't say anything for several seconds, but his knuckles turned white on the steering wheel. "Maybe he did write," he said finally, "but I still don't trust him. Didn't trust him when we went to school together. Don't trust him now."

"You were never close to him in school, and you haven't seen him for years. You have no idea what kind of a person he is." I shook my head. "How can an elder in the church judge someone this way? What happened to 'Thou shalt not judge'?"

"Maybe I am being too critical. I don't know. There's just something about Clay Troyer that sets off alarm bells in my gut."

"I think your *alarm bells* are nothing more than your own jealousy. I'm leaving Kingdom with him, Noah. We're getting married." I hadn't meant to announce my plans yet, but Noah's high-and-mighty attitude made me angry. After the words were out, I felt a sense of relief. Why not marry the man I'd fallen in love with all those years ago? Charity and I would be safe. Besides, I was tired of living hand to mouth. Reuniting with Clay seemed to be God's plan.

Noah kept his eyes on the road, acting almost as if he hadn't heard me. But the muscles in his jaws were working furiously. Finally he muttered, "Well, congratulations. I hope you'll be very happy."

"I'm not sure you mean that, but thank you for saying it. I wouldn't hurt you for the world, Noah. But I have to do this. There's no other choice. I hope we'll still be friends."

He didn't respond, but I could see the hurt in his face. For some reason, it made me want to cry. I tried to keep my focus on the side of the road as I watched for my father's buggy, but the tears in my eyes made it hard to see.

Noah was quiet the rest of the way to the Strauss farm. The wind screeched with fury as it rocked the truck back and forth. We made it to the main highway with Noah driving as fast as he dared. The truck spun out on the icy roads more than once. Each time he expertly fought the sliding tires and brought the vehicle back from the edge of the road.

"That's the farmhouse up there," he said suddenly. "I don't see any lights."

We drove slowly up to the place where the driveway should have been. Problem was, it was hidden under the snow. I shone the light out the window, trying to help Noah. "I think I see it," I said. "It's right there." I pointed toward our right.

"Wait here." He jumped out of the truck and walked over to the place I'd indicated. Navigating our way to the house was tricky because of the drainage ditches that ran on each side of the driveway. One wrong move and we'd end up stuck in a ditch, in trouble ourselves and unable to help my father. It only took one gust of wind for Noah's broad black hat to fly off his head and blow down the highway. He didn't appear to even notice. Gingerly stepping on the snow, he was able to confirm I was right. We'd found the driveway.

He jumped back into the truck and drove carefully past the ditches. Once we cleared them, he stepped on the accelerator and drove quickly to the front of the old, decrepit house.

Built before Kingdom was established, the house was two stories tall with a large wraparound front porch. It was obvious it had been beautiful in its day, but neglect had stripped it of its former glory, and it was surprising that it still stood at all. The windows were dark, and there was no sign of life.

"I don't think anyone's here," I said.

"We need to make sure before we go traipsing out into snowdrifts searching for Matthew," Noah said. "Why don't you check the front door? I'll go around to the back." He reached for the flashlight in my hand. "The headlights will give you enough light to see."

"Okay." I handed him the light, and our hands touched. It sent a chill through me that had nothing to do with the weather. He gazed into my eyes, and I felt that weird sensation of falling, just as I had with Clay. Quickly looking away, I opened the truck door and got out, putting my head down and fighting the snow and wind as I made my way up the front steps of the aged structure.

I heard Noah slam his door and turned to see him heading around to the back of the house. When I got to the door, I tried to turn the handle, but it was locked. The door seemed so old I thought maybe a few good shoves would cause it to open. Unfortunately, I only ended up hurting my shoulder. Looking through the window next to the door revealed a light in the house. It was moving. Noah had obviously been more successful. He pulled the door handle, and I stepped inside, grateful to get out of the storm.

"Is he here?" I asked as soon as he closed the door behind me.

"Just got in. I haven't really looked." He swung the flashlight toward the stairs. "Can you check upstairs while I look around down here? And you might check for any signs he's actually been staying here. If not, we're wasting precious time."

"I understand."

"You take the flashlight. The headlights will give me some illumination down here."

"Okay." I headed toward the stairway.

"And be careful, Lizzie. Those stairs could be in really bad condition."

"All right." I shone the light on the steps in front of me. They looked solid enough, but Noah's advice was wise. Holding on to the banister with one hand and the flashlight with the other, I took each step slowly. The wood underneath my feet seemed strong, but the banister wobbled every time I pulled on it. However, by the time I reached the top I felt more secure. Unfortunately, my first step onto the landing almost sent me to my knees. I swung the light down toward my feet. There was a gaping hole, almost large enough for a person to fall through. I carefully moved to the other side of the floor, praying it was more solid. Then I eased my way down the hall, shining the light in front of me. There were several rooms up here. I opened the door at the end of the hall only to find old pieces of furniture stacked on top of each other, most of them covered with cloth. Backing out of that room, I went to the next. Empty. The third room was the same. The fourth room held a bed, a chair and a dresser. It had obviously once been someone's bedroom, but the dust was so thick on everything it was clear my father hadn't been sleeping here.

I wondered why the other rooms had been cleared and this one left alone. Then I noticed a child's prayer covering draped over the chair in the corner, and a small Teddy bear sitting on the bed looking forlorn and abandoned. This had been Ava's room. A deep sense of sorrow filled me, and I fought back tears. Being the mother of a young girl made the pain this family had experienced all too real. I quietly closed the door.

I made my way back down the stairs, carefully avoiding the large hole in the floor. I'd just reached the bottom when Noah came around the corner from the back of the house.

"I think I've found where your father's been staying," he said, "but it's so dark I can't see much in the room. Bring the flashlight back here, will you?"

I followed him through the kitchen and into another small

room. This bedroom had definitely been used lately. It was clean and dusted, and the bed was unmade. I noticed a Bible on the dresser and flipped the first page open. "It's Father's," I said. "Here's his name." As I handed the Bible to Noah, a piece of paper fell out and drifted to the floor. I bent over to pick it up. It was folded in half, and I pulled it open, shining the light down so I could see it clearly. When I realized what it was, I cried out with surprise.

"What's wrong?" Noah asked. "What is it?"

"It . . . it's a drawing I made for my father when I was seven. I drew our house with Mother, Father, and me standing in front of it. Father scolded me for drawing pictures. Said they sparked vanity in people. He took it away from me, and I cried for a week."

"But he kept it all these years in his Bible. What does that tell you, Lizzie?"

"I . . . I don't know. It seems mean to keep it after making me feel guilty for drawing it."

"I think it says something else," Noah said gently. "But you'll have to figure that out for yourself."

I stuck the picture back between the pages and returned the Bible to the dresser. "Well, at least we know he's been here. But he's not here now. That means . . ."

"That he's out there somewhere in this storm, and we need to find him. Before it's too late."

CHAPTER/22

We drove slowly back the way we'd come, believing Father would have to be somewhere between town and the Strauss place. Using the flashlight helped some, but the snow was so thick the light only cut through the whiteout conditions so much before fading out.

"I doubt he'll be far from the road," Noah said. "Look for the buggy. I can't figure out why we haven't spotted it yet."

As his words sunk in, realization followed. "Noah! The ravine. He must be in the ravine. That's why we haven't seen the buggy."

He slapped himself on the forehead. "What an idiot I've been. That's the first place we should have looked. Hold on, Lizzie. We need to get there as quickly as possible."

I grabbed onto the handle over the window. Noah wasn't kidding. He sped up, sending us careening down the road a lot faster than I thought safe. Somehow he kept us on track. The fact that no one else was stupid enough to be out in the storm kept us from running into other vehicles. It took us ten minutes to reach the road to Kingdom. When Noah first turned the wheel, I was convinced he'd miscalculated, because there was no way to actually see the turnoff under all the snow. Thankfully, he knew exactly what he was doing, and he quickly found the ravine. If Father was down there somewhere, it could take time to locate him. The deep crevasse ran at least a half mile long.

"You stay here," Noah shouted. "I'm going to look for him. If he's not here, we'll move down some."

I started to argue with him. Getting my father out might take the two of us, as he was a big man, but since we actually needed to find him first, I decided to stay where I was. At least for the time being. I could see the light from Noah's flashlight bouncing down the road. A couple of minutes later, he returned.

"Nothing yet." He put the truck into gear and drove a little farther. Then he repeated the same procedure. Still nothing.

The third time, I watched the light as Noah searched the ravine. Suddenly it stopped. Then he held it up, waving it back and forth. He must have found Father. I prayed fervently that he was still alive. Finding my childish picture in his Bible had touched my heart. Maybe Mother was right. Maybe he really did care about me. Instead of being angry, I just wanted another chance to see if we could find a way to carve out some kind of relationship. Maybe we'd never be really close, but at this point, I'd even settle for civility.

Noah's light disappeared as he left the safety of the road. The wind blew the truck with ferocity, and I couldn't see anything except snow. Not willing to let Noah sacrifice himself for my family, I pulled my knit cap down over my ears, dug my gloves out of my coat pocket, put them on, and pulled on the door handle. With the wind blowing directly against the side of the truck, it was a struggle to get it open.

When I finally managed to push the door ajar enough to slide out, I was immediately whipped in the face by blinding snow. It felt like grains of sand against my skin. The headlights shone straight ahead, so I wasn't really worried. All I had to do was watch for the light from Noah's flashlight. I felt my way down the road, being careful not to walk out of the security of the headlight's glare. The wind kept trying to push me sideways, and before long the lights were no longer illuminating the path in front of me. When I turned around, I could barely make them out.

Where was Noah? Why couldn't I find him? There was no light off to my right, and I didn't dare move any farther toward the sharp incline that could lead me to the same fate as Dave Parsons. When I looked behind me again, Noah's headlights had completely disappeared. Fear gripped me. Maybe I should have stayed in the truck, but what if Noah and my father needed help? There was no one else but me. I called out Noah's name into the darkness, but the wind just shoved the words back down my throat. No one would be able to hear me over the roar of the storm.

"Oh, God," I prayed, yelling as loudly as I could into the void that surrounded me. "Please guide me back to the truck. And please, please keep my father alive! Help Noah get him to safety. I need your help, heavenly Father!"

I kept pushing against the strong wind gusts, trying to go toward the place where I believed the truck was parked, but there were still no lights visible anywhere. I had no idea how long I'd been out in the blizzard, but it felt like hours and my strength was waning. All I could think about was Charity. That kept me fighting as hard as I could to get to safety. She needed me, and I had no intention of letting her down.

Suddenly, my foot hit a hole in the road, and I fell. I was so tired, I couldn't get up. I told myself it was okay to rest a bit before trying again, but something inside me told me to get up and keep going, so I struggled to my feet. I'd only taken a few steps when a light shone in my face, almost blinding me.

"Lizzie!" It was Noah's voice calling out my name. I fell into his arms, my energy spent. He picked me up and began walking. It wasn't long before the headlights of the truck shone through the blanket of white that surrounded us. Noah opened the door and lifted me into the passenger seat.

"I told you to stay in the car." He glared at me. "Why do you have to be so stubborn?"

"I . . . I thought you might need help," I mumbled.

"Well, having to rescue you didn't actually help me much. You were way off the road on the other side, by the way. It's a miracle I found you." He slammed the door shut and went around to the driver's side.

"Wh-what about Father?" I asked when he got inside.

"I am here, Elizabeth Lynn," a deep voice said from behind me. I twisted around in my seat and found my father staring at me. His usual black hat was gone, and his hair stood on end, giving him a grunge-rocker look. He had the blanket Mother had given me wrapped around him. He was shivering, and there were smudges of dirt on his face, but other than that, he looked all right.

Noah put the truck into gear and began the drive back to town.

"Oh, Father," I said, tears of joy running down my cheeks. "Are you hurt? What happened?"

"No, Daughter, I am fine. Just very cold and a little bruised. Thankfully, the deep snow kept me from serious injury." He held out his arms and moved them around. "I am thankful my limbs seem to be working." He shook his head. "I should not have taken a chance in this storm. I thought I could make it, but obviously I did not plan well. The buggy slipped into the ravine, and down we went. It fell right on top of me. The horse was able to free itself, but I could not. The more I struggled, the deeper my body burrowed itself into the snow. Has the horse been found? Is he all right?"

"Yes, Father. It showed up at Avery's house. He's the one who contacted Noah."

"But how did you know where to look?"

"Mother thought you might be staying at the Strauss place, so we went there first. When we discovered you weren't there, we figured you had to be somewhere between the house and town. It wasn't until we couldn't find the buggy that we realized you might be in the ravine."

"That ravine is dangerous," Noah said. "Two people have gone off the road in almost exactly the same place within a week's time."

"I certainly agree," Father said, his words stilted by his chattering teeth, "but the ditch helps to drain overflow from the rain. Without it, the road could easily flood and our farmers who live out beyond our borders could not get into town."

"Maybe some kind of fence could be erected," I said.

"A very good idea, Daughter. It certainly would have made a difference for me tonight."

"Are you two getting any warmer?" Noah asked. He'd cranked up the heater all the way and pointed the vents toward my father and me.

"I'm starting to feel less like a Popsicle every minute," I said, smiling.

"I must confess, although I feel better, my body seems to have a mind of its own," Father said. "I cannot stop shaking. However, I am very grateful for the warmth." He hesitated a moment. "I do not have the words to tell you how thankful I am you came looking for me, Noah. You had no reason to put yourself at risk for my sake, but I am grateful you did. The snow had almost covered me by the time you found me. I do not know how much longer I would have lasted."

"We are brothers in Christ, Matthew," Noah said, "and that gives me all the reason in the world."

"Thanks for saving me too," I said. "Seems like you've rescued the Engels family twice tonight."

Noah took his attention off the road for a couple of seconds. His emerald eyes bore into mine. "I promised long ago to take care of you, Elizabeth Lynn, and I intend to keep my word. As long as I can." He turned his attention back to the road ahead, though I had no idea what he saw through his windshield. There was nothing but white in front of us. It seemed impossible to find the way back into Kingdom in this blinding storm, but somehow Noah did it. We were soon pulling up in front of Cora's, the only building in town with light shining through its windows. As soon as we stopped, the front door flew open, and my mother came running out. I climbed out of the truck.

"We found him, Mother," I shouted, trying to be heard over the wind. "He's in the back." I opened the door and pulled the seat forward. Father tried to get out, but he was still a bit wobbly. It took Noah's help to extract him completely from the truck.

"Matthew!" Mother ran to him and was almost knocked

to the ground by a sudden gust of wind. "Thank the Lord you have come back to me!"

Father leaned on Noah and Mother as they helped him inside. I ran ahead and held the door open for them. Once inside, Father collapsed onto a chair while Mother hurried into the kitchen to get him some hot coffee. Charity took in the dramatic scene with big eyes.

"Mama, is Grandpa okay?"

I went over and gave her a big hug. "Yes, Cherry Bear. He's fine."

She wiggled out of my embrace. "Mama, you're all wet. Have you been playing in the snow?"

I laughed. There was a slight tone of petulance in her voice, as if she was upset to think that I'd been having fun without her. "I wasn't playing in it, honey, I got lost in it. Noah found me. This isn't the kind of snow that's fun. You wouldn't like it."

As if emphasizing my comment, the building shuddered against the gale. Charity's mouth turned into an almost perfect circle.

"Mama, that *is* a bad snow." She looked over at Noah. "The prince saved you, didn't he, Mama?"

If my face wasn't already red from the cold, it surely turned crimson at that moment. "Charity, I already told you that Noah isn't Prince Phillip. He's just a regular man."

Noah chuckled. "As a matter of fact, Charity, my middle name *is* Phillip. And if you want me to be a prince, I'll be one. Just for you."

My daughter grabbed my hand. "See, Mama? I told you so. And you didn't believe me."

I frowned at Noah. Encouraging Charity to think he was

our Prince Charming wasn't healthy. Especially since we were leaving Kingdom. All I needed was for her to think we were leaving our "prince" behind.

"We'll talk about it later, Cherry Bear. You wait here a minute while I run upstairs and get some dry clothes. Okay?"

"Okay, Mama."

Normally, she might have been afraid to be in a room with my father, but with Noah there, she seemed perfectly relaxed. She was smiling at him, and he smiled back, obviously taking the whole "prince" thing in stride. Before I could make my exit, Mother came back into the room with Father's coffee.

"I'm going upstairs to change, Mother. I'll be right back."

She nodded, frowning. "Where's the blanket I sent for Matthew? It belongs to Cora. I would hate to lose it."

"It's still in the backseat. I'll get it."

"You stay here," Noah said. "I'll get it."

Not looking forward to another duel with the weather, I quickly agreed. I waited while he retrieved the blanket. It was crumpled into a big, wet wad. I held out my hands.

"I'll run it downstairs to the washer before I change," I said.

"I've already got a grip on it. Why don't you let me carry it for you? Lead the way."

"Thanks. Follow me."

I led him to the kitchen and down the basement stairs. "Just put it on top of the washer," I said, pointing to the old machine in the corner. "I'll take care of it in the morning."

He put it down where I told him. I'd turned to go back up the stairs when he called out my name.

"Lizzie, wait a minute." He stood next to a large wooden support beam in the middle of the room. "I'm probably not going to be able to talk you out of your plans with Clay. But this might be the last chance I have to be alone with you, and I'd like a chance to say my piece."

"I . . . I don't think—"

"I don't care what you think," he said flatly. "It needs to be said. At least I'll always know I did everything I could." He took a deep breath. "I love you, Lizzie. I've loved you ever since we were children. You didn't know it back then, because I was afraid sharing my real feelings would tear us apart." He shook his head. "Maybe that was a mistake. If I'd been honest, it's a good chance you wouldn't have gotten mixed up with Clay Troyer."

His eyes locked on mine. "Regardless, I've always tried to take care of you. Look after you—even when you didn't know it. I realize it's been hard—with your father and everything. You needed someone to protect you when you were young, and you need someone to protect you now. That's why I have to say something to you, whether you like it or not.

"Elizabeth Lynn, marrying Clay is a mistake you'll regret the rest of your life. I'm convinced of it. Stay here, Lizzie. Please. Marry me and stay in Kingdom. Help me make life better for this town. For everyone who lives here. I'm convinced there's nothing you and I can't do together."

I stared at him, trying to find a response, but it was as if my mind was locked up. "I . . . I . . ." was all I could get out.

He came over to me and took my hands in his. Once again I felt lost in his eyes. "You know me, Lizzie. You know me better than you think. And I know you. I know you better than anyone on this earth. Search your heart. If you do, you'll admit you don't really love Clay. I believe you love me as much as I love you."

I knew he was going to kiss me again. I could have stopped

it, but I didn't want to. His lips felt soft and sweet. When he pulled away, I kept my eyes closed because I wanted the moment to last.

"I'm leaving now," he said. "I'll be back in a couple of days. Please think about what I said. You have a choice. Stay here with me or leave with Clay. No matter what you choose, I will love you till the day I die."

I opened my eyes to see him walking up the stairs. The door shut behind him, and I waited for a few minutes, hoping he'd be gone by the time I went upstairs. As I stood there, some of the words from the theme song to *Sleeping Beauty* began to play in my mind. *"I know you, I walked with you once upon a dream. I know you. . . ."* Noah was certain he knew me. Just like Prince Phillip knew Aurora.

I suddenly realized how ludicrous that sounded. "Oh, come on, Lizzie," I said out loud. "You're starting to sound as silly as your six-year-old daughter." I shook my head and laughed. Then I went upstairs. Noah was gone.

Mother and Father sat at the table together with Charity across from them. My father's hands were wrapped around his coffee cup, as if he were depending on it for warmth. His color was back to normal, and he'd finally stopped trembling.

"There you are," he said when I came into the room. "I want to say something to you and your mother before I leave. Would you sit with me a minute, Daughter?"

I was beginning to shiver in my wet clothes, but I nodded. "Sure, but you should stay here tonight," I said. "Both of you. It's too bad outside to venture out again. Especially all the way to the Strauss farm."

"Before we make a decision about that," Father said, "I would like to speak my piece."

That got my attention. It was almost the same thing Noah had said in the basement.

"Elizabeth, when I lay in that ditch with the snow coming down as if it wanted to bury me alive, my mind could only think of your mother . . . and you. I . . . I have tried to be a good father to you. Anyway, I thought I had. It has been difficult for me to understand why you have rebelled against me so.

"I also began to remember how I felt as a child when my father said things to me that may have been . . . unkind." Tears filled his eyes, and my mother reached for his hand. "Although I tried to understand that he was attempting to make me a good man who would serve God and my family with integrity and holiness, I must admit now that over time I grew angry because I could never seem to please him. To live up to his expectations."

He shook his head. "I have come to the realization that my actions may have caused you to feel the same way. If this is true, I must ask your forgiveness. Perhaps I should have led you more by example instead of harsh words." He quickly wiped away a tear that snaked down his cheek. "All I can say in my defense is that I tried to be the kind of father I thought you needed." He stared into my eyes. "I am sincerely asking you to forgive my failures, Daughter. I cannot promise that I will change overnight. But you have my promise that I will do my best to treat you . . . and my granddaughter differently if you will afford me the chance."

He turned his gaze to my mother. "And I will work just as hard to be a better husband, Anna, if you are able to be patient with me. Perhaps someday you will allow me to come home. However long it takes . . ."

My mother put her fingers on his lips, stopping his words. "It takes only this long, Husband. Let us go home now. The wind has died down, and I am sure we can make it safely. You need warm clothes, and I want to draw you a hot bath."

Tears coursed down my father's rugged face. "You can take me back so quickly, Anna? After the way I treated you?"

"Of course, Matthew. You are my dear husband, and I love you with all my heart. Nothing will ever change that."

"You are my heart, Anna," he answered brokenly. "My heart."

As I wiped away my own tears, I felt a tug on my sleeve. Charity stood next to me. "Mama, I don't think Grandpa is a bad man anymore. Can I hug him now?"

I nodded, unable to speak. Charity ran over and wrapped her little arms around my father, who returned her embrace although somewhat stiffly.

"Thank you, Granddaughter," he said. "Thank you for not giving up on me."

"I prayed for you, Grandpa, and I knew God would help you," she said sweetly.

Father gave her a tentative smile. "Please keep praying, Charity. Your prayers are very important to me."

It was too much to believe that my father could change years of negativity overnight, but at least he was trying. That meant more to me than words could express. Maybe we actually had a chance to mend our fractured relationship. My heart, which was soaring with joy, suddenly dropped like a stone. We wouldn't be here for my father to make good on his promise. The ache in my chest was almost physical.

"Father and I are going home," Mother said, rising to her feet. "The wind has calmed down in the last few minutes, but

I am not sure how long it will last." She grinned. "As your grandmother used to say, we had better 'get going while the going is good.'"

I smiled at her. "Grandmother had lots of sayings like that. I wasn't sure what some of them meant, but it didn't matter."

"No, it didn't matter one bit."

She kissed me on the cheek. "Thank you, Lizzie. For everything. If the weather improves I will see you tomorrow." She snuck a quick look at Father, who nodded.

"When the roads are better, perhaps your mother and I will come back and have dinner." He looked around the dining room. "I have heard many good things about this place."

"That sounds wonderful." I went up to him cautiously. Hugging my father wasn't something I'd tried since childhood. Although he seemed a bit rigid, he wrapped his strong arms around me. His beard tickled my cheek.

"I do love you, Lizzie," he whispered, "and I am sorry it has taken me so long to tell you."

It was the first time he'd ever called me by my nickname. It touched me deeply, and I didn't want to ruin the moment, but there was a question that had to be asked. I couldn't let my chance to ask it slip away. "Father," I said quietly, "please don't be angry, but I must know the truth about something. Whatever you tell me now I will accept."

He stared down at me. "As I told your mother, it was a deer, Daughter. You have my word."

I looked into his eyes and saw his complete sincerity. "Thank you, Father."

With that, my parents left. I watched them drive away in their buggy, Blackie prancing in the snow, almost as if rejoicing that his master had returned. As Mother had said, the wind was calmer, even though snow still fell. Maybe the storm was finally moving out. At least one storm in my heart had quieted as well. I believed my father. He didn't kill Dave Parsons. I'd found it hard to believe that my father would ever resort to murder, but I consoled myself with the knowledge that even my mother had been unsure for a while.

So did Dave Parsons really die accidentally? Or had someone else killed him? I shook my head as I stared out at the snow-covered ground. How could that be possible? No one in Kingdom knew the man. The past few weeks had caused me to start looking for monsters around every corner. Sometimes, corners were just corners.

After getting out of my wet clothes, I got Charity ready for bed. She dropped off almost immediately. However, the excitement of the day wouldn't allow me to sleep quite yet. I realized I'd never had dinner, so I went downstairs to make a sandwich and pour a glass of milk.

I felt so confused. Clay's revelation that the police were looking for me, my decision to leave Kingdom, Noah's pronouncement of love and proposal of marriage, my father's rescue and the turnaround in his behavior . . . All of it together seemed impossible to take in. How could I tell my parents I was moving to Seattle? My mind had made a decision, the one I felt was best for my daughter, but what about my heart? Was it selfish to follow it instead of what seemed to be the right choice for my daughter?

A look at the clock revealed it was after midnight. I'd had no plans to open in the morning, but another look outside showed the snow becoming lighter. Surprisingly, the wind had created huge drifts that lined the road, but the street itself wasn't too bad. Knowing the hardy folks in Kingdom, I'd be smart to get some sleep. One of our farmers could be knocking on the door first thing in the morning. As I headed for the stairs I suddenly remembered the blanket on the washer. Letting it sit wet might cause it to mold. I hurried down the stairs and grabbed it, shaking it out first. Something fell out on the floor. Noah must have accidentally picked up something in his truck when he got the blanket out of his backseat.

As I bent to pick it up, I froze, horrified by what I saw.

A blue envelope with my name written on the front.

CHAPTER 23

My legs felt weak, and I grabbed a nearby stool. Slowly ripping open the wet, stained envelope, I found exactly what I expected. Although the letters ran together somewhat, it was clearly another threat.

> *I'm still watching you, Lizzie. There's not much time left.*

I sat there, trying to make sense of it. How did this note get in the blanket . . . which had been in Noah's truck? His declarations of love and his constant promises to protect me suddenly took on an extremely ominous meaning. Had he *protected* me from Parsons? Noah was one of the only people who knew that the man had followed me to Kingdom from Kansas City.

I suddenly remembered something he'd said that I'd forgotten about in the excitement of finding my father. Noah had mentioned that Father had gone off the road in about the same place Mr. Parsons had. How would he have known that? He wasn't around when the body was found. There was only one way he could have gotten information like that—if he'd seen the body himself. But if he loved me and was trying to protect me, why would he write notes threatening me and my daughter? Could this be some kind of twisted plan to make me run to him to seek security? Or were we in actual danger? Maybe he would do anything to keep me close to him. Telling him I was leaving with Clay could have been a horrible mistake.

I felt sick to my stomach. *What should I do?* Phone the police? Tell them that an elder in Kingdom church had gone crazy, had killed a man to protect me and might try to kill me too? As I considered my options, the idea that Noah had anything to do with Dave Parsons' death or the hateful threats seemed impossible. Besides, how could he have sent mail to me in Kansas City? He couldn't have known where I was. And the envelopes all had local postmarks.

Slowly another possibility dawned on me. Could he have hired Dave Parsons to find me and send me the notes? I shook my head as I considered this. Noah's voice echoed in my thoughts. *"You know me, Lizzie. You know me better than you think."* And I did. Noah Housler wasn't a murderer, I was sure of it. So where did the note come from? And how did Noah know where Dave Parsons died?

I let out a big sigh into the semidarkness. What was it with me and men? I'd misjudged Clay and my father, and now I found myself suspecting an elder in the Mennonite church of taking a man's life. I rubbed my head. It was time to get some sleep. Maybe I'd know what to do in the morning.

After putting the envelope into my pocket, I stuck the blanket into the washer, started it, and then slowly climbed the stairs. When I reached the kitchen, I quickly cleaned up the dishes from my impromptu supper and then checked the door. For some reason, tonight I wanted to make sure it was locked. When I finally climbed into bed, I spent time thanking God for saving my father's life and touching his heart. Then I prayed once again for guidance. Even though I didn't believe Noah was behind the threats, it seemed someone in Kingdom wanted to harm me and Charity. Someone who may have killed Dave Parsons.

When morning rolled around, I got out of bed and prepared food for breakfast, although not as much as I usually did. Sure enough, by a little after six, five customers had already made it in, and by nine, we were about half full. Several of the men had come into town specifically to clear the streets. After warming up with a hot meal, they went outside and hooked up snowplows to their tractors, making short order of Main Street. Then they headed out to the side streets.

About one thirty Mother walked into an empty dining room. Everyone seemed to be preoccupied with digging out of the storm. If the skies stayed clear, I had no doubt that tomorrow night would be very busy. "Your father would have come, but he is clearing the snow and doing some work around our home. He admits that it has fallen into disrepair over the last two years, and he is determined to fix it. He was cleaning out the fireplace and gathering wood this morning. Before I left, I saw him standing outside, staring at our outhouse." She giggled. "I believe he is determined to build a bathroom inside, not just for me, but also for Charity."

I laughed. "Sit down, Mother. How about something to eat?"

She lowered herself into a chair. "I don't suppose you have prepared any fried chicken today?"

"Fried chicken is a constant around here. We sell more of it than anything else. I'll be back with a nice hot plate in a few minutes."

She glanced around the room. "Where is Charity?"

"Taking a nap. She found last night exciting but also very tiring."

Mother nodded. "I agree with her. Getting out of bed this morning was quite difficult. However, Matthew's industrious behavior puts me to shame." She took off her bonnet and set it next to her on the table. "Lizzie, I heard your father whistling this morning. It has been so long since—" She stopped and bit her lip, trying to hold back her emotions. "I will not cry today. Before long you will think me a silly, weepy old woman."

"Tears of happiness are a lot different than tears of pain," I said softly. "You can bawl your head off, for all I care."

She laughed. "What a funny expression. Why would I want to lose my head? I think that would not make me the least bit happy."

I grinned at her. "Why, Mother, you made a joke."

"Yes, I did, Daughter. And it felt good."

I chuckled and headed to the kitchen. The mashed potatoes and gravy were still hot, and frying the chicken only took a few minutes. I tossed in a couple of pieces for myself after realizing I hadn't eaten. By the time I carried our plates out to the dining room, I'd made the decision to tell my mother about Clay and Noah. I needed wisdom, and she was the wisest person I knew.

After praying for our food, I first broached the subject of Noah and the note. "He keeps reminding me about a promise he made to me when I was a child, Mother. That he would always protect me. Could his drive to take care of me lead him to kill that detective?"

"Oh, Daughter, I do not think so. I have known Noah Housler all his life. He is a very good man. Not someone who would take a life."

"But what about the note, Mother? And how could he possibly know the exact spot in the ravine where Dave Parsons died?"

She shook her head. "I do not know, Elizabeth Lynn. Perhaps you should be asking him these questions."

I took a big bite of mashed potatoes and gravy while I considered her suggestion. Maybe she was right. Noah was the only person who had the answers I needed.

More than once, as Mother and I visited, I tried to bring up my plans to marry Clay and leave Kingdom, but she was so happy, I couldn't do it. Not yet. I finally decided to wait until our plans were solid before telling her and Father. It would hurt them, and that was something I didn't want to do. Of course, watching me get arrested and hauled off to jail would upset them even more. A verse from Isaiah popped into my head about God making a way in the wilderness and streams in the wasteland. That's what I needed. For God to make a way for me through my mess. A way that would bring joy instead of sorrow. God brought me to Kingdom, and He was the only one who could sort out the muddle I was in.

Charity woke up around two thirty, and Mother played with her for a while. Around four Callie came in, apologizing for not making it in sooner. She'd been snowed in. I sent her home, deciding to close for the evening.

It was almost four thirty before Mother was ready to leave.

She was putting on her cape when she suddenly got a strange look on her face. "My goodness. I almost forgot." She reached inside her cloak and pulled out a package wrapped in brown paper and bound with twine. "The letters Clay sent. Father asked me to give them to you. He said you should do whatever you want with them."

"Thanks, Mother. I'll put them upstairs. Maybe I'll read them someday, but right now I think they'd just make me sad."

"I understand, Daughter. I am sorry they were late in reaching you."

I took the package from her with a smile. "It doesn't matter anymore."

She said good-bye and left. I watched her climb into the buggy and signal to Blackie that it was time to start home.

A few minutes after she'd ridden away, Clay called to find out how late I was working tonight. The roads between Belleville and Kingdom were in pretty good shape, and no snow was forecast for tonight.

"Perfect timing," I told him. "With everyone still digging out, I've decided to close. I'll make us dinner, and the three of us will have the whole evening together."

"That sounds wonderful. I've been stuck in this motel room too long. I'm getting cabin fever."

"Well, not sure how much different being stuck in the restaurant will be, but we'd love to see you."

He laughed. "Trust me. Spending time with you and Charity is what I want more than anything in the world. It might take me a little longer than usual to get there, though. How 'bout around seven?"

"Seven it is. See you soon."

"Love you, Lizzie."

"I . . . I love you . . . too." As I hung the phone up, I struggled with the reason it had been so difficult to say that.

I hurried upstairs to change. Since the restaurant was closed, I decided to dress up a bit. Not being a "dress" person after having to wear long skirts most of my life, I made the ultimate sacrifice. I took off my usual jeans and put on a lovely long-sleeved Nicole Miller print dress I'd found at a garage sale. I'd worn it only once, to a Harbor House banquet. It had muted shades of turquoise, blue, and black and created a pattern that almost reminded me of butterflies. It seemed to set off my dark hair and eyes. The night of the banquet, I'd received quite a few compliments.

I pulled on my only pair of dress shoes, black pumps with small heels. Then I touched up my makeup and brushed my hair. I checked myself in the dresser mirror. Not bad.

"Oh, Mama. You're beautiful," Charity said. "Can I dress up too?"

"If you want to. What about your pink dress?"

She nodded happily. "Just like The Princess. Except she has blond hair and I don't."

I chuckled. "Yes, just like The Princess. Do you need help putting it on?"

She shook her head vigorously. "I'm getting to be a pretty big girl, you know. I can get dressed by myself." She started to flounce out of my room but stopped at the door. "But maybe you better brush my hair for me. I don't do it right sometimes."

"I'll be happy to do that."

"Thank you, Mama." With that she left.

I suddenly remembered a small bottle of cologne I'd bought on sale in Kansas City. Now, where was it? My purse. I'd stuck it in there because it was so small I didn't want it to get lost in all the other junk I'd shoved into our suitcases as we were leaving town. I found my purse and scavenged around in it, trying to locate the bottle.

Before I uncovered the cologne, my fingers closed around my cell phone. I'd forgotten all about it. After finally finding the cologne and dabbing it on my neck and below my ears, I decided to plug in the phone. I had no idea if it would work in Kingdom, so far out in the country. But, since I'd paid for two months of service, it would be interesting to find out if I'd thrown my money away.

Finding the charger took several minutes, but I finally located it in a small bag I hadn't unpacked yet. I unplugged the DVD player, stuck the charger into the receptacle, and turned on the phone. I started to walk away when the phone beeped out a signal that there was a message. I went back, pressed the button to retrieve my messages, and entered my voicemail code. There were six new messages. My stomach clenched. Did I really want to listen? At first I decided not to, but curiosity got the better of me, and I punched in the number that would play back the phone calls. Then I pressed the speaker button. Meghan's voice came through the speaker.

"Lizzie," she said excitedly, "you've been completely cleared! Sylvia found out you'd been let go and launched an investigation. A little research proved you were right. Reba doctored the books, trying to make you look guilty. She was fired. No one is sure why she did it, but everyone knows now that you were framed. Sylvia wants you back. After a few more weeks of rest, she's returning to the director's job." There was a long pause. "I hope you get this, Lizzie. I miss you. Please call me and let me know you're okay. I'm worried about you." The rest of the messages were all the same, although Meghan's plea to contact her became more insistent.

I slid down to the floor, staring at the phone with disbelief. It was over. The nightmare was over. No more running. Relief overtook me, and all I could do was sob. The pent-up fear and frustration of the last couple of weeks slowly drained from my body, leaving me feeling weak but exhilarated. I sat there for several minutes thinking, wondering what this meant for Charity and me.

Finally Charity called out, needing help with her hair. I turned off the phone, got up, and went to help her. After brushing her hair and wiping the mascara off my face, we went downstairs. Charity played with The Princess while I prepared dinner. Steak and potatoes. Salad. As I worked, a deep sense of awareness bubbled up from inside me, and I began to hum a familiar tune.

For the first time since coming to Kingdom, I knew exactly what I wanted.

CHAPTER 24

"Well, that was about the best dinner I ever had," Clay said, polishing off his last bite of steak. "Your mommy is a really good cook, Charity."

She smiled. "You should try her grilled cheese sandwiches. They're yummy!"

He laughed easily. He and Charity had developed a comfortable friendship, and I was glad to see it. "I'll do that one of these days."

"What about dessert, Mama?" she said coquettishly. Charity knew she had charmed Clay and was playing it for all she was worth.

"Yes, we're having dessert," I said, "and after that, you're going to bed."

Her bottom lip stuck out. "But I want to stay up and play with Clay."

"Sorry, Cherry Bear," I said, "but it's very late. Clay can come another time. You can play with him then."

"Okay, but we still hafta eat our dessert. What is it?"

I smiled. "How about hot fudge sundaes?"

"Oh, Mama. That would be just lovely."

Clay grinned. "I think that would be just lovely too."

I started to pick up our dinner dishes when he stopped me. "You've done enough. I'll carry the dishes."

"Thank you. If you'll take them into the kitchen, I'll start on those *lovely* hot fudge sundaes."

"There will be nuts, right Mama?" Charity's question was asked with all seriousness. One episode from an ice cream store in Kansas City when the woman making the sundaes forgot the nuts had caused Charity to become the guardian of hot fudge sundaes. She had no intention of allowing that kind of mistake to occur again.

"I promise you, Cherry Bear, there will be nuts."

"Then it's okay." She settled back with a sigh, content to wait for the highly anticipated sundae to make its entrance.

Clay picked up our plates and carried them to the kitchen while I got the ice cream out of the freezer and began heating up the fudge topping. It was interesting to see how many trips it took him to carry everything when I could have done it in one. There was a way to stack dishes for maximum volume, and Clay obviously needed a lesson. But tonight wasn't the time for instruction in the fine art of waitressing.

I served the sundaes, topped with whipped cream, nuts, and a cherry, to the delight of my daughter and a smile of appreciation from her father. By the time Charity finished her last bite, her eyes were heavy with sleep. It didn't take much encouragement to get her to tell Clay good-night and give him a kiss, so I could carry her upstairs to bed. We prayed together, and then I tucked her in. She dozed off immediately.

On my way toward the stairs, I noticed the cell phone blinking in the living room. It was finally charged, so I decided to unplug it. As I did, something occurred to me. Something

I'd missed the first time I checked the messages. I'd saved all of Meghan's calls, and it just took a moment to find out what I wanted to know. Strange. I turned off the phone and plugged the DVD player back in. It didn't make any sense. What did it mean?

I quickly retrieved the brown paper package Mother had given me and opened it. What I discovered caused me even more concern. Shoving the letters into a drawer, I tried to get myself together before joining Clay downstairs. As I came down the steps, he must have noticed the look on my face.

"Is something wrong?" he asked. "Is Charity okay?"

"Yes, it's not that." I frowned at him. "Clay, earlier this evening I found some calls on my cell phone from my friend Meghan in Kansas City. Seems my old boss raised the roof about the missing money. A little investigation uncovered the truth—that Reba took the money in an attempt to frame me. I've been completely cleared."

His jaw dropped. "But . . . but that's wonderful, Lizzie! I can hardly believe it. You must be so relieved."

I sat down at the table across from him. "Oh, I am. But Meghan's first call came a few days after I arrived in Kingdom. That's over a week before you told me charges had been filed against me."

He looked puzzled. "My information must have been wrong. I'm so sorry. I don't know what to say. My source is usually very reliable."

"It's a good thing I plugged my cell phone in. I'd have never known the truth."

"I'll certainly be calling my friend to find out what happened. I know his information frightened you, and I wouldn't do that for the world."

I drew an imaginary circle on the tabletop with my finger. "It certainly seems odd, though. Don't you think? I thought you said your source knew James Webb."

He frowned, his hazel eyes seeking mine. "Yes, that's right. What are you trying to say?"

"It just seems a little convenient, doesn't it? You want me to go with you to Seattle, and lo and behold your *friend* tells you that the authorities are after me."

"Lizzie," he said, looking at me strangely, "I would never try to manipulate you into marrying me. I only want your happiness. And Charity's. I think you're letting your imagination run away with you."

"Maybe. Seems like I've been wrong about a lot of things. About several people in my life. Especially the men."

His eyebrows shot up. "Men? I hoped I was the only one. How many men are you involved with?"

I leaned back in my chair and crossed my arms. "Well, one of them is my father, if that makes you feel any better."

"Your father? Not much to misunderstand about him. He's certainly treated you horribly."

"Yes, he has. You're right about that." I looked at him through narrowed eyes. The confusion I'd experienced since checking the dates of Meghan's first phone call and the post-marks on Clay's letters began to turn into anger. "But so have you."

Clay shook his head. "Lizzie, I apologized. More than once. And I explained. There's not much else I can do. Has something happened? You seem so . . . so different tonight."

"My mother brought me your letters, Clay."

He looked relieved. "Good. Have you read them?"

I shook my head. "Not yet."

"I don't understand. Why not? If you read them, you'll see clearly how much I love you. How much I've always loved you."

"I don't doubt that they're packed with declarations of love and commitment."

"Doesn't that mean anything to you?"

I leaned forward. "No. Not anymore."

He reached out and took my hand in his. "I have no idea what's bothering you, but I don't like it. We've planned a wonderful life together. With our child. And now . . . Is it Noah Housler? Has he been filling you with lies? Trying to destroy us? You can't trust him, Lizzie. He'd do anything to break us up."

I gazed down at his hand. Well manicured. Clean. Soft. Unlike Noah's hands, which were rough from hard work and many times had dirt beneath the nails from working out in the fields. I pulled my hand from his. "No. The only lies have been coming from you."

"What lies? I haven't lied to you. I wouldn't do that."

"Those letters were sent in the last year, Clay. None of them were postmarked before last January. You didn't try to reach me right after your father's death." I stared at him, feeling as though I was really seeing him for the first time. "You've been lying to me ever since you got to Kingdom. Do you know what you've put me through? If you think I'd leave with you after the way you've tried to manipulate me, you're sadly mistaken."

He didn't say anything. Just sat there. I felt like he was thinking, trying to come up with an explanation that would mollify me. Finally, he stood up.

"I need some coffee. How about you?"

"I guess. However, I'd rather have an explanation."

"And you'll get it. After I get us both a cup of coffee."

After he left, I took a deep cleansing breath. My hands were shaking, but not from fear. I was furious. Furious at being used. Furious at being lied to. As I sat there waiting, troubling ideas began to float through my brain. Bits and pieces that didn't make sense. I was so entrenched in my thoughts, I didn't hear Clay return. When he set a coffee cup down in front of me, I was startled.

"So you've made up your mind? You're not coming to Seattle with me?" he asked.

"No. But I'd already decided not to go before I made the connection about the phone calls and the letters."

"And why is that?"

I didn't like the look on his face. His expression was void of emotion, and his tone of voice disturbed me.

"Because I realized the main reason I was going with you was to protect Charity and give her a father. I would do anything for my daughter. Unfortunately, it wasn't because I loved you."

"But you said you did."

"I think I did . . . once, but I've realized I'm not the same person I was when I knew you before, Clay. I've grown up. I want something different in my life."

"Like Noah Housler?"

"Yes, like Noah Housler. And Kingdom. The truth is, I don't want to leave this town. I love this old restaurant, and I want to run it. Also, I want to bring Charity up around my parents and all the other wonderful people who live here."

"What about me?"

"You have to do whatever's best for you. It will take me

a long time to trust you again." I picked up my coffee cup. The pot must have been on way too long. It was bitter, but I drank it anyway. I needed a shot of caffeine to stay on my toes.

"What if the best thing for me is to take Charity to Seattle?"

The coffee cup almost slipped from my hands. "Take Charity? Away from me? Of course not. But you can see her, Clay. Even if I don't like what you did, she *is* your daughter."

He took a sip from his own cup and put it down. "I'm afraid that won't work for me. My mother would never accept that."

"What does your mother have to do with anything?" I finished the coffee in my cup and wished I had more.

Clay sighed and leaned forward, resting his head on his hands. "She has something to do with everything. You see, she has the money. My father left her all of it. Every last dime. And unless I bring her granddaughter to her, I'll have nothing. She's threatened to write me out of her will."

I shook my head slowly. "I don't understand . . ." But that wasn't true. I *was* beginning to understand. And if I was right, the truth was horrifying. "Clay, who was Dave Parsons?"

He raised his head, and I was shocked to see the wild look in his eyes. "Dave Parsons was a cheap detective hired to find you. He did a great job, letting me know you were in Kansas City. But then he became a problem."

"A problem?" The room seemed to be spinning slightly. I guess I hadn't realized how tired I was. I shook my head, trying to clear it. "Wh-what do you mean?"

Clay smiled oddly. The corners of his mouth turned up, but the eyes that studied me were cold and dead. Like a shark's. "He found out about the notes I was sending to you, and he wanted out. Felt sorry for you. Poor old Dave just didn't have the killer instinct, you see."

"You sent those vile threats?" My tongue felt too thick for my mouth. "Why?"

He laughed. "I told you. My mother wants her grand-daughter. I guess she's given up on me. She thinks she can groom Charity to carry on the family name." He shrugged. "I don't care, as long as I get the bulk of her estate. She promised me a tidy sum as well as a place on the board of my father's company if I succeed in bringing her long-lost seed home. I thought about how to accomplish the task for a long time. I'd heard you'd left Kingdom, so I sent your parents some letters vowing my unending love. When I didn't hear from them, I hired good old Dave to locate you. After that, I started sending those notes to frighten you."

"The threatening notes . . ."

He laughed. "Good move to start them up again, wasn't it? I didn't want you to think the threat was past after Dave died. So I stuck one under the door the other night." He frowned. "Had another one, but I lost it somewhere."

"In . . . in Noah's truck . . ."

He snorted. "Noah's truck? Now how in the world did it get there?" He chuckled like I'd just told him a really funny joke. "The other night when we had dinner, I was going to drive back to town after you'd gone to bed and put it under the door—just like the other one. But when I looked for it in the car, it was gone. It must have fallen out when I got the roses out. I'm guessing your boyfriend found it and stuck it in his truck."

All I could do was stare at him. *Oh, God, how could I have been so foolish? Why didn't I realize Clay couldn't be trusted? And how could I have doubted Noah, even for a second?*

I suddenly realized something else, although for some reason it was getting harder and harder to think clearly. "So it wasn't Roger who told you where I was?"

"No. Roger didn't call me. But I was glad when you jumped to that conclusion. It was a much better explanation than the one I'd cooked up."

"You had me set up in Kansas City, didn't you?"

"Yep. I needed to put you in a situation where you'd run to me when I showed up in your life again. When Dave found you in Kansas City, it was easy to call in a few favors. Well, actually I pulled some old skeletons out of several closets. You see, my father had all kinds of people in his back pocket. Luckily, Councilman Webb was one of them. A little pressure, some intimidation thrown in, and he put his girlfriend in at that place you worked. What was the name of it?"

"Harbor . . . Harbor . . ."

"Harbor House. That's right." He grinned, but it reminded me of the Cheshire cat from *Alice's Adventures in Wonderland*. "A little creative thinking and *poof*. Threatening notes. No job. No prospects. Possible imprisonment. And then I sweep in. Your protector. Your knight in shining armor. But before I could *accidentally* run into you in Kansas City and save the day, you took off for this flea-bitten, one-horse town."

"And Dave?" My voice was little more than a whisper. What was wrong with me? Why did I feel so strange?

"Dave was on his way to see you when I intercepted him. Lucky break on my part." Clay shook his head. "He told me you were almost killed in Kansas City when you ran out in front of a car. He felt like the whole thing was his fault. He even called 9-1-1 for you. I guess you threw one of my notes on the ground, and he found it. Read it. Put two and two together. He gave me back my money and quit. Said I was sick and needed to be put away. He was on his way to tell you everything. A little push down the ravine, and old Dave was history."

He grimaced. "Poor Dave. His problem was that he had a conscience. I sent one of Dad's minions to his run-down apartment to clean up after me. By the time he was done, there was nothing left to tie us together." He leaned closer, peering into my face. "All you had to do was leave everything alone, Lizzie. Originally, I'd planned to just get rid of you and take Charity. But the funny thing was, the more time I spent with you, the more I wondered if we might actually have a future together. So I changed my mind and decided to marry you. Take you both back to Seattle. Mother might not have been pleased to have you there, but I was willing to risk her anger for you. Too bad. In my own way, I think I might actually love you."

"You only love your mother's money." I put my head down on the table, cradling it in my arms. "What's wrong with me, Clay? I . . . I don't feel well . . ."

"I'm sorry. It's the sleeping pills I put in your coffee. You must have the constitution of a horse. I'm out after two. You've had six."

I tried to raise my head but couldn't. "Why?"

Another odd laugh. "I've been carrying those pills around since I got here. My original idea was to knock you out and then . . . Well, let's just say that I had another plan. Good thing I forgot to take them out of my coat pocket. Now it's not too late to stick to my previous strategy."

"What . . . what . . ."

"What am I going to do?" He reached over and stroked my hair. "I'm going to leave, Lizzie. But then I'll remember

I left something here. My wallet. My coat. It doesn't really matter. When I return, I'll find the kitchen on fire. I can't get to you, so I run upstairs and save my daughter's life. After your tragic death, no one will argue that it's not my right to take Charity home with me. You won't be able to stop me or tell anyone the truth. My mother will be very happy, and I'll be back in her good graces. Problem solved."

Even as I began to lose consciousness, I realized how dangerous his plan was. If he didn't reach Charity in time, she could die. Using every bit of strength in my body, I tried to get up. I had to save my daughter. But my legs felt like wet noodles, and I felt myself slump to the floor. Just as I drifted away, I heard an odd sound, almost as if it were a faraway echo. Screaming. A loud crash. And then everything went black.

CHAPTER / 25

They kept me in the hospital overnight, but the sleeping pills Clay gave me wore off fairly quickly. Mother let everyone know the restaurant would be closed for a few days, but no one complained. Kingdom residents seemed concerned only about my welfare. So much food was delivered for Charity and me that I could have opened a second restaurant. Even Frances Lapp brought chicken and dumplings and offered to help me in any way she could. The people of Kingdom were incredibly gracious, and although I had some residual weariness, I felt better every day.

By Saturday morning, I woke up feeling like my old self. I sent Mother home, thanking her for taking care of us. I made the decision to reopen the restaurant on Monday and put a hand-drawn sign on the door. Charity drew a picture of us waving at the bottom of the note. Just the right touch. We spent the remainder of Saturday resting and watching videos. *Sleeping Beauty* was front and center, of course.

After being treated and released for a rather nasty bump on the head from when Noah hit him with a chair, Clay was booked into jail in Washington. We heard from Sheriff Ford that he would soon be transferred somewhere else, and that the investigation into Dave Parsons' death would be reopened. Clay's mother sent a high-powered attorney down from Seattle, and the word was that Clay might be released pending trial.

I didn't care. I was the only one who could testify against him, so I realized it would be my word against his. Even if no one could prove he killed Dave or tried to kill me, he would never get Charity. According to their lawyer, who actually seemed like a rather nice man, Mildred Troyer had withdrawn her plans to raise my daughter. Seems Clay had his own skeletons, and too much scrutiny directed toward him could bring some embarrassing and very unwelcome attention to the Troyer family. It was safe to say that they were out of our lives for good.

Fortunately, Charity had slept through the whole horrible scene Thursday night. I made certain she didn't hear that Clay had tried to kill me and take her away. That was something she never needed to know. She didn't seem the least bit concerned when I told her Clay had gone away and wouldn't be coming back. That was the last time I planned to ever mention him again.

As it grew dark outside, I went through the food in the refrigerator, settling on a beautiful pot roast that Myra had brought by. I heated it up until the juice bubbled around the tender, browned potatoes, carrots, and onions. Then I put some rolls in the oven to warm up. I heard the front door open and smiled.

"Have a seat. I'll be right out." I grabbed a coffee carafe and two cups. My coffee drinking had been cut way down since Clay tried to do away with me, but tonight, the memory of the drug-laced brew seemed far away and unimportant.

"Here, let me get that," Noah said, when I came walking out. "Just in case you're thinking about dumping coffee in my lap."

I laughed and handed him the tray. "I'm doing fine now, really," I said, smiling. "Funny how long it took to feel like myself again. Remind me to stay away from sleeping pills."

"Stay away from sleeping pills," he said softly, leaning over and kissing me softly.

I laughed. "You're a funny man. You know that?"

"If you say so. I'm just so grateful you're okay."

"Me too. Want to help me carry in our dinner?"

"Well, I guess, since you're feeding me."

"Yeah, I worked really hard heating it all up."

He grinned and followed me to the kitchen. A few minutes later we were seated, a candle burning in the middle of our table. Charity was eating supper at my mother and father's house.

I smiled at him. "Tell me again why you came by that night."

"We've been over this several times," he said.

"I don't think I'll ever get tired of hearing it."

He took a deep breath. "I drove into town to visit with Abner Wittsman and his wife. Abner's recovering from a bad fall, and the church has been giving them a hand, since he isn't able to work right now. They needed food and their horse had to be fed. I'd just finished up with them and was getting ready to drive home, when something told me to go to the restaurant."

"*Something* told you?"

He shook his head. "Okay, you're right. *Someone* told me."

I stuck a piece of pot roast in my mouth and smiled. "Go on."

"It's not polite to talk with your mouth full."

"I'm recovering from a traumatic event. Don't give me a hard time."

Noah sighed dramatically. "And how long are you planning to use that excuse to get your way?"

I pointed my fork at him. "As long as it takes."

"I don't doubt that."

"Go on."

He shook his finger at me. "Patience, woman. I'm getting there." He rolled his eyes. "Now where was I . . . ?"

"Someone told you to check on me."

He nodded. "That's right. So I drove over here, and when I looked through the window, I saw you falling on the floor while Clay simply watched. It was obvious something was wrong."

"Maybe it was just a really boring date. You could have really embarrassed yourself, you know."

"That's true. Maybe I shouldn't have interrupted you two."

I snorted. "Well, if you hadn't, I'd be cooked more than this pot roast."

"Not funny."

"Sorry."

"Anyway, I checked the door, which of course wasn't locked, even though I told you a hundred times to lock it."

"Good thing I don't listen to everything you say."

He gave me a dirty look. "It may have worked out this time, but in the future . . ."

"Go on."

"Quit saying 'Go on.'"

"Okay. Go on."

He raised one eyebrow. "Now *you're* being funny."

"Sorry."

"I burst in, picked up a chair, and conked Clay on the head before he had time to react. And you looked dead, by the way."

"But I wasn't."

"Yes, I'm aware of that now."

"Go on."

His eyes narrowed as he stared at me.

"Sorry."

"The look on Clay's face . . ." Noah shivered. "Crazy. I've never seen anyone look like that. Hope I never do again."

"You made him scream like a little girl."

"Who's telling this story? You or me?"

"I'm not sure."

Another look. "I made him scream like a little girl."

I shook my head. "Inappropriate behavior for a Mennonite elder."

He shrugged. "I wasn't really worried about my reputation at that moment. Saving your life, should you not actually be dead, seemed a little more important."

"Thank you."

"You're welcome."

"So you knocked the stuffings out of him."

He frowned. "I'm not sure what *stuffings* are, but he didn't move after I hit him."

"Good thing you didn't kill him. I might have had to visit you in jail, and I'm a little busy right now."

"I would have hated to inconvenience you."

"Thank you. So after you cleaned Clay's clock?"

"He had a clock?"

"Stop it."

"Sorry." He scowled at me. "I'm really hungry. When can we quit talking and eat?"

"Soon. So then what happened?"

Noah leaned back in his chair, his emerald eyes twinkling with amusement. "I looked to see if you were alive. You were, by the way. Then I ran upstairs, checked on Charity, cut the drawstrings off your drapes—"

"I'll probably have to get new drapes."

"I don't care."

"Go on."

He sighed deeply. "Came back downstairs, tied Clay up, called for an ambulance and the sheriff, and then waited for them to come. After they carried you both off, I woke Charity up and drove over to your parents' house to let them know you were on your way to the hospital. They got in my truck, and we all drove to Washington to check on you. End of story."

"Thank you."

"You're welcome. Now if you don't mind, I'd like to eat my dinner in peace."

"I don't mind."

He took several bites, then put his fork down. "So you actually thought I might have killed that detective? Unbelievable."

"Well, you kept telling me how you were going to *take care of me.*"

"Notice I didn't say I would *kill* for you. Mennonites don't believe in that, you know."

I shrugged. "I'm pretty sure they don't believe in conking people over the head either."

He sighed again. "Yes, you're right. Apparently I wasn't thinking clearly."

"I guess not."

He shook his head. "I still can't believe you thought I was a murderer."

"Well, men in Kingdom confuse me."

"Obviously."

"With your declarations of protection and knowing where Mr. Parsons died . . ."

"Because Avery pointed it out to me."

"*And* finding the note."

"Which I found stuck halfway under the bottom stairs outside."

"Now I know why it took you so long to make it to your truck that night. You were busy retrieving the envelope and tossing it into the backseat of your truck. You know, I wouldn't have suspected you if you'd just given it to me right after you picked it up."

He raised one eyebrow and speared a potato. "Sorry. Saving your father's life seemed a little more important at that moment than completing a mail delivery." Noah put his fork down with a little force. "Seriously, Lizzie. You really thought I'd killed someone?"

I stared down at my plate. "No, not really. Maybe just for a minute. To be honest, I was so confused about everything. I couldn't trust Sheriff Ford's conclusion that Mr. Parsons' death was an unfortunate mishap. It was obvious he didn't want to mess with the KBI and would do just about anything to agree with the coroner. I just couldn't wrap my mind around the coincidence that he had just *accidentally* fallen down that ravine right after my mother told the elders about him. I knew in my heart something was terribly wrong with that scenario.

"When I saw that note, I guess my mind tried to put the

319

pieces of this weird puzzle together in a way that would make sense out of everything. It didn't take long for me to clearly see you couldn't have done it. I mean, I know you, Noah. I really do." I smiled. "And then I found the call from Meghan. Once the pressure from the situation at Harbor House was gone, I could see everything more clearly. I not only knew beyond a shadow of a doubt that you weren't capable of hurting anyone, I also knew exactly what I wanted more than anything in the world. And where I belonged. A part of me never left Kingdom, you know. It just took me a while to realize it. "

"Even though Meghan told you Sylvia was offering you a job at almost twice what you had been making?"

I nodded. "Didn't tempt me even a little bit. I'm just glad my name was cleared at Harbor House. I hated thinking that my reputation had been ruined. Of course, Meghan and Sylvia never doubted me. And I finally got to thank Sylvia for everything she's done for me. That meant more than I can say."

Noah raised his coffee cup. "I think a toast is in order."

I laughed. "Good Mennonite boys aren't supposed to toast stuff. Are they?"

His eyes grew moist. "When they're getting ready to marry the most wonderful woman in the world, all the rules become meaningless."

"Oh, I see." I raised my cup and touched it lightly to his.

"To the future God has for us."

"And to God for bringing me home. He knew exactly where I was supposed to be. I'm so grateful He never gave up on me even though I gave up on Him."

Noah nodded and took a sip from his cup while I did the

same. "As an elder's wife, you do plan to wear an appropriate dress on Sundays, right?"

"I'll think about it, but I'm not sure about a prayer covering. Black's not really my color."

"But you'll think about that too, right?"

"I will."

He sighed. "My life is going to get very interesting. Isn't it?"

I grinned. "Count on it." I suddenly remembered something important. "Wait a minute. I have something for you." I got up, hurried into the kitchen, and grabbed a folded piece of paper lying on top of Charity's small table. I took it back to the table.

"What's this?" he asked as I handed it to him.

"It's from Charity. She drew it just for you."

Noah carefully opened it. A prince stood in the middle of the picture, a large-rimmed black hat on his head, topped by a yellow crown. She'd dictated the caption that I'd written at the bottom. *Prince Noah Phillip. Mama's prince and my new daddy.*

"Oh my," he said softly, his eyes growing moist. "I'm certainly not a prince."

"Don't be silly," I said, reaching for his hand. "You're definitely *my* prince. As my daughter said the first time she met you, we've been waiting for you such a long, long time."

"When I left the restaurant that night, I prayed God would allow me to be your Prince Charming."

I wiped away a tear of happiness that slid down my face. "Boy, when He answers prayers, He does a good job. You will always be my prince, you know."

"You're not going to sing the song from that video you and Charity made me watch, are you?"

"I love that song. 'I know you,'" I sang softly. "'I walked with you once upon a dream.'" I smiled. "I did walk with you once upon a dream, you know. I was in a boat, lost in a storm. A man came to rescue me. Told me that if I'd come to him, he'd save me." I put my hand on Noah's cheek. "That man was you."

He reached over and took my other hand in his. "You go right ahead and sing that song as much as you want. In fact, as far as I'm concerned, you can sing it every day for the rest of our lives."

"The rest of our lives. What beautiful words."

"Yes, they are."

And with a sweet, tender kiss from a very handsome Mennonite prince with emerald-green eyes, our very own fairy tale began.

Discussion Questions

1. Why did Lizzie run away from Kingdom? Should she have stayed, or did she do the right thing? Can you think of a time when you ran away from something rather than facing it?

2. When she had to deal with pressure in Kansas City, she fled to Kingdom. Was she just running away again, or was there a difference this time?

3. Even though Lizzie believed she was going back to Kingdom to protect Charity, she also felt drawn to return. Was she hearing from God?

4. Some people believe that if we aren't perfect, God won't talk to us. Is that true? Lizzie made the decision to turn her back on God. Did He reject her too? Do you ever feel cut off from God because you have sinned?

5. Matthew Engel, Lizzie's father, seems to be a very hard, unforgiving man. Why is he this way?

6. Unhappy past events shaped Lizzie and her father in very negative ways. As Christians, should we allow the past to affect us? What's the best way to keep past hurts from influencing our future?

7. Cora Menlo is a strong character who refused to allow others to dictate her life. Do you identify more with Cora, Lizzie, or Lizzie's father?

8. Was Anna, Lizzie's mother, an abused woman? Although she said Matthew never hit her, what about some of his other actions? Were they abusive? Did Anna do the right thing when she told Matthew to leave?

9. Were Lizzie's motives right when she decided to marry Clay and move away from Kingdom even though she had deep feelings for Noah? What would you have done?

10. How do you feel about Kingdom? Do you understand the desire for a place of safety where families can live away from the evil in the world? Is that really possible? Is it right? If given the chance, would you like to live in a town like Kingdom? Why?

Acknowledgments

My undying thanks to Judy Unruh, Alexanderwohl Church Historian in Goessel, Kansas. You've held my hand throughout this Mennonite journey, letting me know when I have it right and when I have it wrong. Your wisdom and direction show up in every book I write. You're my Mennonite guardian angel! God bless you, Judy!

Thank you to Raela Schoenherr, who brought me into the wonderful Bethany House family. You probably had second thoughts the first time we met. Thanks for turning your car around to prove to this weeping author that the Canada geese crossing the road had safely made it to the other side! LOL! I love working with you, Raela, and hope to live up to your high expectations. I'll always try my best.

To Sharon Asmus, editor extraordinaire: Thank you for all your hard work. I couldn't ask for a better editor. I am so blessed to work with you. You make me better than I really am.

To Bethany House Publishers: Thanks for taking a chance on me. I'll do my best to make you glad you did.

Most of all, thanks to the One who decided to make me a writer. I'm not sure why you did it, but I'm so grateful. I love you, Father. It's all for you.

Turn the page for a sneak peek
at Nancy Mehl's next book!

UNBREAKABLE

ROAD TO KINGDOM #2

Available Spring 2013

CHAPTER / 1

"All I know is that you folks in Kingdom need to be careful." Flo neatly folded the piece of fabric I'd just purchased, running her thin fingers along the edge to create a sharp crease. "Two nights ago a church near Haddam burned to the ground. Someone is targeting houses of worship in this part of Kansas, and they don't care about the denomination. They just hate Christians."

She put my purchases into bags and handed them to me. "Please, even if you think I'm being paranoid, speak to your church leaders. Urge them to take precautions." Flo, usually a rather dour person, gave me a rare smile. "You're very special to me, Hope. I don't want anything to happen to you."

I smiled back, rattled by her words of caution, yet appreciative of her concern. Flo and I were as different as night and day, yet over the years we'd developed a deep friendship.

I patted her hand. "All right, Flo. I'll talk to one of our elders when I return."

As she came around the side of the counter, I put my packages down and gave her a hug. "You are such a blessing to me. Thank you for caring so much."

Most people would probably think we looked odd. An older woman with bright red hair and overdone makeup hugging a plain Mennonite girl wearing a long dress with a white apron and a white prayer covering on her head. But Flo and I had moved beyond seeing our differences.

She let me go and swiped at her eyes with the back of her hand. "You take care of yourself, and I'll see you next month."

I said my own good-bye and went outside, where Daisy, my horse, waited patiently, tied to a post near the door. I put my sacks in the storage box under the seat in the buggy, and then I unhitched her. "You are such a good girl," I said, rubbing her velvety muzzle with my hand. She whinnied softly, and I climbed up into the carriage seat. "It's time to go home, Daisy." Lightly flicking the reins, I guided Daisy toward the street.

I loosened my hold on the reins and relaxed back into the seat. I could nod off to sleep and Daisy would still be able to deliver us safely home without any direction from me. We'd been making this monthly trip for a long time, and I was confident she knew the way as well as I did.

I took a deep breath, filling myself with the sweetness of spring air and deep, rich earth. The wheat in the field was tall enough to wave in the gentle wind, and I was struck once again by the beauty of Kansas. Usually, my ride to and back from Washington was a peaceful time when I could be alone with my thoughts, but my concern over Flo's warning left me feeling troubled inside.

From the other direction, I saw a buggy coming my way. As it approached, I recognized John Lapp, one of the elders who'd left the church in protest. I nodded at him as he drove past, and he returned my gesture with a barely discernible tip of his head. John's wife, Frances, had been ill for quite some time. I'd heard whispers that her illness was caused more by her laziness than by any actual physical disability, but I tried to ignore those rumors. It was a little difficult in Frances's case, though. Poor John was constantly driving to Washington for medicines and supplies his wife insisted she needed.

As Daisy's hooves clip-clopped down the dirt road that led home, the buggy swaying gently in time with her gait, my mind went back to my conversation with Flo. Who could be behind these vicious attacks? Most people in the towns surrounding Kingdom treated us with kindness, care, and respect. I wanted to take Flo's warning seriously, but this kind of hate was beyond my experience. Kingdom was so secluded, so remote, that the idea anyone could even find us, let alone try to harm us, seemed extremely unlikely. However, since I'd told Flo I'd say something to our leaders about the situation, I began to rehearse exactly what I would say.

Suddenly, the roar of an engine shook me from my contemplation. I automatically pulled Daisy as far to the side of the road as I could. Glancing in my side mirror, I saw a bright red truck barreling down the dirt road, a wave of dust behind it. Only seconds before it reached us, I realized with horror that it was aimed straight for the back of my buggy.

Not knowing what else to do, I pulled tightly on the reins, guiding Daisy into the ditch. The truck roared past us, spraying us with gravel. The buggy teetered for a moment and then began to tip over on its side. Before it fell, I was able to jump out into the ditch, landing hard on my hands and knees. Daisy staggered under the weight of the stricken buggy.

I forced myself to my feet even though my right arm hurt and my knee burned where it had been badly scraped. I stumbled over as quickly as I could to unhook her from her harness, pushing against the weight of the buggy so she wouldn't topple. Breaking her leg could put her life in jeopardy, and I had no intention of losing her. I cried out as I struggled to release her from her restraints, holding tightly on to her reins. Fear caused her to fight me. She whinnied and tried to rear up, and I held on for dear life while trying to calm her.

Once I finally got the harness off and she was freed from the buggy, she began to quiet down. I took her reins and started to lead her back up to the road. Over her soft, frightened nickering I heard the sound of an idling engine. Surely the driver of the pickup was coming back to help me, regretting his carelessness. Thankfully, his momentary lack of judgment hadn't cost us more than a damaged buggy, a nervous horse, and a few cuts and scrapes. I hoped he was aware that the situation could have been much worse and that he would be more careful when approaching any other buggies he might encounter on this road.

Although it was still difficult to see through all the dust, I peered through the haze and discovered that the red truck was parked about fifty yards down the road with its motor racing. As Daisy and I strained to make it up the incline, I waved at him. Maybe he would at least help me get my buggy out of the ditch and back to Kingdom. One wheel had come completely off and the axle was bent. There was no way I could drive it home.

It wasn't until he put his vehicle into gear again and stepped on the accelerator that I became aware he wasn't concerned about my condition. This man had another intent entirely. A scream ripped through me as I realized there was nowhere to go. No way out. Whoever was driving that truck was trying to kill me!

NANCY MEHL is the author of twelve books and received the ACFW Mystery Book of the Year Award in 2009. She writes from her home in Wichita, Kansas, where she lives with her husband, Norman, and their puggle, Watson.

If you enjoyed *Inescapable*, you may also like…

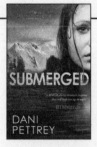
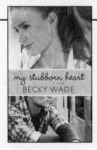